The disappearance of New York Supreme Court Justice Joseph Crater from the streets of New York City in 1930 was one of the greatest puzzles of the 20th century.

What happened to Judge Crater?

What took him on that hot August night on his short two-block walk to the Belasco Theater?

After decades, the answers have finally surfaced...

in

JUDGE CRATER TAKES A POWDER

Cover Design by Glenn Lazar Roberts

JUDGE CRATER TAKES A POWDER

by
Glenn Lazar Roberts

ADVENTURES OF THE RADIATED LESBIAN NUN
Part 1

Dark Lotus Books
home of the
JUST PLAIN WEIRD

www.darklotusbooks.com

If you enjoy
JUDGE CRATER TAKES A POWDER
please post a
REVIEW
on the following websites:
www.amazon.com
www.goodreads.com
www.siriusreviews.com
www.authorsden.com

DEDICATED TO
ROBERT CRUMB
"MR. NATURAL"

ISBN 978-0-9675809-5-1
www.darklotusbooks.com

from DARK LOTUS BOOKS:
A tale of the fantastic
and macabre...

THE GLOW

by

Glenn Lazar Roberts

Sam Trencher has a problem. To keep from exploding into flames, he must keep the exact same coins in each pocket. Six years ago he left his home town and his girl. Now he's coming back to find her–but can't tell what's real and what's not…and his temperature is rising.

"Non-stop chills from Glenn Lazar Roberts."
—Sirius Reviews

From Dark Lotus Books

JUST PLAIN WEIRD

Life at the touch of a button…or death!

FRENZY

by

Glenn Lazar Roberts

The hurricane party went well–until someone locked the doors. Now the partygoers' only escape from the Research Center's basement is through a labyrinth of rapidly flooding tunnels with drug gangs, psychics, a stock fraud, and one-minute piranhas created by experimental 'genechips'. Weird sci-fi run amok.

"A terrifically fun read! Glenn Lazar Roberts squeezes a lot of horror, mystery and plain old fun into his new novel... Grab a copy as fast as you can and read this face-paced novel."

—Jerry D. Mohrlang, author of Sarawak.

"A plot worthy of the movies..."

—Michael Fox, author of Theater Boy.

Heroic Fantasy in the tradition of
Robert E. Howard &
Edgar Rice Burroughs

THE MAALSTROM SERIES:

BOOK 1

MAALSTROM

by
Glenn Lazar Roberts

In the midst of war with the tyrant Nesos, Flores of the Turlicum is trapped in the Temple of Vensa where he falls under the spell of the priestess Amina, the most beautiful gila of the Three Valleys. First half of the The Selk King.

"If you enjoyed Game of Thrones or Joseph Campbell, you'll love Maalstrom."
—John Picha

"Glenn Lazar Roberts is one of the finest writers of unconventional prose in contemporary fiction. His wonderfully inventive plots and mastery of the language place him in the company of Calvino, Burges, Gass..."
—C. Thorman

More Heroic Fantasy
from DARK LOTUS BOOKS

THE MAALSTROM SERIES:

BOOK 2

THE SELK KING

by

Glenn Lazar Roberts

Flores of the Turlicum pursues his lost love Amina across the alien planet Maalstrom to the Island of the Sun-God, or Heavenhell. In another plot with twists and turns, Flores discovers the Black Pillar and climbs its spiral ramp from the nether-world to the selks' glass city in the clouds, encountering further unfolding of the mysterious relationships that link Maalstrom's bizarre inhabitants. Strewn with eccentric characters and gruesome combat, *The Selk King* is a triumph of mythological speculation and psychological insight into the nature of the Sacred.

"Compelling. Any sci-fi enthusiast would love this book." —*Writer's Digest*

"A unique and visionary epic."
—*Sirius Reviews*

And more fevered dreams
from the mind of
Glenn Lazar Roberts...

ADVENTURES OF THE RADIATED LESBIAN NUN

PART 2

'CROSS-DRESSERS FROM PLUTO'

by
Glenn Lazar Roberts

Pop the Thunderbird wine and break open the nopalitos. Because Maggie, the Radiated Lesbian Nun is igniting fires and breaking hearts from Santa Monica to across the galaxy! Political correctness may never recover from this *no-holds-barred* mercilessly satirical novel.

"Nuts!" —Sirius Reviews

AND COMING SOON...

More from the warped mind of
Glenn Lazar Roberts...

ADVENTURES OF THE RADIATED LESBIAN NUN

PART 3

'THE RADIATED LESBIAN NUN MEETS EVIL MIMES'

Maggie, the Radiated Lesbian Nun and Queen of her all-girl Warriors roller derby team, rules the mean streets of Los Angeles. Insanity reigns in this satirical take-off of the

1979 cult classic movie
THE WARRIORS.

Political Correctness meets its match in this work of eccentric genius!

TRIGGER WARNING!

Snowflakes, Politically Correct, and the Easily Offended...

There are no Safe Spaces past this page.

CAUTION!

You may injure yourself laughing.

Article in the *New York Times*
September 4, 1930:

WIDE HUNT IS BEGUN FOR JUSTICE CRATER

The police of two cities and the New York State Attorney General's office began yesterday efforts to determine the whereabouts of Supreme Court Justice Joseph Force Crater, who disappeared last August 6...Though many theories were advanced, the one most generally accepted is that the justice has been "done away with." A few acquaintances, however, indicated that they felt no great concern for the justice's safety and believed he had decided to take a few days of vacation...

*****

JUDGE CRATER TAKES A POWDER

'HOW MAGGIE GOT HER POKELICIOUS FROM BRAT-WURST & THE FUCK IN THE BACKSIDE INSTITUTE'

Episode 1

"Son, I'm not going to tell you again. Don't you *ever* interrupt me." The man in the black robe seated behind the dais glared supernally down from his high seat, the gleam from his partially receded pate adding to the confusion evident in the lawyer's eyes. The judge pointed his wooden gavel. "Didn't they teach you anything in law school?"

The lawyer gulped. "Not if you say so, Your Honor."

"Good answer. Now get the hell out of my courtroom. I've got a show to catch."

As the bailiff raised muscle-bound arms to shoo spectators and the lawyer out of the Judge's court, the Judge gathered his black robe about his midriff like Marie Antoinette stepping over a puddle and climbed down the few short stairs from the dais. He disappeared into the anteroom and shut the door. He tossed the robe onto a coat-rack and turned to his young law clerk.

"I need a burn-bowl."

"Burn-bowl, Your Honor?"

"You heard me. And some lighter fluid."

"There's an old barbecue pit in the maintenance area…"

"Perfect."

The Judge sat at his desk and slid open several filing drawers and rifled through voluminous paper files. Periodically he withdrew a manila folder and put it on his desk. The stack grew large.

"That's everything. Bring them, please."

His clerk grasped the stack and followed the Judge outside to a small fenced side yard. A glance around revealed no witnesses and with a curt gesture from the Judge, Joseph plopped the entire bundle into a barbecue pit. He sprayed lighter fluid on top and lit it. The Judge stirred the pit until nothing but ashes remained. Another gesture and the clerk followed the Judge back to his office.

"I need you to cash two checks for me, Joseph." Drawing a checkbook from his desk, Judge Crater handed them to his clerk, whose brows arched in surprise.

"Your Honor! These checks total $5,150!"

"A small fortune! So don't lose em." The Judge extracted a briefcase from below his desk. "The bank is just around the corner. Take this. I expect you to be back here in thirty minutes with the cash locked inside. I've already phoned my banker. He's expecting you."

"As you say, sir." The clerk took the briefcase and exited at a run. In twenty-nine minutes he was back. He handed the briefcase to the Judge, who unlocked it and quickly counted its contents.

"Well done, Joseph. Now get my other briefcase as well. Bring both."

"Yes sir, Judge."

Joseph grabbed the two worn briefcases from the Judge's desk and together they hurried to the Court's parking lot. They entered a black Stutz Limousine. Joseph sat behind the wheel. Turning toward the back seat, he looked up at his boss.

"My apartment on Fifth Avenue. And step on it."

The engine revved. Once they arrived, an attendant swung open the chain link gate topped with barbed wire, and the Stutz entered the flow of traffic and before long arrived on Fifth Avenue.

The Judge got out, holding a locked briefcase in each hand. "Joseph, I know I just came back from vacation, but I've decided to take off a few more days. You may take my car back to the lot. Then you're done. I'll call you when it's time to come back to work."

Joseph grinned. "Thank you, sir!" The car disappeared in the heavy noon traffic.

Hours passed. As the sun set, the Judge approached a restaurant and paused under a sign emblazoned 'Billy Haas Chopshop' to re-read the theater ticket in his hand: 'The Belasco Theater presents: Dancing Partner'.

He nodded to himself–it was all he needed. In the window he saw the outline of a voluptuous flashy blonde, the kind who belonged in dives with hi-hat horns frequented by patrons intent on getting rich quick, but who usually achieved the opposite. Next to her sat an old lawyer friend. The Judge smiled and entered, carrying a bundle wrapped in newspaper under his arm.

At exactly 9:00 p.m., a taxicab pulled in front of the restaurant. While the cabman stared, three figures rose from their window table and exited. The woman and the third man waved to the Judge as they slid into the cab.

He waved back. "Sorry to run, Sally. See you soon, Bill."

Sally blew him a kiss. "Bye, love."

"Enjoy the show, Judge," said Bill. "It's about time you took a break."

"More than you know!"

The cab veered into traffic. As its yellow back vanished bearing his friends away, Judge Crater turned. Adjusting his package, he strode confidently in the direction of the Belasco Theater, only a short distance away–two blocks over and one down.

The traffic had dwindled; few pedestrians remained to loom out of the darkness. The desultory gas lamps strewn at odd intervals gave their ghostly glow, only occasionally interrupted by newly installed electric advertisements. He turned south and crossed to 44th Street. Sweat grew under his armpits. Better than most he knew the risks of wandering the streets of New York after dark. The Belasco Theater appeared on his right, its neon sign a welcome relief, signaling safety. In the side street by the theater he paused. He would enter–but not yet. First, he had some business to take care of. Luckily, he remained alone, the side street clear of loiterers.

Before long, his suspicions were allayed–or confirmed–depending on whether his mind was more relieved or more alarmed with each passing moment.

A black car appeared. Nosing slowly from 44th onto the side street, it glided quietly, its interior invisible to prying eyes. The Judge pressed himself against the brick wall of the theater. The car slowed to a stop and a back door opened.

"Get in," growled a voice.

The Judge put one foot inside.

"Don't forget your package!"

The Judge clutched it and slid into the back seat. A chauffeur in wool coat and cap stepped out and shut the back door, then re-entered, and the car motored back into the light traffic of 44th Street.

"Wha–" the Judge began.

"Sssh! They could be watching." The speaker remained shadowed in the back seat until the car entered the secure bottom floor parking garage of a high-rise apartment, also on Fifth Avenue. Stopping in a reserved space, the chauffeur jumped out and opened the back door on the car's other side, then opened the Judge's door.

A short stocky man whose jaw seemed stuck akilter

stepped out, a too-large thick coat encompassing his body. “Say nothing till we’re in private. We can’t be too careful.”

The Judge nodded. His coat was slight compared to the other man’s bulky attire.

The chauffeur led them through a series of locking metal doors and into an elevator. Moments passed and they entered a darkened corridor that led to a private suite with solid double doors of intricately carved wood veneer. Two young men in suits and ties eyed them as they approached. They swung the double doors wide.

The short man growled again. “I know I own the floor. But I can never be sure if I own my agents.”

The doors swung shut and they were alone, the chauffeur remaining outside with the two gate-guards. The stocky man approached curtains that opened on a forest of skyscrapers, the Empire State Building arching far above the rest.

Turning to the Judge, he squinted at him almost sideways, his jaw still maintaining its angled pose. “Ribbet.”

The Judge’s eyebrows rose.

The eyes stared upward more sharply. “Ribbet!”

“Director? Sir?”

Throwing off his bulky coat, the shorter man flopped backwards on the couch by the curtains and–to the Judge’s surprise–was dressed in a woman’s evening gown. Fuschia. With a pearl necklace. As the Judge watched, the Director exchanged his formal shoes for mid-high heels and proceeded to attach ruby ear-rings to his ear lobes.

"One more thing I need to do. Over here, please, Judge."

The Judge approached hesitantly.

"Drop em."

"Mr. Director–sir?"

"Don't panic, Judge. Just trust me on this. Drop em."

The judge dropped his pants. Before he could react, the Director slid one hand into the Judge's shorts.

"Turn your head and cough," he growled.

He turned his head to one side. "Uh-haack!"

Frowning, the Director leaned back. "It's okay. You're not one of–" He peeked behind him where the open curtains revealed a glittering New York night. "–*them*."

The judge belted his pants again. "So what's this all about, Mr. Hoover?"

"Judge Crater, we're in trouble. *Big* trouble. But first I want to thank you for the undercover work you've done for your country. You helped us set up that punk Scarface by accepting his bribe. Now we've got him. It's just a matter of time before we convict that dago and put him away for keeps."

Crater interrupted. "Here's the money he bribed me with and that he didn't pay tax on." He placed the newspaper-wrapped package on a coffee table. "I burned all my files showing your involvement, just like you asked."

J. Edgar Hoover briefly nodded and went on. "And I want to thank you for helping uncover Capone's power-base among the Masons in Cicero. It was a big surprise to learn that Capone was really working for Mussolini." Hoover leaned forward, his visage expanding. "But here's the real shockeroo: I guess you've heard that Mussolini recently recognized the Vatican?"

"Last year wasn't it? 1929?"

Hoover nodded again. "Just before the Depression hit. People like to think Mussolini put the Pope in his place. Think again. The truth is that the Pope now owns Mussolini–lock, stock, and barrel. We've also learned that the Vatican is now in control of the Masons, and Mussolini, and…"

Hoover paused.

"–the *Chartreuse Gang!*" said Hoover.

Crater caught his breath. "We *are* in trouble!"

"So the F.B.I. needs to send you undercover again–deep undercover. Tonight. And there's even more: we thought that Herr Hitler and his Nazis were finished after the last election. But the latest intelligence says that next month he will win the coming German elections by a landslide. And you know what *that* means."

"Bratwurst and beer for everyone?"

"No! It means the Vatican will be running both Germany and Italy. Unless we stop them!" Hoover glared at the Judge. "That means you, Crater. So I'm making you my chief spy-catcher and I'm sending you to–"

"–Rome?"

"No, Judge. Nevada."

Crater stared. "Nevahda?"

"Nevaada," corrected Hoover. "As in 'vat'. They hate

it when you say ‘ah’.”

“But why…Nevaada?”

“Because that’s where our reports put the Mormon seminary.”

“Mormons!”

“Yes, the Mormons! Who do you think runs those goddam Masons for the Pope? *Of course* the Mormons. We think there’s a seminary of Mormon Nazis there that you need to infiltrate. You have to gain their trust before I can send you to Rome.”

“*Nevahda…*”

“*Nevaada.* Slap-dab in the middle of nowhere. But you can’t trust anyone. The Chartreuse gang work for the Masons who work for the Mormons who work for Mussolini who work for the Vatican. Or maybe the other way around.” He stuck out his gown-bedizened chest. “But sure as hell none of them work for the United States of America!”

“But what about my court?”

“Fuck your court, goddam it man! I’ll double your salary and find someone else to trip over your goddam black robe all day.”

Crater stared at the ceiling and sighed. “It’s true I’m not getting along well with my wife–”

“Fuck your wife, goddam it man! Your country needs you. What do you think will happen when that goddam Pope sends his Fascists and Nazis into Salt Lake City and they have thousands of babies with hundreds of Mormon women? How long will this country last if that happens?” Hoover jumped up and grabbed Crater by his lapels, balancing with surprising ease on his mid-high heels. "Do you want to see this country over-run with young men in crew-cuts and short sleeves knocking on doors saying '*Do you haben a moment to discuss ze Lord?*' Have you no *heart*, Crater?" Hoover shook him hard.

"I would have to let my man Joseph go."

"Fuck your man, goddam it wife! We'll give him an all-expense paid vacation to Panama. What do we care?"

Crater adjusted his hair. He blew out his cheeks. "Well, I guess that's about it."

Hoover stared upwards into Crater's eyes, his massive jaw still crooked. "You're goddam right that's about it. Don't go home. Don't visit your office. Don't call anyone. Just go." He smoothed his gown and picked up an envelope from the coffee table. "This will get you started. And don't forget to write. It's essential that you stay in touch with me. Nobody else–just me. We don't have anyone else on the inside with these goddam subversive organizations flooding into this great U.S. of A. You made a great start, so you're it."

Drawing himself up straight, the Judge could not resist saluting at the diminutive red-gowned Hoover.

"Oh, could you zip me up, please."

Hoover turned his back to the Judge and Crater zipped up his gown. Pocketing the envelope, he zipped his own zipper, turned and strode out of the room. The doors opened. The agents guarding them entered and, as Crater disappeared down the elevator, he overheard a voice growl, “Clyde! Call the airport. Fast!”

Escorted to the parking garage by a silent suit-and-tie, Crater slid into the back seat of a nondescript auto, and soon found himself back beside the Belasco Theater on 44th Street. Without his clandestine employer present to ensure cooperation, the agent failed to exit and open his door, but merely pointed. Time to get out.

No problem, thought Crater, and as good a place as any. He still had time for his last rendezvous–if *she* was still waiting. But the Dancing Partner had danced and the patrons were streaming out. He decided to wait in the alley for her to exit, and his heart swelled with affection. He was head over heels and knew it. Since he had met her, all other women had faded away, including his wife–even his hi-hat mistress Sally. But how to break the news? His country called. He felt in his jacket pocket for the envelope and was reassured since this undercover stuff could get expensive and from now on he would have no more Judge’s income to supplement the Bureau’s largesse. He drew his jacket tighter; although it was early August, the day was not a hot one and the temperature was cooling rapidly. Silently he watched the people exit–but, with a tear in his eye, watched especially for *her*.

Tires spun.

Glancing behind he saw what looked like the same black Stutz Limo that Hoover had driven and Crater exhaled in relief. *Hoover must have a postscript to deliver*, he thought. Turning, he pasted a smile on his face. Like before, the car jerked to a stop. The back doors popped open and two men in coats and wide-brim hats grabbed him by his lapels.

My lapels are getting quite a workout. I'll have to clean and press them next time I'm not being abducted. He was shoved into the back between his two abductors.

As the car accelerated, Crater ventured a joke to the Bureau agent on his left. "Ease up, Bugs. The boss won't like you shoving around his favorite spy."

The heaving bulk turned a bone-thick jaw towards him. A voice too deep for anything but a gorilla said, "How'd you know my name?"

"Uh, lucky guess?"

The thug looked forward to the front seat. "Fat Tone. How'd this guy know my name? Did you tell him?"

"Not me, Bugs. Maybe you spilled it when you grabbed him."

Bugs squinted as if searching barely functioning memory banks. "I don't think I did." He turned to the looming bulk on Crater's right side. "Did I, Paulie?"

The other stared out the window at the passing lights. Came a high wise-cracking voice. "Did youse what, Bugs?"

"Say my name."

"What name?"

"My name."

"Your name? It's Bugs."

Traffic honked.

"It's what?"

"Bugs. That's your name. Don't you remember it?"

"Remember what?"

"Your name. It's Bugs. How many times I gotta tell ya, ya creep."

"Oh yeah, that's right. Bugs."

"And don't forget it again."

"Thanks, Frankie."

"That's Paulie, Bugs."

The Stutz braked to avoid hitting the car in front. Leaning out the window, the driver yelled back at them, "Ya fuckin dago, what the hell's the matta wit ya? Ya get your license out of a box of Cracker Jacks?" An arm extended out of the driver's window of the car in front and elbowed up in an Italian salute.

"Did he just do what I think he did?" asked Fat Tone.

Paulie answered. "I think he did just do what you think he did. You gonna let that joik get away with that? I mean that's...disrespectful. He ain't no good citizen, that guy."

Fat Tony snapped the gear into park and jumped out of the Stutz, evoking honks from two autos stopping behind him. Two more arms saluted in his direction.

"Can you believe this, Frankie? I'm tellin ya–what's the world comin to when a law-abidin guy can't pick up a guy off the street and take him for a ride to his consigliere without gettin goddam fists and fingers stuck in his face by disrespectful strangers?" Fat Tony pulled a pistol from his front jacket.

"That's *Paulie*."

Tony halted and looked back inside. "That's what?"

"That's Paulie, ya joik. I'm Paulie. That's Frankie in

front of ya, ya moron. Frankie, your brudda. The guy you're about to plug."

Fat Tony peered into the darkness. "I don't give a fuck who it is–nobody can disrespect me like that and get away with it." He looked again. "Who'd you say that guy is?"

"Your brudda, ya goddam joik. And that's your cousin Frankie behind us, with his bruddas Paulie and Tony. Can we get this jalopy movin already? The Boss won't like it if you get into another ringside match with those relatives of yours. He never can tell who's who."

"Family. That's important, Frankie. You remember that. Family." Fat Tone slid his gun back into his jacket and got behind the wheel again. He turned towards the back.

"Bugs."

No response from the gorilla on Crater's left.

"*Bugs!*"

Still no response.

From Crater's right, Paulie reached over Crater with his left arm and smacked Bugs on the shoulder. Bugs jerked. "He's talkin to ya, ya goddam moron." The car resumed moving.

"Talkin to *me?*" came the deep voice. "I gotta name, ya know. Why don't ya use it?"

Paulie smiled at Fat Tony. "And what is your name?"

Silence again.

"Would it be somethin like…*Bugs?*"

Bugs looked hurt. He pushed out his lower lip and stared out the window.

"Yeah," continued Paulie. "It's *Bugs!* Now don't make me tell it to ya again. Bugs! Ya got it now?"

"Yeah. I got it."

"Repeat after me. My name is Bugs."

The cavernous chest echoed. "Repeat after me. My name is Bugs. And I woik for the Chartreuse Gang."

Both Fat Tony and Paulie rocked back in their seats, their jaws dropping. Paulie put his hands over Judge Crater's ears. "Ya goddam moron! How many times we gotta tell ya, ya never say that name! Forget that creep, Crater. He don't know what the hell he's sayin."

Crater stared out the window. At the mention of the unnameable name, sweat exuded from his neck. "So you're with the Chartreuse Gang…"

"Yep. That's us." To Crater's surprise, everyone stared calmly ahead.

After a while they approached the Lincoln Tunnel. Without pause, they rumbled through and plunged into the wilds of New Jersey.

"Gentlemen," said Crater, "you're leaving New York!"

Fat Tony and Paulie laughed. "Lookit the genius!"

"But I have…uh, court in the morning."

"Not now, you don't." Paulie breathed down his neck. "Sorry, Crate. But when the Boss says bring the Judge, we bring the Judge. Don't matter what he got goin on in the mornin."

"I see…"

"By the way, Crate. Don't you got any kinda… friendly type name? 'Crate' sounds kinda…low-class, if ya know what I mean."

The others chuckled.

"We got Skinny Vince, Fat Tone, Bugs Bugliosi, Rat's Ass Rudy, Pussy Louie. Don't you got any friendly type name that we can call ya?"

"I don't know."

"Ain't you got anything that really says: *you?*"

"Other than having my life constantly interrupted?" He sighed again. "Like *coitus interruptus*."

"What's your foist name?"

"Joe."

"That's easy!" said Fat Tony. "You're No-dick Joe!"

Paulie shook his head. "He didn't say he got no dick, Tone. He said he just can't use it. Don't you know no goddam Latin?"

"No. I ain't never been to school."

"Well, youse been to jail–a couple thousand times. If you ever heard a judge talk, then you know Latin."

Fat Tony thought about it. "I guess that's right. *In loco delicious*. That's what they told me last time." He smiled.

"There. See? You do know Latin. Me too. The last judge looked right at me and said: 'You need to file a *pro forma moron*.' And you know what? He was right." Paulie thought again. "Dickless Joe."

"Dickless Joe?" said Fat Tony. "That's what I just said."

"No, you didn't. You said he ain't got no dick at all. I said he's got one but ain't usin it."

"Ain't no difference."

"Sure there is. Ain't ya ever heard of Shoeless Joe, the ballplayer?"

"Master of the World, that one!"

"He got shoes. Somewhere. He just don't wear em on the field. Like our friend here. Dickless Joe." He reached over and gave Crater a big hug with his left arm. "Much better than Judge *Crate*."

Crater slumped. "Thanks."

Paulie patted him on the shoulder. "De nada." Fat Tony looked back at Paulie and they both laughed hard, even Bugs joining in.

When the hilarity eased, Crater spoke again. "It's getting late, gentlemen. Or rather early. How long are we going to keep driving?"

"Wouldn't ya like to know! Relax, Dickless. It's gonna be a while. You may as well take a powder."

Bugs added, "Yeah. Take a powder. It takes a couple days to get to Cicero."

"Hey hey, ya moron! Watch that big mouth of youse!" Fat Tone slapped Bugs, who stared into the distance, his lip protruding again. Tone looked at Crater. "Seems you missed a summons to your lodge and the Worshipful Master wants to know why. Ain't right to do dat."

Outside the window, a sign loomed out of the dark informing them that they were entering Hackensack. The traffic began to back up. A truck blocked their progress. Crater glanced at the truck's side reflection and recognized a picture of a purple mannequin as it passed retail glass windows. On the back of the truck was a company logo that read Purple Retail, Inc.

"Fat Tone, where's your cousin Frankie?"

"Did he come wit us?'

"Yeah, ya moron. He was in front a while ago and now he ain't."

"Maybe he took a breather. We all gotta go, ya know."

"Not when the Boss gives us a job, ya don't! Ain't nothin interferes when we got a job."

"That's right, *amico mio*. Not rain, or sleet, or snow –"

"That's the mail, idiot! We ain't deliverin no mail!"

"But what we're deliverin is just as important."

"It ain't more important than the mail. Nothin's more important than the mail. Didn't they teach you nothin at school?"

"I already told ya, I didn't go to school. And the mail ain't neither more important than family!"

"No. That's right. Family. Ain't nothin more important than Family."

"Except the Boss."

"Except the Boss."

The traffic slowed and Fat Tone screwed down his window again. "Goddam Hackensack. I knew we'd have trouble here. There's always trouble in Hackensack."

"I don't like it, Tone. We're a long way from Cicero."

Tony paused, one arm ready to give a time-honored one-fingered salute. "You're right, Paulie. This ain't Chartreuse country."

"I know what ya mean, Tone," Bugs spoke up. "The

Boss said we gotta watch out for that *other* color which we don't want *nuttin* to do wit."

"Ya got that right, Bugs."

"Oh, there's youse brother, Tone. He's right behind us."

Before Tony could withdraw his arm, the truck in front jammed on its brakes, catching Tony with his head turned. Tony jammed his brake pedal into the floorboard.

Still staring behind, Paulie grabbed his seat and yelled, "And he ain't stoppin!"

The car in back slammed into the Stutz's rear, which shook like a giant had pulled the road out from under. The impact thrust the Stutz into the back of the box truck stalled in front, and the back of the truck sprang open, expelling a stack of purple mannequins mixed with pieces of dismantled furniture–legs and rods landed on the Stutz with a staccato clatter.

Fat Tony and Paulie shot panicked looks at each other.

"It's the Purple Gang!"

"They got a chopper!" yelled Bugs. "Run for it!"

More mannequins spilled noisily from the injured truck, and the Stutz's doors swung open like the starting gate of the Preakness to release a line of stumbling thoroughbreds who bolted into every dark corner and alleyway which the night mercifully offered, not pausing as the third car of gangsters plowed into the back of the second car.

Cries of "The Purple Gang!" rang through the night

and the street soon cleared of thugs in heavy overcoats leaving an armory's collection of guns and knives dropped helter-skelter on the street.

Episode 2

Judge Crater calmly exited and for a moment stood dumbly staring. He stretched his arms. Casually whistled. As a police siren sounded in the distance, an unshaven man with a cigarette and blue overalls descended slowly from the Purple Retail Inc. truck and picked up the purple mannequins and casually threw them into the back. Crater shrugged his shoulders and began to walk, hands in pockets.

A Yellow Cab approached. Crater signaled from under a streetlight. It made no effort to slow, although he could plainly see the cabbie staring at him, so he whipped out a green bill and flapped it in the light and the cab screeched to a halt, barely avoiding causing another series of collisions.

"How would you like to make a quick ten?"

"Do I kill him or just break his legs?"

Crater hopped in the back seat. "Fifth Avenue by 3:00 a.m. and I'll double it."

The tires smoked.

Within the hour they were back in Manhattan. Construction signs diverted them once, twice, and again. But finally they were back on 44th Street.

"Good enough. I'll walk from here." An exhausted Judge Crater slid out, his coat draped over his arm. He threw the other ten down and the cab merged and disappeared, and the Judge resumed his previous night's walk toward Fifth Avenue.

The shadows lengthened and darkened. *Lucky I still have my wallet*, he thought. *And my wristwatch*. He read 3:20 a.m. and sighed. Despite his tiredness his feet kept moving, knowing every step of this, his stomping ground. Not that he had ever stomped anyone–but there were plenty of characters and convicts who may believe otherwise after his years on the bench. He pursed his lips and glanced behind. Not safe for a judge to walk anywhere alone, least of all mid-town Manhattan.

At the end of the block he became aware of several figures following. He hurried his pace. But they seemed not to lag and after a block they overtook him.

A slim figure in rags thrust a dirty hand under his nose. "Dime for a cuppa coffee?"

"Just one, my friend." To delay him, Crater placed the coin on a concrete wall paralleling the sidewalk and increased his pace while the bum picked it up. The others, however, were not delayed and quickly caught up. The lines that he often saw during the day of unemployed queueing for free soup vanished at night, but seemed about to re-form behind him.

"I'm sorry, friends, but I'm all out of dimes."

"How bout a nickel?"

Crater looked back quickly but saw only a motley collection of bearded dirty men in worn overcoats, more approaching.

"I'm out of change, friends, sorry." He picked up his pace.

One grabbed his coat. "I know you got a nickel in there!"

He yanked it back. "No! I got nothin! Leave me alone!" He walked faster.

The crowd followed. "Come on, buddy. Throw us a bone. We're veterans and we still ain't got our bonus."

"I gave at the office! I got taxes to pay!" Crater skipped.

"Oh, he got *taxes* to pay! Don't your heart bleed for this guy?" They nipped his heels. One growled, "Cough up, Mac, or we'll strip your socks."

Another sniffed. "I can smell your change!"

Crater took off.

With a roar, the crowd launched after him. More bums streamed from alleyways, a high-pitched shriek resounding off the brick and concrete buildings. "Change!" Overhead a peal of thunder cracked and a sudden downpour added to his discomfort, pushing him from concern to desperation as his clothes soaked.

Up ahead–an arm from a doorway, barely visible in the weak streetlights. Before he could dodge, the hand clutched him and yanked him inside. Huddled in darkness, Crater hugged the wall as the narrow door clicked shut. He put his hands on his knees to catch his breath.

"Lucky for ye I happened by, me son." A man in a black cassock stood in a corridor barely lit by lights seeping from rooms at its other terminus. "Thank God they didna see the door or those desperate people might be breakin into God's holy house at this very moment." The man shook the water off his hands and quietly locked the door. Heavy steps echoed outside as the mob continued its pursuit.

Crater's gaze settled on the priest's collar encircling his neck leaving a rectangular patch of white like a Hitler mustache in negative.

"Father?"

"O'Malley." He smiled broadly, offering his hand. "This way, me son. Let's find a place where ye can dry off so ye donna catch your death of cold."

"Best idea I've heard all night." Crater squished to the end of the hall and entered a wide comfortable room furnished with plush chairs and couch and a well-used fireplace. A pleasant smell of pipe tobacco percolated. A clattering drifted from the next room, which Crater gathered was part of the main rectory.

Crater approached the fireplace where embers glowed.

"Ah, let me stoke the fire once more, me son. No need to worry. We'll soon have ye dry." Father O'Malley smiled at Crater while he stirred the ashes with a poker. "Wet in New York is never a good idea, not even in this high season of August." Father O'Malley peered through the further door. "Conan, me child! Bring more wood! Quickly!"

Crater removed his jacket and warmed his hands on the last emanations of the previous night's fire. "Please don't put yourself out, Father O'Malley. I can manage. I just need a few minutes to rest and I can be out of here."

"Nonsense! I won't be hearin of it. Ye bein me guest now, ye'll insult me if you try to leave without givin a Father a chance to play the host."

Shrugging, Crater folded his arms and waited, water dripping off his shoulders.

O'Malley stood for a moment rocking on his heels, his gaze wandering to the door. "Excuse me." He stepped toward the door. "Can ye be hurryin it up, Conan, me lad! Our guest here got caught in the downpour and we need to be startin a fire to dry him out!"

Crater squeegeed one ear with a finger.

The Father returned. "Here, ye can be hangin your jacket on the coat rack in the corner. That's perfect, me son. One canna be too careful when it comes to ye health; a stitch in time, and all that." The conversation lapsed as O'Malley's eyes directed back to the door of the rectory. More clattering could be heard beyond.

"Conan, me boy!" Father O'Malley smiled reassuringly at Crater, then called out again. "Let's not keep our nice guest waitin, if ye don't mind! There's a good boy, Conan!"

Crater rubbed his hands one over the other to warm them up. "It's not really necessary, Father. I can wait for a few moments, then just be on my way."

"I won't hear of it, me son. We'll have the wood in just a moment. Believe me, it's no inconvenience at all. It's all part of the great work that Christ in his eternal grace has charged us with doin, and it bein the greatest joy and privilege for us who have answered his call to serve."

The door to the rectory darkened. A boy of about ten stood at the threshold frowning, several split lengths of logs in his arms soiling his altar clothes of white satin gown and overarching green silk vest.

After a moment of silence, the altar boy walked swiftly to the fireplace. “One side, please,” he muttered. “I wouldn’t want you to get any *dirt* on your clothes.” He glared at Crater, sideswiping him with the corner of one log. After plopping the load in the fireplace, the boy turned and walked quickly back to the rectory.

Turning to Crater, O’Malley rubbed his hands together, his face impassive. “Well, now, that’s a fine start to a fine fire. I’ll just sprinkle some holy water over it.” He produced a squeeze bottle of lighter fluid and sprayed it on the logs. “And lay some newspaper on top to get the flame going nicely.”

O’Malley took a newspaper from an adjoining chair, crumpled several pages of The Catholic Gazette, and laid them in the fireplace. In another minute, a flame spread a wave of warmth over Crater.

Crater turned his backside to the fireplace and rubbed his hands together briskly. “Oh, what a relief!”

“Excellent! But can I be askin ye a question now, Mr…?”

“Crater.”

“Mr. Crater, sir. Not to be importunate, but are ye Catholic, me son?”

Crater thought a moment. “My mother was.”

O’Malley breathed a sigh of relief. “Ah, your dear saintly mother belonged to the true faith. That’s good to hear. But have ye had the water of Christ on your body, now I’m askin ye? Did your kind saintly mother, or your dutiful father fulfill their obligations to the Lord and bring ye in for Communion as they were supposed to when you were still at a tender young age?"

"I don't recall, Father, but I don't believe they did."

Father O'Malley caught his breath. Slowly he let it out. "Well, now, that's a problem, me son. Yes, it is. But not a problem that canna be fixed."

Despite the growing flame, Crater shivered. Sitting on the couch that sat at right angles to the fire, he removed his shoes and stripped off his wet socks.

O'Malley joined him by the fire. "Here, why don't ye let me take these damp clothes of yours and have them dried out."

"Don't mind if I do, Father. That's very kind of you."

"It's the kindness of Jesus, me son. I'm only His humble servant on Earth."

"As you say, Father."

Crater unbuttoned his shirt and handed it to O'Malley. A moment later O'Malley had his pants as well, leaving Crater standing almost nude, dressed in only his boxers. He backed against the fire again, rubbing his hands on his bare legs.

O'Malley turned to the open door. "Oh Conan, me lad! Will ye come and take our guest's wet clothes, please? They need dryin most urgently, I'm sure!"

The clattering in the rectory ceased. For a quarter minute total silence followed while O'Malley rocked on his heels.

The priest looked back to Crater. "You know it's part of the sacred obligation of every saintly mother and dutiful father to bring in their little lads and lasses to Christ's Holy Church and have the water of Christ put on their tender little bodies. They canna get to Heaven without it, as our Holy Vicar of Christ in Saint Peter's magnificent basilica has repeatedly told us."

O'Malley glanced back at the rectory door. "Excuse me again, Mr. Crater, sir." The priest walked back toward the rectory and peered through the doorway. "Conan, me boy! It's not proper to be a poor host to a stranger who's stumbled into our humble kirk! Can ye come get his clothes, please, and place them in the dryer so Mr. Crater here donna catch his death of cold?"

The clattering resumed, louder. Then quieted. At length footsteps sounded as they approached the threshold and Crater looked at O'Malley, who continued to smile blandly at him.

The boy appeared at the door. His satin and silk vestments were covered by a kitchen apron tied around his neck and waist and he was drying his hands with a towel. Throwing the towel on the floor, he walked in. With a frown, he picked up Crater's damp socks, damp shirt, and damp pants and strode out of the room, dragging the pants on the floor behind him. Pausing in the doorway, Conan let fall a harsh glare at Crater. The door slammed.

Without a word, O'Malley stood smiling broadly at Crater, rocking back and forth on his heels, hands on hips and elbows relaxed behind.

"Now bein as how you're almost half-Catholic now, me son, ye have made a most excellent start, but ye really must finish the job, so to speak, and bring your soul within the embrace of the Most Holy Church. All ye need is a little water of Christ upon your body and your sins will all be forgiven and ye can sit back and be most assured that when the great day comes your soul will rise up with the other saved souls, and go right past Limbo like a rocket in the sky, not even pausin for stop signs or yellow lights, and sail right on through to the great Pearly Gates of the Most Holy Hereafter."

Crater rubbed his hair. "I think I'm warmed up now, Father O'Malley. You think my clothes might be ready?"

"Of course, me son," beamed O'Malley. "But now ye be thinkin about what I just said, and how will ye make it to the Great Hereafter if ye haven't been gathered into the embrace of the Holy Church of Christ, seein as how ye can't make it to the one if ye haven't made it to the other. Now I'm certain your dear departed mother would most happily agree."

Crater stared at the floor. "Yes. Certainly, Father."

O'Malley walked to the rectory door and opened it to a renewed clanging of pots and pans. He looked through into the other room and the clattering and clanging ceased. "Oh Conan, me son! Sorry to be interruptin ye again, me child, but our guest is in dire need of his clothes. We canna be leavin him standin here all night almost bare naked, now can we?"

For a moment, the clanging resumed louder than ever–then abruptly stopped. O'Malley smiled and came back to Crater, leaving the door open. A full minute passed and the clothes still had not arrived.

Another long silence followed.

Finally, O'Malley stepped again to the doorway. "Will ye be bringin us a spare set of clothes then,

Conan, please? We canna leave our guest standin here naked all evening." Reassured, O'Malley returned to Crater and for another minute the two observed each other in awkward silence, their eyes alternating hesitantly between each other and the vacant open door. For a long while nothing could be heard from the rectory and its kitchen.

Suddenly the door darkened. A bare bum thrust backwards into the room, Conan's altar vestments pulled up and gathered in front to expose his derriere. Conan directed a fierce glare at Father O'Malley. "Is that what you want? *IS THAT WHAT YOU WANT?* Just go ahead and fuck me, you ass-jockey! You son of a donkey-bangin whore! You goddam hippo surfer! Why don't you go back to fuckin Jesus in the ass instead of makin my life pure hell, why dontcha?" Conan stepped back into the rectory and dropped his gown.

The door slammed shut.

O'Malley stared at Crater, with the corners of his mouth crinkled and eyebrows raised. For a long moment they stood and stared at each other to the echoes of a lone cricket.

"So, Mr. Crater, sir, what brings ye to our little slice of heaven in mid-town Manhattan in the wee hours of an August morn?"

Slowly, Crater shifted his boxered rear away from O'Malley and towards the fire. "Uh…if I told you you wouldn't believe me Father I can barely believe it myself if you had a mirror I would pinch myself just to see if I'm really awake." His mouth seemed to rattle on of its own accord. "And–and I'm not entirely sure I'm awake even now."

O'Malley cracked his knuckles. "It's certain that I hear a lot of oddities in the confession box, Mr. Crater, things ye would na believe. The role of a priest requires much patience. Yes, lots of patience. But Christ hears all and sees all. If ye don't want to speak to one of his priests, then maybe ye should try speaking directly to Him."

Crater eyed the hallway that led back to the street. "Oh yes, uh–well, I can speak to Jesus, Father, but–but will He answer?"

"Ah!" said O'Malley, "Now that depends on what's in your heart."

"I–I'm on a secret mission Father I wish I could tell you more but I can't… though I do admit I'm a little confused."

"Secrets are dangerous, me son. If you want to receive the grace of God, you must unburden yourself." O'Malley glanced down at Crater's shorts. "Are ye certain ye have not unburdened yourself to a priest before this?"

"Confession? When I was young I was briefly an altar boy but really I think I've had no confession since then."

"An altar boy! Oh, me son, why did ye not say that earlier?"

The door to the rectory swung abruptly open. Conan thrust his auburn-hair into the room, an angelic smile on his freckled face, the previous frown entirely gone. His altar clothes and apron had been replaced by short pants and a loose-fitting white shirt with wide V, lined with frills. Open-toed slippers graced his feet. Conan angled in, moving gracefully across the room till he stood directly before Crater and beamed an innocent smile up at the older man. "Good evening, sir!" he said batting eyelashes, "Is there anything I can do to make your stay with us…more *comfortable?*"

Crater directed a look of surprise at O'Malley. "Why…why, I think I don't need anything at all, young man."

"Are you certain, dear sir?" Conan batted his eyes again and smiled even more. "Isn't there something I could do to help you…relax?" He sidled up to Crater and put his arms around Crater's waist. He smiled and opened his mouth bringing it closer to Crater's.

Crater looked in alarm at O'Malley and tried to step back. "I–I think I'm quite dry now thank you Father maybe if I could just get my clothes back I could go ahead and head back to my apartment on Fifth Avenue. I really don't mind if they're wet…"

"Um…" Father O'Malley glanced hesitantly at Conan.

The frown returned. The boy stepped back. Hands on hips, he shouted at Judge Crater in a high pre-pubescent voice. "You cock-suckin son of a bitch! You lame duck-fucker! The curses of Mary and Jesus be on you! What's the matter? I'm not good enough for ya?" Conan ripped off his shirt, sending buttons and frills flying about the room. He rubbed his hands over his chest. "Take a look! Who wouldn't want this? Who are you stickin it to? Why don't you bring it home!"

In shock, Crater stepped back further and stepped into

the fire, his backside erupting in flame. Fearful that he was about to become totally nude, he slapped at his rear until the fire went out and he backed up again till he hit a corner of the fireplace mantle.

O'Malley shook his finger. "Now, Conan, me boy, that's not the proper language to use when a guest enters our little kirk here in Manhattan–"

"Fuck you, you fuckin son of a whore! You child banger! You want me to shut up? I won't, you cocksucker, with you bringin in someone new every goddam day! Why don't you just fuck em right here on the floor in front of me, you Irish tickler! Why don't I get out your Irish flute and play one of your goddam Irish tunes while you fuck a new one here in your goddam church every goddam day?"

Crater looked at the floor. Then the ceiling. "Oh, yes I should definitely be going."

Conan's smile returned, directed up at Crater with half-closed eyes. He sidled close again and connected with Crater's side, open mouth purring. One hand slid to Crater's underweared front while the other roamed his scorched rear. Conan sweetly whispered, "Let's do it, Mr. Crater. Don't let *him* stop you. He doesn't own me." Conan's hips began moving rhythmically thrusting against Crater's leg. Crater tried to shake him off but Conan's grip tightened.

"Ah, now there ye go tryin to hump the guests again, ye little rascal! Why don't ye let them be!" Hurrying forward, O'Malley took hold of Conan's shoulders and tried to dislodge his grip from Crater, while Conan continued to pump, accelerating his thrust while Crater ran about the room, pausing every few feet to shake his leg in vain attempts to dislodge the altar boy's grip.

O'Malley grabbed the rest of The Catholic Gazette and rolled it into a cylinder. "Get off him, I said, ye little hot dog. How many times have I told ye not to hump the guests!" He began to rain blows on Conan. "Get off him, I said!"

Crater shouted. "My clothes, Father! Can I please get my clothes? It's time I really must be going!" He tried to untangle Conan's arms, but only succeeded in transferring Conan's grip to his waist.

"I do blow jobs for a dollar!" grinned Conan.

"Off, ye little rascal!" O'Malley landed a blow on Conan's head who ignored it and locked his lips on Crater's nipple. "Get down, I said! Jesus help me, he's at it again." Newspaper blows landed on Conan's back and rear.

Crater stumbled. Before he could crawl away, Conan had him down with one arm pinning Crater's left arm and the other pinning Crater's right leg. O'Malley threw the newspaper aside and wrapped his arms around Conan's waist trying to pull him off but the priest only managed to slip and land on top of both.

"Fuck me! Fuck me!" yelled Conan, his lips attempting to transfer to Crater's lips, his hands holding Crater's hands on Conan's rear in a grip of surprising strength.

O'Malley produced a bottle of water and splashed it on Conan. "Power of Christ!" The water had no effect and Conan sat on top of Crater rubbing his rear against the judge's boxers, his short-shorts unsnapped and coming down, the overpowered Judge lying outstretched on the floor.

"Off him, ye rascal. How many times have I told ye we donna be rubbin our Jesus cheeks on the guests!"

Rolling over, Crater succeeded in dislodging Conan and the judge managed to struggle to his feet. "I think," he panted to catch his breath, "I think I hear someone calling. Yes, I hear someone calling me, it's definitely time for me to go."

Conan jumped up and blocked him like a linebacker. Contacting the fireplace, Crater's boxers again burst into flame and with a high-pitched shriek he ran into the hallway towards the exit, dodging Conan. "Can't stay another minute Father just send my clothes when they're done!" A trail of smoke followed as Crater penetrated the hallway, a burning luge in an ice chute.

Springing the door wide, Crater was relieved to discover that dawn was breaking, and he launched himself into a dead run down 44th Street, his boxers flaring until the last remnants were gone, Conan running after with his short-shorts unbuttoned and zipper held up only by his rapid pace. Behind trailed Father O'Malley swinging his rolled up Gazette.

"I love you, Mr. Crater! Kiss me! Take me with you! I'll leave him, I will!"

"Put your clothes back on, ye little hot dog! Sweet Jesus give me strength!"

Diving into an alley, Crater spun around a forest of trash cans and re-emerged on 44th heading in the opposite direction. He already had images of policemen cuffing him and the headlines that would result. He paused to ransack dumpsters for spare clothes to cover his nakedness, extracting from one a discarded muslin tarp that he wrapped about his bare body, grateful that at this early hour, with the sun not yet verging the horizon, none others were up and about to see his nakedness.

From around a corner, two figures dressed in bulky black-clothed tents emerged–they grabbed him in vise-like grips. Dragging him to a large cab hauling a truck of lumber and paving stones, they effortlessly thrust Crater up and into the back seat of the cab. Sitting one on either side of the Judge holding him in a tight grip, the doors shut and the truck rumbled down the alley, soon lost in growing morning traffic.

Episode 3

"Oh, my goodness!" A high voice tittered. "Oh, my my my." A black-shrouded figure on Crater's left spoke in falsetto to its counterpart on Crater's right. "Quickly, Maria, I can't look. Is he covered?" The black-shrouded figure riding in the forward passenger seat glanced back and one eye peeked through fingers covering a face devoid of makeup.

"I believe so, thanks be to Mary and Joseph." The eye winked out and she turned to look forward. "Last night I confessed with three Hail Mary's, five Our Mother's, and a Luminous Mystery. But after all this–my my my–I'm certain I must do five Hail Mary's and five Our Mother's."

The laden truck barreled west on 44th Street.

"A Luminous Mystery, Marie?" said the driver. The nun chuckled to herself. "Oh my my. But last night was Friday. Friday is Sorrowful Mysteries."

"Oh my my my. You're right, Marina. I should have said the first Sorrowful Mystery. Well, here goes: I am a voice crying in the desert, making the Lord straight. He is mighty and coming after me. I baptized you with boiled water. He will baptize you with the water of God. Behold the lamb-rack of God. This is my Sun in whom I am well pleased, so I am sending down a basted dove sufficient to feed the Trinity."

"Maria–no! That's Luminous! Anyway, today is Saturday. That means the Joyful Mystery!"

"Oh yes yes yes. Thank you Marie for reminding me."

"Marina, Maria. I'm Marina."

"Yes yes. But I'm Maria, Marina."

"Oh my my, yes of course. How silly of me."

"Well, here goes: The Embodiment is at hand, God prepared Mary to have the Last Word, Hail full of Grease, the Lord is with thee, Mary is wonderful, Fear not for you shall conceive and give birth to Jessie whom no man shall touch by the power of Christina the Holy Spirit, and She shall be called the Sun of God, Behold the lap dance of the Lord, the Word is lusty and dwells among us."

Loud honks sounded from all round as Marina guided the large truck through the Lincoln Tunnel. An exhausted Judge Crater sat and bounced with the swaying of the truck, wondering what to say. As they emerged in New Jersey, Marina leaned out the driver's window and thrust an arm upward at another driver in the time-honored salute of drivers everywhere. "Oh, my my, there I go again! How silly of me. That's two Hail Mary's. Well, here goes: Hail Mary, full of geese, the Lord is with me; blessed are you by women, blessed is the fruit of thy loom, Jessie Christina. Holy Mary, Mother of God, pray for us folksingers, now and at the hour of our rest, amen."

"Careful, Marina, don't forget to watch the road. The Grace of our Lord won't stop sinful men from drinking their whiskey and running into us."

"Yes, that's right, Mary. We poor nuns can hardly get through a day anyhow. It's only through the strength of Virgin Mary, Queen of the Universe, that we make it from day to day."

A screech announced a failure to negotiate a turn and the truck lurched to a stop, sending several enormous lengths of wood spilling onto the shoulder of the road.

"Oh my my my. Marina, look at us now. What are a few poor helpless nuns supposed to do with a load of lumber fallen off a truck in dangerous New Jersey? Look–there are *men* here!" Maria, Marie, and Mary slowly climbed out of the cab. Using strips of rawhide they tied their voluminous brown and black habits about their waists and lifted the cut wood. With ease of long practice, they swung the heavy lumber back onto the truck, the energy of their tosses sending the enormous blocks to the top of the stacked lumber like so much styrofoam. When they were done, they swiftly re-locked the heavy chains and climbed back into the cab.

"Thank you Jessie, Mary, and Joseph for giving us the strength this time, but what will we do next time? Think of it–a few helpless nuns stuck on the New Jersey turnpike, helpless prey to any sinful man that happens along."

Marina gunned the engine and the truck leaped forward inducing several autos to lurch to one side to avoid being crushed.

In his exhaustion, Crater dozed off, but soon re-awakened as the heavy truck bounced.

"Sisters," he finally blurted, struggling to keep his eyes open. "I must demand to know why you have abducted me."

"Oh my! I'm not sure we can speak directly to a sinful man. What do you think, Maria?"

"Five Our Mother's are in order if you do. And at least three Hail Mary's."

"And another Mystery."

"You mean a Rosary don't you, Mary?"

"That's only for evening, Marie. Rosaries are too long for daytime."

"Oh, it's so confusing!"

"It certainly is! Oh my my."

Crater shook himself awake. "Sisters, please! I will have to insist on your stopping this truck and letting me out at once. And you must tell me why you have kidnapped me!"

"Oh my. When the head of Opus Dea asks us to bring a guest, we have a sacred duty to obey. Thus saith the Virgin Mother of God, our Lord Jessie Christina."

"But Sister, I am a judge. I have court…sometime soon." He stared out the window.

"Oh, Mr. Crater, the Sacred Precinct works for the good of all humanity. I'm afraid that a matter has come up that is more important than anything you have on your schedule. Oh, yes."

"Sacred Precinct? And where is that?"

"Oh my my. Who doesn't know that? It's in Nevada."

"Nevahda?"

"Nevaada. As in 'vat'. That's how we like to pronounce it."

The truck roared on. "Parts of our convent are still under construction. Maybe when we bring our cargo we can finally finish our nunnery."

"Won't that be nice!" said Marie.

"Yes, indeed!" added Maria.

The truck slammed across several potholes, jarring the nuns. "Look to our lumber, Mary. Check to see if it's coming loose again."

The two nuns in the back passenger seat looked at their load through the window in the back of the cab. "I think we're okay."

"Thank you Jessie, Mary, and Joseph. We have a long way to drive before us."

"Oh yes yes yes."

In the front seat, Maria looked back at Crater. "Yes, and I'm afraid we really must check you, Mr. Crater sir. I hope you don't mind, but we can't take any chances."

He looked puzzled. "Chances? Check me?"

Maria looked at him directly, no longer peeking

through her fingers. "Ribbet." Getting no reply, she repeated louder, "Ribbet!"

"Ribbet?" Crater shook his head in confusion. "What the hell does that mean?"

All four nuns tittered. "Oh oh oh oh! Three Hail Mary's if you please, Mr. Crater!"

"What? After you strong-arm me into a truck, kidnap me, and try to drive me all the way to *Nevahda*, you want me to recite a Hail Mary?"

"NevAada, if you please, thank you Mother of God."

"Nevaada, if you please."

Four vise-like grips squeezed his arms and Crater immediately broke out in a high staccato, "Hail Mary full of goose the Lord is with thee, basted art thou, blessed is Jesus–"

"Oh no no no! That sounds like those bad You-Know-Who's! The proper wording is: 'Blessed is J.C. Christina'. But it sounds much better if we just say 'Jessie'. Please try again."

"Hail Mary, full of grace, the Lord is with thee. Blessed are you women…"

Several broke out in titters.

"Oh no no!"

"Oh my my!"

"I'm sorry, Mr. Crater, but that's just not the proper way to say it! Here: Hail Mary baked in grease, the Lord is thy recipe, blessed are you by women, blessed is the fruit of thy broom, Jessie Christina. Holy Mary, Mother of Virgins, pray for us folksingers, now and at the happy hour of our best, amen."

"Amen!" the nuns all repeated.

Crater stared past the black and brown-clothed figures beside him at the shuddering scenery and wondered how far away Nevaada was. He had not believed in Hell before this. Now he was beginning to suspect he had been wrong.

"I'm afraid we simply must check, though."

He blinked and looked back at Marie in the front seat as she turned to stare directly at him.

Reaching over the seat, she placed her hands between Crater's legs. "Turn your head and cough, please Mr. Crater, sir."

Catching his breath sharply, he could think of nothing else but to comply. "Hack!"

"Oh yes. He's a man, Maria."

"As only a sinful man can be."

"Oh my yes. As normal as any sinful man can be."

A metal sign appeared announcing the city of Hackensack. Before Crater knew it the truck was barreling down the same street where he had been just a few hours earlier. He squinted out the side windows. Surely his former abductors could not still be chasing him....

The truck hit another pothole and, with a savage bounce, ground to a halt, boards and paving stones spilling off the truck.

"You really must try my new recipe for lemon meringue pie, Maria," said Marina as she slid to street level. "It was revealed with the white pins at Fatima."

She was soon joined by Marie, Mary, and Maria. "Oh yes, we must." Tying back their habits with rawhide, they wrestled several heavy boards back onto the truck and swung the heavy paving stones back into place.

"Oh, Jessie, Mary, and Joseph. What are we helpless women to do? There's always trouble in Hackensack."

"Well, we can't wait for those sinful men to do us any good. We know what's always on *their* minds."

"Yes, indeed we do!"

They paused in the street to brush dust off their clothes, their voluminous habits surrounding them like enormous tents.

A Stutz Limo pulled suddenly in front. Jerking to a stop, the doors burst open, expelling four men, joined a moment later by a second and third car, from which spilled more frowning thugs. Several brandished baseball bats. Others brass knuckles; more had knives and lengths of chain.

For a moment they stood facing the four nuns in silence.

A high voice wise-cracked "Okay, Bugs. Give it to em."

No one moved.

"I said: Give it to em, Bugs."

Still no one moved.

Paulie turned to the hulking brute next to him and smacked him on the shoulder. "That's you, ya moron! Your goddam name is Bugs, rememba?"

The brute looked at Paulie. His cavernous chest rumbled "Oh yeah. Repeat after me. My name is Bugs. And I woik for the Chartreuse Gang." Bugs turned back toward the nuns. "Ohhhh…" A two by four bounced off his nose and he fell backwards like a building under demolition.

More boards flattened several more thugs as Marie

and Marina swung like veteran ballplayers. Mary and Maria followed the assaults with well-aimed paving stones.

The rest of the thugs scurried for the protection of alleyways. "Run! It's the Black and Brown Gang!"

"Oh my my my!"

"Yes, indeed! What are we helpless women to do?" Mary smacked one thug on his back, angling her board like Babe Ruth. Down he went. "How can we survive? These sinful men won't leave us alone. How are we supposed to live?" More pavers sailed through the air to land unerringly on the heads of the remaining thugs, all of whom fled as if their lives depended on it–as indeed they did. The street was soon littered with discarded brass knuckles and baseball bats.

"Come on, Sisters. We had better make sure they don't come back."

"Yes, indeed, Marina."

"That's Maria, Mary."

"I'm Mary, Marie."

"That's Marina, Mary."

"That's Marie…"

Crater slid down from the back of the cab and watched the nuns' backs disappear in pursuit of the routed Chartreuse Gang. For a minute he stood in silence looking about him, hands on hips. None remained in sight.

He scratched his head.

Up the street a yellow cab appeared. Absently, Crater groped for his wallet–nothing. It was in his missing clothes! Glancing about, he glimpsed an open purse and–swallowing his shame that a judge would resort to such–stole a couple of tens. As the cab cruised slowly by, he spilled from the truck and waved the green bills.

The cab jerked to a stop.

"Ten bucks to get me to 44th Street. And ten more bucks if I get there before Noon."

"You got it, Mac!"

At 11:55 they arrived on 44th Street. Crater thrust his other ten into the cabbie's hands, and cautiously peeked out the window of the Yellow Cab before exiting, one foot resting on the pavement. His eyes peered east; his eyes peered west. Finally, seeing nothing but the usual noontime traffic of mid-town Manhattan, slowly he exited the cab and quietly shut the back door.

He watched the yellow tail of the cab until it vanished in the flow of traffic and realized that he stood in the middle of a concourse of pedestrians while dressed in only a discarded soiled tarp. Crater–his presence garnering the attention of an increasing number of passersby who stared wide-eyed and open-mouthed–began to panic. He rushed into an adjacent clothing store.

"No bums inside! No bums inside!" A thin man in his fifties rushed forward, his toupee edging forward as he hurried to intervene and toss the intruder out.

"One side, my good man!" shouted Crater. "I ain't no… I mean, I am not a bum! I am Judge Crater and I'm due in court–"

"Good story! That's the best I've heard all day!" The thin man turned and shouted. "Lazlo, help me get this bum out of here before we lose our paying customers!"

Lazlo grabbed one arm and the thin man grabbed the other, and Crater found himself dragged toward the street.

"The alley! The alley, gentlemen! I can't be on the street looking like this!"

Briefly the thin man and Lazlo exchanged glances, and, as Crater dug in his heels, they reversed direction. In another moment, Crater found himself in the same alley standing by the same trashcan from whence he had earlier retrieved the black plastic tarp that still covered his nakedness. With a final warning glare, the clothing attendants re-entered their store and left him alone in the alley.

For a minute he stood uncomfortably. Again scratched his head.

What next? He could not wander around in public dressed in nothing but a tent. How long could he evade every cop in mid-town Manhattan? His mind conjured newspaper deadlines in giganto-type: CRATER NABBED FOR INDECENT EXPOSURE. Or worse: JUDGE IN ALTAR BOY LOVE NEST.

He looked around, and sighed.

His eyes lit on the large open-top dumpster. What choice had he? Pulling up a wooden crate, he stood atop and stared inside. There! In the far corner was a pile of clothes discarded by the very store that had just ejected him. Head and shoulders inside the trashcan, Judge Crater leaned as far as he could manage in an effort to reach the pile of clothing. The clothes were just out of reach.

Backing out, he sighted a stick. He snatched it, conscious of the need to accomplish his task as quickly as possible before the inevitable happened and he was discovered. Returning to the dumpster, he leaned over the edge, head and shoulders thrust forward so that his feet barely touched the ground.

A noise sounded from the alley's entrance.

In a flash, the headlines reappeared in Crater's mind, sailing across his brain like a Times Square news flash. He dove in. Another second and he had closed the cover upon him, encasing himself within the dumpster, where he huddled in silence, hoping to be overlooked.

Noises rumbled outside the dumpster–more croak than speech. At first Crater was relieved since the owner of the voice was clearly not a policeman. His anxiety returned as he suspected the owner may be one of the Bonus Army who had pursued him earlier. Or–worse–a jealous Irish altar boy named Conan. But the voice was not a voice but a grunt. And the grunts were not just grunts, but speech, intelligible to someone who had now begun to answer, though obscure to Crater as he strove to listen from within his hiding place between a stack of cardboard boxes and out of style clothes.

His eye wandered to the clothing illuminated by a pencil of light seeping in from one corner, revealing shirts, pants, and boxers, along with several other items he could not categorize.

Clang!

Something knocked the side of the dumpster with a metallic ring and as the reverberations eased he pulled the pile of clothes over himself. He was glad he had done so because no sooner had he covered himself than the metal top of the dumpster was thrown open. Crater began to panic, convinced that he was about to be tossed out with the trash, so to speak–but, as no truck appeared, he calmed.

A body descended into the dumpster.

He dared not move. Was it someone who had seen him enter, intent on robbing or killing him? Or was it the managers of the clothing store about to sweep him out with the rest of the bums? Or could it be the Chartreuse Gang still in pursuit of an errant lodge brother? Or–horror of horrors–the nuns of Opus Dea, intent on sharing their recipes?

Face covered, he lay and listened.

A second body entered the dumpster and took position beside the first body, and the metal top of the dumpster closed. More croaks sounded–this time from directly beside Crater, and clearly emanating from whoever had entered. He tried to understand. Failed. It was speech, but none he was familiar with. For a full minute the two intruders exchanged croaks and grunts as they puttered with items that scraped like metal on metal.

Humming echoed, transforming their speech into a communication that sounded more like buzzing than croaking. The dumpster shook. With a rocking like an earthquake, Crater found himself jarred against one side. He flattened as gravity seized him in a vicious grip.

Episode 4

"Korplash! Viski Dixie Doodle!"

"Nunu Xplak! Klaatu barada nikto! *Urk!*"

The dumpster shook and the pencil of light expanded to an array of bright rays as the metal top shook and rattled. Sounds rang like a creaky washing machine. Peeking from under the clothes, Crater stared–couldn't be. He rubbed his eyes and looked again. No difference.

Dust drifted and he sneezed.

Chameleon eyes bulged as they swiveled and settled on their unexpected cargo. Crater gazed on scaly skin, bloated bodies, down-turned jawlines, and parallel slits where noses should be. The two strange figures looked at each other, then back at Crater. With a jerk, the dumpster swirled and dipped. The first figure grabbed a metal lever set in the side. Deep voices emanated from enormous guts.

"Garengi matakup, Xplak!"

"Catalong derido, Korplash! *Urk!*"

The second figure pulled a black device ringed with cables from under a stack of brightly colored rubber objects behind him. Stretching forward a webbed hand–or was it a foot?–it thrust one device on its head and another on Crater's head.

With a start Crater realized he now understood the croaking. A chameleon eye focused on him.

"My eye sees unpleasantness. What climbs inside cosmodrones without announcing its intentions?"

"A stowaway it is, Korplash. What is ugly and wraps itself in plastic?"

"Ugly thing in ugly plastic. Is it our cousin, Xplak?"

"No, Korplash. Is it fat and green?"

"No, Xplak. Is it a bad-speaking tibbet?"

"No, Korplash. Is it shuman from Bonus Army?"

"It is shuman from Bonus Army. Xplak splash shuman from Bonus Army?"

"Xplak no splash shuman from Bonus Army–"

A rumble interrupted.

"Korplash rumble. Korplash croak?"

"Korplash no croak. Xplak bring shuman Gork?"

Listening to this bizarre exchange, Crater stared from his corner of the dumpster, wondering what might be the import of these enigmatic gutturals. Concluding that Xplak and Korplash–if these were the toads' names–had forgotten him, he stripped off the tarp, and, taking advantage of comparatively smooth sailing of the dumpster, proceeded to dress himself in the by now long admired pile of clothes in the corner. In short order he donned black trousers, white shirt, tweed jacket, and a pair of scuffed dark shoes, all of which fit better than he had any right to expect.

The guttural rumbling repeated, louder. Xplak stared at Korplash, eyes bulging.

"Korplash rumble. Korplash croak?"

"Korplash no croak. Xplak bring shuman Gork?"

"Xplak no bring shuman Gork. Korplash bring shuman Gork?"

"Korplash no bring shuman–"

Korplash ceased speaking. Xplak turned a chameleon eye on Korplash who sat, webbed hands on metal levers set in the side of the dumpster, a rumbling gathering strength as it traveled up Korplash's esophagus.

An ear-splitting crash thundered.

Crater put his hands over his ears as the dumpster spun and swirled, tossing its contents over Crater and his two companions.

Xplak's wide round jaw hung open, staring at his toad comrade with both bulging eyes. Xplak closed his jaw. "Korplash croak," declared Xplak.

"Arroo!"

From somewhere came a barrage of sharp barks as if the dumpster were suddenly pursued by junk yard dogs. Xplak threw open the side panel. Craning forward, Crater glimpsed a blur of brown and blue crisscrossed with small brown loops and ox-bows–rivers on a distant landscape. His stomach tried to exit his throat and he jerked back grabbing for dear life a handle welded in the interior of the dumpster. But he could still see out the aperture left by the sliding metal panel, and what he saw floating beside the dumpster made him doubt his sanity.

Directly in the dumpster's wake a second craft levitated, saucer-like in shape, with a second smaller circular cupola on top. Half a dozen dog-like snouts thrust through open windows in the cupola, barking and howling, beady eyes focused intently on the dumpster.

"Aarf! Arf, arf, arf! Woo, woo, woo, woof!" The muzzles in front snapped as their craft came closer. Jaws in the back hung wide open, dog ears blowing in the wind, bright eyes taking in the expanse below, tongues lolling happily.

Inside the dumpster the deep croaking resumed.

"Korplash croak. Xplak swim for cover?"

"Xplak swim for cover. Korplash swim for cover from siridogs?"

"Korplash swim for cover from siridogs. Shuman swim for cover?"

They glanced at Crater. Shaken by the rising volume of the barks, Crater was silent as the dumpster lurched.

"Shuman must respond… response, shuman?"

"Yes, shuman must respond… shuman response?"

His eyebrows raised. "How's this for a response: *Get me the fuck out of here you goddam toads!*"

Glancing at each other with mouths open, Korplash and Xplak suddenly closed their mouths and spun dials and flipped levers and the dumpster jerked more strongly than before, spiraling in an effort to evade their dog pursuers. Crater found himself upside down.

The toads resumed. "Xplak and Korplash swim for cover from siridogs. Shuman swim for cover from–?"

At that moment, hanging upside down by one hand from the handhold in the side of the dumpster, Crater screamed. The top of the dumpster–now become the bottom–had fallen open strewing its contents into the stratosphere. Korplash and Xplak clung easily to the sides with their webbed feet and hands, for all appearance hardly noticing the fact that they were now flying upside down while the dumpster's top hung open.

"Korplash: shuman scream like girl. Shuman scream like girl?"

"Shuman scream like girl, Xplak. Shuman scream like little girl?"

"Shuman scream like little girl. We bring shuman to

Gork?"

"We bring shuman to Gork. Xplak–"

Crater failed to hear the required response as his fingers lost the handhold. Twisting through air he plunged earthward, his throat screaming like girl–like little girl.

With a thud he landed on what felt like thick astroturf. Rolling, he groaned and sat up, one hand slowly crawling to his lower back to feel for breaks.

He froze.

He was inside the other craft. Surrounding him was a phalanx of two-legged dogs, snouts pulled back to reveal wicked-looking sets of teeth. They were not smiling. To his surprise he still wore the language translator device.

"Windinface," growled one, "how many times do I have to tell you not to leave the top hatch open? Look what the Croaks dragged in. What kind of a siridog are you?"

"I didn't leave it open, Bigtooth." A shallow whine followed, long furry tail wagging behind. "You–you're not mad at me, are you?" The whine turned into a whimper.

"Leave it open again and you'll see how mad I am." Bigtooth rolled up a magazine and slapped Windinface on his nose for emphasis.

"Arooo!" Windinface scuttled forward and threw himself on his back, his tongue lolling down his neck. "Don't scold me, Bigtooth! I'm your most loyal slave, I am."

"As long as you know that." Bigtooth lay a pretend bite on Windinface's neck. "Now get up. Here–" Bigtooth threw him a bone. "Munch on this."

"Oh thank you, thank you, grand poobah. I will treasure this bone forever. I will have it set in silver. I will have it set in gold. I will–"

Crater jumped.

A snout rose from his tail end.

"What are you doing?" Crater yelled.

"What are *you* doing?" The siridog threw his question back at him. "Turn around so we can find out who you are." The dog-thing stepped around him again and put his long snout-nose to Crater's rear.

"You could ask me!"

"You could lie!" Several more snouts joined the first. "Ass-prints don't lie!" Loud sniffs followed, and the stern expressions of Bigtooth and several other big dogs persuaded Crater to submit to the humiliating treatment. "Now turn around. Nothing gets past Noseupass."

"Crater," announced Noseupass. "First name Joseph." He sniffed. "Judge in mid-town Manhattan." Sniffed. "Married." Sniffed again. "Girlfriend Sally Ritz. Showgirl." Again. "Crater's friend William…dogging Crater's showgirl Sally when Crater not around."

Several siridogs barked. "Arooo!" called out two and panted loudly. "Dog her good, Billy! Arooo!"

Once more Noseupass sniffed. "Crater seeing another young woman. Short hair. With freckles. In a theater." He looked up at Crater. "Ruff! You sly dog, you!"

"You–you can tell all that from sniffing my hind end? That's pretty good."

"More." Noseupass and the others looked at Bigtooth. "Bog smell. Croaks were taking him to Bogland."

Bigtooth confronted Crater. "We heard a burp from inside our territory and came to investigate and to our surprise we find a human in the company of Croaks. Why were you going to Bogland?"

"Bogland? What the hell is that?" Crater felt his eyes growing heavy. He stamped a foot. "Wait just a minute! I've had no sleep for a day and a half. I don't know anything about any Bogland, or anything about Croaks, or anything about anything except that last night I was on my way to my apartment on Fifth Avenue when I was abducted, and every time I find my way back to 44th Street in Manhattan I get kidnapped again! All I want is to get back to my apartment so I can flop down in my own bed and sleep forever! Now where the hell are you taking me?"

"A planet around the star Sirius, of course. Where else would siridogs' 'running ground' be? It's only seven light-years away. Any other questions?"

"Yeah," said Crater, slumping with fatigue. "Where's the nearest hydrant? And when do I get a bone of my own?"

"We raise legs over there." He pointed. "And here's a bone." Bigtooth tossed him a bone that had scraps of meat on it. Hungrily Crater stripped it clean in seconds.

"I must be high status," he muttered to himself. Dragging his exhausted body to a small live tree in a pot, he peed, then collapsed onto the floor. Paws like fingers were laid on his arms and he was dragged to a blanket in the corner on top of astroturf. In another moment, his snoring filled the room.

With Crater's snoring in the background, the craft continued on course and, using their near-lightspeed drive, arrived at Sirius within a day. As Pinktongue pumped the tank with mid-grade anti-matter, Crater continued to sleep, oblivious. He missed the glorious running grounds where the siridogs used their break to launch themselves en pack at small furry animals, reverting to all fours for the chase. He missed the parade of triumph as Bigtooth rode in honor on a palanquin supported by his crew for his success in bringing home cow innards from Earth. He missed the illegal but inevitable gang fight that Bigtooth's crew engaged in behind the stadium after the parade in retaliation for their rival Fang nipping Bigtooth's information guru Noseupass, and trouncing Fang's pack, who were jealous of Bigtooth's success on Earth, but who would have initiated a gang fight in any event. And he missed Bigtooth's celebratory orgy after the gang fight, where Bigtooth dogged all the pack's females, followed by the rest of his crew, and Thumper got stuck in the female siridog Octotit and had to be separated by cold buckets of water.

Having refueled, and the cow innards entirely consumed at the post-orgy feast, Bigtooth and his crew piled back into their vehicle. In another day they had returned to Earth and were cruising Wyoming looking for more stray cows to give up their tasty organs, taking the usual steps to avoid the unidentified crawling objects that erupted from their primitive structures like ants to challenge them whenever the siridogs smelled udders and livers and descended to harvest them for brunch.

A kick awoke the Judge.

"Errr–Arooo!" Bigtooth could not help letting loose an energetic howl on occasion for the least cause. It worked. Crater blinked several times and sat up.

For a moment he was stunned. "Am I awake and dreaming? Or dreaming I'm awake?" He looked around and rubbed his eyes.

"On your paws, Croak-lover. You have no udders and even I can tell by your smell that your liver is poisoned by ginger soda. If you stay on board any longer I will have to charge you Credits. I don't suppose you have any Galactic Credits?" He glanced at Crater's straight thin legs. "No, I didn't think so. You stickwalkers never do."

Bigtooth looked at another siridog. "Droolonfloor, navigate us to the place they call Manhattan. I want to dump this freeloader. He's had free leglifting for three days of spacecraft time, which is seven years in stickwalker time. No more free leglifting for him."

"Seven years?" asked Crater, confusion on his face. "But how–?

Bigtooth paused. "I don't suppose you know anything about the slowing of time during space travel?"

"Space what?"

"I thought not." Bigtooth turned. "Lower the hatches, Droolonfloor. This stickwalker will understand what it means to travel near light speed soon enough."

"Arf arf, Bigtooth." Droolonfloor spun knobs and pulled cranks and in another few moments they were hovering over 44th Street.

Turning back to Crater, Bigtooth pointed through a glass pane set in the bottom of the craft where 44th Street was visible. Light motor and pedestrian traffic typical of late night in Manhattan meandered past.

Crater hesitated. "44th Street? Um…maybe a different street would be better. How much to take me to Fifth Avenue, or 40th Street? Or anywhere else at all?"

"No can do. We can't put you back in the same time, but we can put you back in the same place. From 44th Street you came, so it's to 44th Street you go. Those are the rules. Now grow a tail and stop whining."

The window in the bottom of the craft slid to one side and Thumper and Pinktongue extended a ladder into the opening and Crater was none too gently pushed onto its rungs. Before he could react, the ladder dropped like a stone and when he was three feet from the ground an electric shock forced him to relinquish his grip.

He fell.

Standing, he brushed himself off and looked up. The craft was gone. He looked around. He was back in the same alley beside the Belasco Theater, in the same spot where three evenings earlier he had been picked up by J. Edgar Hoover of the F.B.I., and, as before, dressed in a suit, though this time the jacket was grey instead of black, and fit a bit better, which he was thankful for, though it struck him as odd. He remembered Noseupass' comment about his friend William and grew serious. *Screw my showgirl girlfriend, will he? I'll show him! Just as soon as I get back to my apartment and get cleaned up. And I've got a hell of a jetlag.*

Proceeding cautiously down 44th, Crater paused at the intersection and peered carefully around the corner. Something looked different. He half expected strong-arm nuns or hulking wiseguys to spring out of the darkness, or priests and altar boys to snatch his clothes, but none appeared. Still, he could not relax. There was something about the traffic and look of the storefronts that failed to conform to memory. The Theater looked suddenly in need of an uplift and paint job. The advertising on the side of the building had vanished to be replaced by graffiti. Then he noticed the cars.

Although it was late, nearly midnight, the gas streetlights had in places been replaced by electric lights, and in their steady glow he glimpsed a series of unfamiliar automobile styles. There were still a few Model T's rumbling past, but they were now outnumbered by larger rounder styles with epaulettes that announced unfamiliar names like Packard and Plymouth. It was confusing.

He approached the curb and noticed that the bums were fewer than before, though a few lounged in corners seeking to grab some sleep under newspapers, as always. Something about one of the headlines caught his eye.

He stepped closer.

"Famous Pilot Amelia Earhart Missing…" blared the headline. He rubbed his neck. Didn't they mean Famous Pilot *'Charles Lindbergh'*? But last he heard, Lindbergh wasn't missing. He resumed reading: "… ships and Planes Search Pacific." Another headline shouted: “President Roosevelt Warns Reorganization of Courts.” His eyebrows rose. “President Roosevelt? What happened to President Hoover?” Remnants of another front page blew into his path. “Hitler Brags of Huge Army in New Speech.”

“*Hitler?!* What the hell is going on?” Crater looked closer. The date at the top of the newspaper said July 19, 1937. Crater staggered, then steadied himself on a lamp-post. “*Seven years?*” He looked at the reports on Earhart again and almost burst into tears. He stood up straight and scratched his head, which had not been washed since August of 1930. “Just how long did I sleep?”

A car pulled up beside him. Two large men with shoulders like medieval knights jumped out and surrounded him, glaring.

Episode 5

Crater threw up his arms as they stepped closer. “Alright. Who wants me next? Just do it and let’s get this over with.”

Like giants preparing to split a chicken, the two grabbed Crater and threw him into the back of a new sleek round Packard. Gunning like a racecar, they soon left 44th Street behind. Next thing Crater could tell he was crossing the 59th Street Bridge toward Queens.

The silence was deafening–and perplexing. “Uh…I hear they’re planning a new tunnel at 42nd Street.”

One of the giants thrust his blond crewcut head in his

face. He frowned in superior fashion. "Vat do ve care about your puny little Model T tunnels, little Amerikanisch…you mit your *Jean Harlow* unt your 'sving'," he sneered. "Ven ve Herrenvolk take over your veak little sister country, ve vill make ze pips squeak, ya!"

For another minute they rode in silence while Crater sat stunned, trying to understand his latest abduction.

The other giant spoke, almost if not quite as large as the first giant. "Heinz, you got to say 'sving moosic'. He don know vat you say ven you say 'sving'."

"Vat is wrong mit 'sving'?"

"You don say it correctly, Heinz. Your English is not ze good English, it is ze bad English."

Heinz looked put out. He frowned out the window. "I zink nozing is wrong mit 'sving', Herr Huntz. Every one of ze bodies knows vat 'sving' is saying."

Huntz turned to Crater. "Look at his face, Heinz! He don unnerstan you. Maybe if you move your body ven you say sving, he vill unnerstan."

Heinz frowned more deeply. "I do not move my body, Mein Kommandant. I am German. I don move *my* body. I move *his* body ven I kick him in ze *keepem-fromdroppin!* But because I am German I do not move *my* body. I am Herrenvolk, not some dancing arount vaving my arms in ze air like some Amerikanischer circus clown."

"Heinz, try svinging your body. It is not hard to do. See, vatch me."

Huntz bent over the steering wheel in a half-raised position and wiggled his hips while Heinz stared at him with an intently studious gaze. Through the window Crater watched a sign announcing Queens appear and be left behind.

"Ya, I zink you sving your body goot, Mein Herr. But don tell me to sving my body. I am German! I don sving!" Heinz set his jaw.

"Then it don mean a thing, Heinz."

"It don mean a thing if I don sving, Huntz?"

"Ya, Heinz! It don mean a thing if it ain't got that sving!"

"Ah!" Heinz nodded. He put his chin in his hand and thought deeply. "Zey no tell me zat in ze Spying on ze Amerikanischer School in Munchen."

"Unt vat did they teach you in ze Spying on ze Amerikanisher School, Heinz?"

Heinz stared up and out the window as Long Island suburbs sped by, heading east. "Zey teach me I must alvays land at Amagansett because nice guys in vite suits vill stop unt give me ze goot directions."

"Ya, vell, that is right, Heinz. They taught you vell ven they told you that."

Crater interrupted. "Is that where we're going? Amagansett? Where the hell is that, somewhere on Long Island?"

The larger giant turned and looked at Crater. "Ya. On ze little bitty, little sister finger of Long Island. Ve have much bigger beaches in Deutschland mit lots of beautiful svamp, unt, how you say…little sister stones."

" 'Gravel', Heinz," said Huntz.

"Ya. Lots of goot gravel on our goot superior beaches."

More suburbs raced by, including Hamptons by the dozen: Westhampton; Hampton Bays; Southampton; Bridgehampton; East Hampton; North Hampton; Nexttolasthampton; Youpassedithampton; and Whythehamptondon'tyougoback. Finally they arrived at a pristine sandy beach, the sun setting far to the west. Exiting the Packard, they walked to the beach.

A minuscule light flickered on the south horizon. Following the stares of Huntz and Heinz, Crater said. "What's that light out there?"

The smaller giant replied. "Nuting for you to vorry your little sister Amerikanischer head about," said Huntz. "Ve Germans operate on, how you say…*need to know* basis. Unt you don need to know nozing about our Unterseeboot out there vich is on ze secret Amerikanischer spy mission."

"You speak ze good English, Herr Huntz," said Heinz, rubbing his blond close-cropped fuzz, "Zat you do."

"Vell, you just listen to me, Heinz, unt I vill teach you ze good English too."

Heinz lit a cigarette.

For a long moment Huntz stared at him.

"Heinz…"

"Ya, Huntz."

"*Vat* are you doing?"

"Smoking ein excellent Amerikanischer cigarette, Huntz." Heinz thought a moment. "Ah." Heinz dropped it on the sand and stepped on it. Extracting another cigarette from his pocket, he lit it. "I mean to say, smoking ein excellent *German* cigarette, due to fact zose Amerikanischer cigarettes are no good little sister cigarettes that ve herrenvolk don smoke." He stood straight and smiled broadly.

"Not that, Heinz!"

Heinz looked at Huntz; then looked at his German cigarette. "Ah." He switched his fingers to hold it from the underside instead of between his fingers. Looking at Huntz, he smiled confidently.

Huntz slapped the cigarette from Heinz's hand. He yelled. "Heinz, did ze Spy School in Munchen say you light ze cigarette ven ve iz doing ze secret business at night on ze secret Amerikanischer beach?!"

Heinz rubbed his close-cropped hair again. "Ah!" With his foot he buried the German cigarette in the sand next to the American cigarette.

The light off-shore was closer and Huntz pulled a flashlight out of his pocket. He flashed it twice. Waited five seconds. Then flashed twice again. Nothing happened. Finally he flashed shave-and-a-haircut–two-bits. He got an instant response.

Huntz looked sadly at Heinz. "Ze Unterseebootmen vent to ze same spy school in Munchen as you, did zey not, Heinz?"

"Yavvol, Huntz! Das ist good, ya? Now ze Unterseeboot can pick us up unt take us to Panama." Heinz grinned and moved his hips in time with imagined tropical music, throwing his arms in the air as he turned. "Da da da…daa!"

Huntz yelled, his eyes bugging. "Heinz! How many times I got to tell you–keep your *keepemfromtalkin* shut!" Huntz looked back at Crater in alarm. "Now he knows every one of ze secret things!" He looked back to Heinz. "Unt don move your body like ze circus clown, because you are *German!*"

Heinz stopped dancing. He kicked at a sand dune morosely.

Huntz sighed and stared into the distance. He took a deep breath. "Heinz–you know you are ze stupid dumkopf."

"Ya, Mein Kommandant." Heinz pouted.

Huntz looked at him and stared upward. Finally he took a breath and patted him on the back. "But ve shall have bratwurst unt beer for every one of ze bodies ven ve get on board ze Unterseeboot."

Heinz straightened and brightened. "*Danke*, Mein Kommandant!"

As twilight turned into night, a motorboat approached, quietly riding the black-green waves.

"You… you're not really taking me to Panama, are you?" said Crater. "Why the hell Panama?"

Heinz turned and shouted at Crater. "Vat did I just tell you, veak little sister Americanisch! You don give ze orders to ze Master Race; ve Herrenvolk give ze orders to veak little sister Americanischers!"

"But Panama is American, not German! Are you crazy?"

"Ya! Heinz ist crazy! Unt Herr Huntz ist crazy too! Unt if you keep up mit your little sister crying act, Huntz vill fuck you in ze *keepemfromdroppin!* Zat is vat ve do to crying little Amerikanischers! Iz zat vat you vant, little crying in ze baby finger fist Amerikanischer?" Heinz rubbed his curled up fists in his eyes.

"Waaah! Waaah! You vant Huntz fuck you in ze keepemfromdroppin now?" Heinz's eyes bugged out as he shouted loud enough for the Coast Guard to hear.

Huntz looked shocked. He raised his hands and grabbed Heinz by the throat. "Heinz! I no fuck Amerikanishers in ze keepemfromdroppin! If any one of ze persons fuck Amerikanischers in ze keepemfromdroppin, it is *you* who fuck Amerikanischers in ze keepemfromdroppin, not Herr Kommandant Huntz who fuck Amerikanischers in ze keepemfromdroppin! Iz that unnerstoot, Heinz?!" Huntz turned red. Finally he relaxed and let go of Heinz's neck.

Heinz rubbed his Adam's apple. He glanced at Crater's backside and angled his head to one side. "Are you sure, Huntz? Don you zink he has a *nice* keepemfromdroppin?"

Huntz looked where Heinz pointed and calmly stared. "Ya. I agree. He has a nice keepemfromdroppin." Then he looked back to Heinz. "But I still no fuck Amerikanischers in ze backside, Heinz! You no move your body because you are German, and I no fuck ze Amerikanischers in ze backside because I too am German! *Iz that unnerstoot, Heinz?!*"

"Yavvol, Herr Kommandant..." He kicked the sand dune.

"Act? What act?"

Huntz looked back at Crater and smiled knowingly. "Don play ze stupid mit us, Herr Crater! Ya, ve know who is ze stupid ones–unt it is not us!"

"Ya, it is not us!" added Heinz.

"Ve know that your little sister J. Edgar Hoover put

you in charge of finding ze German spies in ze U.S. of A. Unt ve know that this is being your job now for seven years! Vat do you say to that, Herr Amerikanischer Spy?" He directed a look of triumph at Crater.

Crater looked dumbstruck. He muttered to himself: "July, 1937." He scratched his head. "Last time I saw Hoover he said he was appointing me his chief spy-catcher…"

"Ya, that is correct, Herr Spy! Ve are on to your little game. Now ze boot ist here. Unt now ve take you to our base in Panama. No more running about ze country on your little bent Amerikanischer legs grabbing ze German spies. Ve are here to tell you that you don do that no more! Ve ist putting ze end to that little sister game of yours!"

"You…you have a secret base in Panama?"

"Ya, zat ve do. Ve have ze secret base in Panama." The boat undulated in front of them. "Now, get in!"

Crater climbed into the small metal skiff, his hand-me-down dumpster shoes sucking up seawater like a sponge. Behind him Heinz bumped shoulders with Huntz, who glared at Heinz till he backed down and reluctantly allowed Kommandant Huntz to enter the skiff first.

The motor puttered and soon they crossed to the submarine, where Heinz and Huntz again bumped shoulders trying to exit the skiff at the same time until another stare from Huntz persuaded Heinz to retreat. Huntz stepped on board, and Crater followed. Several German sailors pulled the skiff onto the surface of the submarine and chained it upside down behind the tower. Huntz lunged and elbowed Heinz in the Adam's apple before Heinz could bolt first onto the conning tower ladder and left Heinz rubbing his windpipe. Hacking and coughing, Heinz followed closely on Huntz's heels.

After they entered the submarine, the sealing hatch slammed shut, sending reverberations shuddering through the vessel–and through Crater's soul. Not nuns, priests, gangs, jealous altar boys, or interplanetary spacecraft could bring him back now. He smiled in relief.

A very short thin man with an implacably clean blue blazer and white captain's cap sidled up to them as they stepped off the ladder inside the conning tower. A wispy short beard moved to and fro in opposite time with the gentle rocking of the submarine. He glanced surreptitiously left, then right, then glared up at Huntz and Heinz through half-closed eyes. Huntz took off his leather jacket and laid it down in the only empty space he could find. Two sailors wormed past the narrow gangway as the engines gathered steam for the trip to Panama, temporarily but totally obscuring the short man in the blue blazer.

Once they had passed, the short submarine captain looked at Crater and addressed Huntz in a high voice. "Yavvol, Herr Huntz. I see zat you have created yet another mess for me to clean up. Who is zis zat you have brought on board my Seaboot?"

A pair of giant shoulders pushed forward between the Captain and Huntz, jostling both. "It is ze little sister Amerikanisch who goes WAAH WAAH WAAH!"

Heinz screwed his fists into balls and rubbed his eyes.

Huntz slapped him. “Stop it, Heinz! Did I ask you to give ze report on our prisoner? No, I did not! Now, be quiet unt have some respect for Kapitan French.”

Heinz’s eyebrows crawled up his forehead as he stared down at the minuscule submarine commander with his ever-shifting eyes. His mouth opened and he stepped back. “Kapitan *French?*”

Quiet snickers sounded from obscure corners of the submarine.

Snapping his head around, Kapitan French stared fore and aft, his little white beard wiggling ferociously. He stepped toward his sailors and shouted in a high voice. “Who made zose sounds? I am varming you, I insist on knowing vich of you *schweinhunds* keeps mit ze making of zose sounds!”

None of the sailors responded but continued looking to their tasks.

“I am telling you, I vill get to ze bottom of zose bad sounds! Unt ven I find out who is ze making mit them, he vill not be happy!” Raised to soprano, his voice rebounded through the submarine. “Ya, he shall be valking all ze vay back to Deutschland! Unt he vill be very not happy zen!”

More snickering sounded.

Glaring again at his sailors, Kapitan French looked back to Huntz. His voice returned to its normal falsetto. “I am sorry, Kommandant Huntz, but as you can see zese dummkopfen of meinen are very unreliable. Ze sooner I get zeir tailenbetweenlegen back to Deutschland, ze better for ze everyone.”

Sniggers echoed.

Kapitan French sent stabbing glares fore and aft. The soprano voice returned. "But ze tailenbetweenlegen vill not save you from *ze svift kick in ze hind end ven ve get back to Germany, you schweinhunds!*"

French looked back, glared upward at the much taller Huntz, his beard twitching. "Vell, Herr Huntz, you can zee vat I have to put up mit here. But you can be certain," he waved a small finger, "that I am *up* to ze task."

Giggling rose from several directions, their sources immediately lost in the merging of echoes.

Kapitan French glared until the sounds finally stopped.

"Now vat have ve here…?" he stepped in front of Crater. Halting two inches from him, he stared upward into his face. For a moment, French made as if to light a cigarette, holding it from the underside, but then realized he had none and shook his hand open.

Huntz replied. "Kapitan French," Huntz suppressed a smile, "this is the Amerikanischer spy! Ve caught him mit the redden handen catching the goot German spies in the U.S. of A!"

A pair of giant shoulders pushed Huntz aside, almost knocking him down. "YA! Zis is ze little sister Amerikanisch who is doink ze catching of ze German spies, for zat little sister *Ya Egger Hooper of ze Fuck in ze Backside Institute!*" He curled his fists again. "*WAAH! WAAH!*"

Huntz shoved Heinz back to avoid Kapitan French being trampled by the Nordic giant.

"I zee…" Recovering his color, Kapitan French

stepped back to Crater. “Ein spy, eh?” He stepped even closer, his up-ended wispy beard tickling Crater’s breadbasket. “You know vat ve do mit ze bad spienen, bad Amerikanischer spy? Eh? You vant to know vat ve do mit ze Amerikanischer spy, you schweinhund?” Crater tried to step back but was blocked by Heinz’s enormous body. “Eh?” French’s voice rose ever higher. “You vant to know, you bad bad Amerikanischer? You really vant to know vat ve do to ze bad bad people just like you, ven ve catch zem doing ze bad bad zings zat ve really don like?”

“Wha…what?”’ Crater stared downward at the Kapitan as if at his toes.

French shrugged his shoulders. “Ve take zem to Panama.”

Crater let out his breath.

“Panama!” Heinz threw his hands in the air and danced as if he were on his way to Rio. “Da da da daa…da!”

“Stop it, Heinz!” Huntz slapped him.

Heinz stopped. Morosely he kicked at a bulkhead.

“Come, Herr Huntz, I vill show you your quarters.” He led the way aft, in exasperation thrusting his elbows into the hips of several sailors who did not see him, finally stopping at a metal door. Putting his ear to the door, he turned to look up at Crater. “Kindly be putting ze hands over ze ears, bad Amerikanisch, so you no hear ze secret code.” Heinz immediately intervened, pushing aside Huntz’s hands as he attempted to put them over Crater’s ears and substituting his own.

Kapitan French knocked on the metal door: shave-

and-a-haircut–two bits. More sniggering followed. French answered with another glare. “Zat is ze secret code zat is used everyvere. It is ze *goot* secret code unt not ze *bad* secret code.”

The door opened.

“You vill move to von side, Karl. You have company for ze rest of ze trip. But do not zink zat your punishment is over! You vill stay in solitary until you apologize for being so bad!”

A frown answered. Karl blew a curled paper party favor that buzzed in French’s face then withdrew into the darkness. Snatching at the party favor, but missing, French looked back to his guests like nothing happened.

“Zis vill be your quarters vere you vill do ze sleeping, Herr Huntz unt…Heinz, is it? Ze doing your business end business room iz at ze business end of ze boot. As for *my* sleeping quarters,” French pointed below to where another metal door lay on the floor. “If you need any-zing from me, my quarters are down here…*unter* ze bridge. It may not look like much, but believe me, I assure you zat vatever ze problem, I am still being *up* to ze task.” He rocked on his heels, tiny hands on hips.

Heinz squirmed, trying to conceal a grin. More giggles arose behind him. French’s eyes half-closed again as his accusatory glance shifted fore and aft and he jerked his neck around to look behind. Finding no one there, he darted his glance forward.

“Unt zere is nozing wrong mit ein Seeboot Kapitan sleeping under ze bridge of ze Seeboot!”

Barely suppressed snickers rose.

"I am telling you, sleeping under ze Seeboot bridge no make ze Seeboot Kapitan ze sleeping Troll unter ze Bridge!"

The snickers turned into chuckles.

He stamped a foot. "I am not ze Troll on zis Seeboot!!"

Laughter erupted.

"*Unter*-seeboot," said Heinz, suppressing a smile.

The Kapitan put his hands on his hips. "You call zis ze Unterseeboot. I call zis ze Seeboot. It iz all ze same."

"But, Kapitan. Ze Unterseeboot goes *unter* ze vater. Ein Seeboot goes on *top* of ze vater." Heinz rippled his hand by way of demonstration.

The Kapitan stared up at the towering Nordic giant and ground his jaw, his little beard twitching more than ever. He shouted. "If I say ze Seeboot goes *unter* ze vater, zen ze Seeboot goes *unter* ze vater! Unt I am ze Kapitan of ein Seeboot, not ein *Unter*-seeboot!"

Heinz's efforts to control his grin began to fail. "Yavvol, Herr 'seeboot *unter* ze See' Kapitan."

Giggling rose from the sailors.

"Zat is better, Heinz." Captain French calmed.

Heinz grinned. "Yavvol, Herr *Seeboot* Kapitan *French*."

From somewhere a raspberry sounded, echoing through the submarine. Several sailors let loose tears of laughter.

Eyes stabbing about him, Kapitan French thrust his arm out in a Nazi salute, almost reaching Heinz's chin. Heinz answered with a similar salute, forcing French to jump back to avoid being knocked over. Kapitan

French retreated behind Huntz and thrust his head out as if from around a tree trunk.

"Gooten day, Herren. Dinner is in ze mess hall at 0700 hours."

The time passed swiftly. At 0700 a bell rang and those sailors not already awake stumbled out of their bunks, dressed quickly, and entered the central mess area, which consisted of a single long metal frame table paralleled by two metal seating benches. One of the sailors wore a white apron, already soiled by hours preparing the special meal ordered by Captain French at the request of Kommandant Huntz.

As the guest of honor, Huntz sat first, in full Navy uniform, followed by several sailors as the cook rattled ladles in cauldrons, and their guest Crater took the seat across from Huntz. Captain French, in his spotless blue blazer, sat close to them at the head of the table in a special raised seat just for him. At Captain French's right hand and between French and Huntz was an open seat, which the sailors seemed reluctant to take.

A metal door clanged shut and Heinz entered the mess dressed in suspenders and lederhosen with a feathered cap. Before Huntz or the Captain could react, he occupied the narrow space between them like an invading army, jostling Huntz and almost knocking Captain French off his special seat. Utensils and cups scattered as Heinz spread his enormous arms over the width of the table. With a broad grin, he intermurled his fingers and popped his knuckles.

"Gooten morgen, Herr Huntz!" He glanced across the table at Crater. "Gooten morgen Little Amerikanisch

Sister." Then glanced to his left at the head of the table and looked downward with a big toothy smile. "Unt Gooten morgen, Seeboot Kapitan French!"

Snickers sounded from the sailors.

Heinz grabbed a knife and fork. Licking his lips, he looked at the cook and called, "Unt vere is die famous bratwurst unt beer zat Herr Huntz promised?" The sailors perked up when they heard this and several grabbed their own knives and forks, smiles spreading among them. None had been told of a special feast.

Huntz glanced ahead without smiling. He turned his glance to Heinz. "Why, it is almost ready, dear Heinz. Our Cook Fritz almost has it prepared…" Huntz looked toward the cook. "Our 'bratwurst' is almost ready, is it not, Herr Fritz?" He risked a squint of warning which was answered by the cook with a raised eyebrow.

"Ze links: zey are almost done." Fritz put his circled fingers to his lips and smacked loudly, grinning with satisfaction, then returned to stirring his pots, stewed pleasantness filling the room.

Heinz banged his knife and fork on the metal table. "Wunderbar! Unt vere ist ze beer?" he called.

Huntz motioned to Cook Fritz, who swiftly distributed large metal mugs to the sailors–and a special smaller mug with an engraving of a tugboat for Seeboot Kapitan French.

Dropping his utensils with a sound like Chinese nicknames, Heinz grabbed the first mug and eagerly held it out. Fritz filled it with pale liquid.

Heinz inspected the thin brew. He stopped smiling. "Herr Huntz." He looked in his mug. "Zis is not ze goot yellow German beer. Zis is ze bad pale beer from I don know vere." He looked at Huntz with a narrow expression, his brows contracted. Some of the sailors' faces displayed similar disappointment as their mugs were filled in turn by Fritz.

Captain French interrupted. "It is beink ze goot beer, Heinz," he said in his high voice.

Heinz leaned over the captain and frowned at him.

Captain French shrank back. "My goot incredibly *big* Heinz…" French squirmed, trying to get out from under the giant's shadow without falling off his special seat.

"I am sorry, dear Heinz," said Huntz, "but you know ve cannot get ze goot German beer in ze middle of ze sea, so ve got ze goot Amerikanischer beer instead."

Disappointment settled over Heinz like snow on an igloo. "Little sister *Amerikanischer* beer!"

"Ya, Heinz. After all, beer ist beer."

For a long moment, Heinz stared straight ahead with a blank expression, his hands in his lap. As a minute elapsed, the rest of the table looked at each other with growing discomfort.

"Heinz…Heinz?" Huntz brought his face close to Heinz's face and inspected him for signs of life. "Heinz, are you in there?" He passed his hand in front of his eyes. "Is any of ze bodies home?"

Heinz stood. Stepping away from the table he straightened, turned round and marched out of the mess room to his bunk. From the corridor came the sound of a metal door slamming shut, the echo reverberating sharply from one end of the submarine to the other, seeming to split every eardrum.

"Ach! He vill make ze drum of ze ear deaf for life!" Captain French squealed and put his hands over his ears as the metal door slammed again and again, the submarine shuddering from the impact.

Huntz shouted over the din, "Heinz! Come back! See, I have a little of ze very goot real German beer zat I vas keeping just for you, goot Heinz! But please no more making mit ze banging of ze metal door!"

The submarine grew quiet. In another moment Heinz emerged from the corridor, his enormous girth filling the narrow aperture. He displayed a hesitant face to the room.

"See, Heinz! Look at zis!" Huntz pushed forward a small bottle of beer that Captain French was holding in reserve, and who now glared at Huntz through his typically half-closed suspicious eyes.

A broad smile took hold of Heinz and he resumed his place between Captain French and Herr Huntz. Popping off the top of the small bottle effortlessly, Heinz drained the beer bottle in two gulps. He burped. Snatching up the metal mug that he had previously rejected, he drained it too, then banged the metal table with the metal mug.

Ein Pro-sit! Ein pro-sit!
Der Ge-mut-lich-keit!
Ein Pro-sit! Ein pro-sit!
Der Ge-mut-lich-keit!
Eins-Zvei-Drei-Drink!

The rest of the sailors joined in as Crater yelled at Huntz. "What is he singing, Herr Huntz?"

Huntz shrugged. "It is merely being ze goot German drinking song zat all of ze goot Germans alvays sing ven zey have ze goot German beer in zeir bodies." Huntz picked up his mug and swayed from side to side. "*A toast; a toast; to fun unt good times! One-Two-Three-Drink!*" He pushed Crater's beer-filled mug towards him.

"But, Mr. Huntz, I don't drink alcohol."

Heinz put his mug down. He stopped moving and frowned at Crater. Like sudden death, the singing stopped.

Crater leaned back. "That is–unless it is for toasting, and for fun and good times." Crater took a sip and quickly smiled.

Heinz grinned and returned to swaying. The mugs lifted.

Ein Pro-sit! Ein Pro-sit!
Der Ge-mut-lich-keit!
Ein Pro-sit! Ein Pro-sit!
Der Ge-mut-lich-keit!
Eins-Zvei-Drei-Drink!

Even ze Seeboot Kapitan French paused from his suspicious glaring at his sailors to drain his glass.

"Unt how is ze cooking of ze links coming along, Herr Fritz?" Huntz asked, looking cautiously at Crater.

"Zey are *reeady!*" Fritz picked up a large bowl and brought it to the table. At Huntz's direction, he placed the bowl in front of the Captain directly between Heinz and Crater.

Heinz drained his mug and slammed it down, picking up his knife and fork once more, then directed his gaze into the bowl. For a long moment he stared without moving, no change in expression visible, no sound emanating from within to give the others a notion of what might be transpiring in his huge Nordic head. The room gradually became silent. At length the others fidgeted uncomfortably again, worry crossing their faces.

"Uh, goot Heinz," inquired Huntz. "Is zere any of ze problems, by any chance? As you can zee, zese is pieces of ze good meat, ya?" He poked at the little pale lengths with a large trident fork. "Zis is goot for us, ya?"

Heinz stood. Stepping away from the table, he spun on a heel and marched off to his bunk.

Crang! Clang!

Again the metal submarine door banged shut over and over, sending the submarine into what Huntz believed must be a tailspin, the vessel lurching from one side to the other, while the sailors grabbed plates and containers to prevent them sliding onto the floor, and others grabbing their seats to avoid slipping off–Captain French unfortunately missing his hold and catapulting to the floor, where his impeccably clean blazer emerged somewhat less pristine.

As he regained his own seat and his composure, Huntz called out. "Heinz! My dear Heinz! Please, you must understand zat zis is ze very best zat ve can do! Please come back unt join us at ze goot merry table for our fun unt good times!"

The banging stopped.

When no one appeared at the door, Huntz called, "I'm sorry ve have no more of ze goot German beer, unt ve have no goot German bratwurst to give you, unt I am very sorry for zat. But ve still vant you here mit us, my very goot boy Heinz!" Huntz looked at Captain French with a mixture of alarm and hopeful relief.

Captain French was glaring at his sailors as if the whole situation was merely another trap lying in wait to besmirch his dignity, which he was determined to avoid.

Finally a face appeared cautiously at the door. Heinz looked up at the ceiling. Standing straight he said quietly, "You promised bratwurst."

Huntz stood and walked cautiously but quickly over to Heinz. "Ya, I know zat, my dear Heinz, I know zat I promised you bratwurst."

"You promised bratwurst."

"I know zat I promised you bratwurst, but after all ve are in ze middle of ze sea."

"You promised bratwurst." The ceiling continued to absorb his expressionless gaze.

"Please Heinz, vat ve got ve got just for you, our very special Heinz, our very goot boy Heinz, who ist being our very best, very goot German boy Heinz!"

Heinz angled his head on his neck. "You promised bratwurst…" A giant leg kicked the side of the door.

"Look! Look here, goot Heinz! Look vat ze goot Kapitan French has for you!" He looked at Captain French who was helping himself to the contents of the bowl while glaring alternately at the sailors and his plate as if the sailors were not above poisoning him.

Heinz stopped kicking the door. He took a breath. "You promised bratwurst." Heinz's voice rose as he glanced at the bowl with a sneer. "Zose…are Amerikanischer *hot dogs*."

"Ya, my goot Heinz. Zey are Amerikanischer hot dogs. Kapitan French got zem special for you on account of ve cannot be getting ze goot German bratwurst on account of ve ist being ze goot German spies spying for ze Fatherland, unt ve are not here at sea in Amerika for ze buying of ze German bratwurst."

Huntz took Heinz by one giant arm. "Now please to join us, my goot boy Heinz, because ve is not being able to make goot mit ze fun unt good times mitout our goot boy Heinz!"

Heinz allowed Huntz to bring him back and return him to his seat at the table next to Captain French.

"Unt now please be ze goot boy unt eat some of ze nice Amerikanisher hot dogs." Huntz looked quickly at Crater and repeated his earlier apprehensive look at Fritz the cook.

Eager to avert another threat to the seaworthiness of the vessel, Judge Crater selected two hot dog links for his own plate and took a bite. "Mmmm! Now that's what I call a good American hot dog!"

Heinz took a look then stared straight ahead. "Zese are *not* ze goot German bratwurst. Zese are only ze plain Amerikanisher hot dogs."

"Ya, Heinz. But zey are still ze goot hot dogs. See? Our guest, Herr Crater, likes to eat zem!"

"Mmmm! Darn tootin good, too!" Crater wolfed down two more. "They're especially good with good American ketchup, like this nice bottle of Hunts Ketchup! Watch me!" He reached for a bottle of ketchup, one of several bottles of American condiments that Fritz had placed on the table for the occasion, but before he could get the bottle, Captain French grabbed it. Within seconds, he had turned it upside down and, to Huntz's dismay, emptied all of its ketchup on his own hot dogs.

Heinz looked blankly at Captain French, then stared straight ahead. "I cannot eat zese hot dogs. Zere is no more ketchup." He moved one leg as if preparing to stand.

Looking at Crater with alarm, Huntz grabbed another red bottle. "Look, Heinz! Zis one is ze ketchup too! Zis is ze goot Amerikanischer ketchup zat all of ze bodies like on ze goot Amerikanischer hot dogs! Try it!"

Heinz glanced at the bottle, then stared up at the ceiling. "*Zat* is ze wrong bottle."

"Wrong bottle? But look, goot Heinz. It says right on ze bottle: 'Heinz Ketchup.' Zat is goot, ya? Zis is your very own bottle of ketchup mit your very own name on ze bottle!" He pointed to the label.

"I don vant *Heinz* Ketchup. I vant *Huntz* Ketchup." He spoke quietly, angling his neck.

"But, my dear Heinz, Kapitan French ate all of ze Hunts Ketchup. All ve have left is Heinz Ketchup."

"I don *vant* Heinz Ketchup. I vant *Huntz* Ketchup."

Huntz looked at Crater in exasperation. "Heinz, be reasonable. Ve don have no more of ze Hunts Ketchup.

Ve only have ze goot Heinz Ketchup. Ketchup ist ketchup. Zese ketchups ist all ze same goot ketchups unt zere is no more difference between zese two goot Amerikanischer ketchups so please make mit ze eating of ze goot Amerikanischer *Heinz* Ketchup!"

Heinz blinked. "I don vant Heinz Ketchup. I vant Huntz Ketchup," he said calmly as if reading a weather report.

Everyone at the table ceased eating while waiting for a resolution to the impasse. Even Captain French paused in his downing of hot dogs to stare suspiciously at Heinz and Huntz as if it were only a screen for another conspiracy directed at him.

"Look," said Crater, "as an American I happen to know that the factory that produces ketchup makes exactly the same ketchup for both the Heinz Ketchup Company and the Hunts Ketchup Company." He removed the tops from both ketchup bottles. "Let's just pour some Heinz ketchup from the Heinz ketchup bottle into the Hunts ketchup bottle, then we will have some good Hunts ketchup and everybody will be happy and we can sing *Ein Prosit!*"

Heinz looked at him blankly.

Taking the Heinz bottle, Crater carefully poured half of the ketchup into the Hunts bottle while Heinz watched. He replaced the cap and carefully pushed it across the table toward Heinz with a smile.

"Look Heinz! Ve now have ze goot Amerikanischer Heinz Ketchup in ze goot Amerikanischer *Hunts* bottle just for you, my dear Heinz! Das ist goot, ya? Now ve can finish our goot Amerikanischer hot dogs unt sing our goot German drinking song vile ve eat ze goot hot dogs, ya?"

Heinz's stare returned to the ceiling. "Zis is *not* Hunts Ketchup in ze bottle. Zis is Heinz Ketchup in ein Hunts bottle. Unt I don vant to eat ze hot dogs mit Heinz Ketchup." He rippled his lips while he stared.

Kommandant Huntz tore at his hair. "Heinz! Ze ketchup iz all ze same!"

"It is *not* ze same. I vant ketchup from Herr Huntz–not from Heinz."

Huntz looked at Kapitan French. "Look, Heinz. Ve also have some goot Amerikanischer mustard. Zat is how ze Amerikanishers like to eat ze hot dogs. Vould you like to try some of zis goot Amerikanischer mustard on your Amerikanisher hot dog?"

Huntz held up the yellow bottle for Heinz to look at.

Heinz read the label. He rippled his lips again and looked back to the ceiling. "*Zat* is Kapitan French's mustard. I don vant Kapitan French's mustard."

Crater looked at the yellow bottle: it read 'French's Mustard.'

"But Heinz, zat is not Kapitan French's mustard! Zat is ze name of ze company zat makes ze mustard, unt it is not Kapitan French!"

"I don vant French's Mustard. I don vant Heinz's Ketchup. I vant Huntz's Ketchup."

"Be reasonable, Heinz! Ve don have vat ve don have!"

"You promised bratwurst unt beer. Zere is no bratwurst but only plain Amerikanischer hot dogs. I vant Hunts Ketchup on my hot dogs. I cannot eat ze

Amerikanischer hot dogs mitout I have Amerikanischer Hunts Ketchup."

"Vell, vat do you expect us to do, Heinz? Turn ze boot around unt go back to Amerika to buy some Hunts Ketchup so you can eat your Amerikanischer hot dogs?"

He thought. "Zat might vork."

Huntz pulled more hair out in exasperation.

Captain French frowned. He spoke up. "You don vant French's Mustard?"

"I don vant French's Mustard."

"Unt vat is wrong mit French's Mustard?"

"Nozing is being wrong mit ze French's Mustard. I just don vant French's Mustard."

"Are you saying zat you don vant nozing from Kapitan French?" Captain French fumed, his face growing red.

"I vant Herr Hunts' ketchup. I don vant Heinz Ketchup. Unt I don vant Kapitan French's mustard."

"I zink zat is not a goot zing unt I zink you should not be saying such a bad bad zing on ze Seeboot of Kapitan French! If I say you are eating ze French's Mustard, zen you are eating ze French's Mustard!" Captain French removed his special seat support and stood on top of his bare seat so that his face was even with Heinz's face. His voice rose from falsetto to soprano. Several sailors grinned.

Huntz looked at him in alarm. "Maybe if ve can find another goot bottle of ze goot German beer, zen Heinz can finish his hot dogs…"

"Kapitan French no gives his goot German beer to

just any of ze bodies zat you drag onto his Seeboot!" He stamped his foot and thrust the bottle of mustard at Heinz. "You vill eat ze French's Mustard or you vill be doing ze valking back to Deutschland, unt zen you shall be very sorry!"

The giant voice yelled out, "Nein! I don vant French's Mustard! I don vant ze hot dogs mit French's Mustard!"

Kapitan French grabbed Heinz's nose in one small hand and popped the top off the mustard bottle with the other. "You vill eat ze French's Mustard because I am ze Kapitan of ze Seeboot unt not ze Troll unter ze Bridge unt if ze Kapitan gives ze orders to ze German spies unt ze German sailors, zen zey vill obey ze Kapitan!" Jumping to the table top, Captain French upended the bottle and splattered mustard on Heinz's hot dogs. Grabbing one hot dog drenched in yellow, he aimed it at Heinz's mouth.

"*MUTTER!!*" Leaping up, Heinz grabbed Captain French in one ham-like hand and twirled around, the Captain simultaneously clinging to the hot dog and to Heinz's enormous neck.

"Eat ze hot dog, you schweinhund! How dare you refuse your Kapitan's mustard!"

"I don vant French's Mustard! I don vant ze hot dog!"

"You vill eat it!!"

"Herr Huntz, help me! Ze Kapitan French–he ist ze *spleenig kopf!*"

"Put him down, Heinz!"

"He hurting me ist, Herr Huntz! Ze *nutty head* ist hurting my nose!"

"You must put him down, Heinz!"

Spinning round, Heinz put both hands around Captain French and leaned over the Captain's seat. Prying his small hands off his neck, Heinz spun and sent the Seeboot Kapitan French sliding the length of the table, his tiny beard picking up ketchup and mustard from one end of the table to the other, where he landed on the floor with a thump. No blue could any longer be seen on his blazer through the layers of red and yellow.

The sailors rolled on the floor, devastated with happiness.

Heinz shouted, tears streaming down his cheeks. "NEIN! NEIN! You can't make me eat ze hot dogs! I don vant ze mustard! I don vant ze ketchup!" He lumbered out of the mess room and back to his room where the metal door resumed its banging.

Red lights flashed and a siren blared.

Episode 6

"Ze Seeboot!" yelled Captain French through layers of French's Mustard. "Heinz vill send ze Seeboot to Davy Jones' bottom!"

Water sprang from the sides, inundating the floor and quickly rising to knee-level. The metal door continued to slam, shaking the submarine from end to end.

Somewhere in the watery depths below, a seated short man in white uniform with black trim, looked up in alarm from his close examination of an undersea map and stared cross-eyed through thick round glasses at another short man in blue blazer and white cap. The seated man removed his earphones.

"Kyaputen Girusu! Disu sailoreru hearing strangeru noiseru in wadaru above us!"

"Ah so… Sailoreru Benjirou, you have idearu of causu of disu strangeru noiseru?"

"No, Kyaputen! Soundingru ryike earthshakeru, endu disu sailoreru hearingu phrasu 'nutty head' from some-one crying 'waah waah!' "

Captain Girusu of the Emperor of Japan's Imperial Navy contracted his brows and thought. "Handu me-u the mikruphonu." He listened to the microphone, a look of puzzlement settling over him. Finally he nodded. He handed the microphone back to his crewman. "Disu iz Amerikanhito trick! Continue-u our cours-u to Panama-ru."

"Kashikomarimashita!"

"Sailoreru Benjirou–"

Sailor Benjirou saluted, smiling broadly under his crossed spectacled eyes.

"You study Engrish in Imperial schooluru, ryike-ru me-u. Pleaseru to sayeru only 'Yes sir.' "

Benjirou bowed deeply from his seat. "Kashikomari-mashita!"

The Captain frowned.

"Kashikomarima–"

"Psst!"

"Kashikomari–"

The Captain's hand raised.

"Kashiko–"

"Don-yu sayeroo it!"

Benjirou opened his mouth…

"Don…" The frown deepened.

"Kashi–"

Deeper.

Benjirou stopped smiling. "Yes sir," he muttered.

"That iz bedderu." The Captain looked away.

"*Kashikomarimashita*," Benjirou whispered into his palm.

Another crash radiated from the microphone so even the sailors around them could hear. The Captain looked up in alarm. "What the hellerou iz happening above the Emperor's sacred-u submarine-u?"

Before he could react a great weight landed on top of the Japanese submarine, shaking it from end to end, tossing its submarine crew to the floor. As if entwined by spooky action at a distance, the Imperial Navy Captain emerged with mustard on his blue blazer. "Ah? Who is eateringu wasabi? Just rook at the Emperor's sacredu blazeru!"

Beneath the unexpected weight, the submarine continued to sink, then, seemingly at the last moment, stabilized. Attempting to raise the view scope but failing, the Captain again frowned.

"Disu Captainu no understendo what iz on top of the Emperor's sacredu submarineru. This Captainu will rook againeru." This time he managed to raise the view -scope. His eyes grew big.

"We aru vely rucky that we aru in the Emperor's sacredu hugeru giganteru submarinu, because it rook rike rittle submarineu on top of disu submarineru iz triyingu to pottu its johnsonu in disu submarineu."

He looked through the view-scope. “We cannot ret the Emperor’s bigu sacredu submarineu get screyuwudu by horny rittle submarineu. We are close to Panamaru. So we musto go to Panamaru as fasteru as the Emperor’s propelleru can takeru us. Sailoreru Benjirou…put-u the pedal-u to the metal-u.”

As one, Benjirou and the sailors saluted and rushed to obey. Chugging slowly, the submarine gradually picked up speed and soon arrived at a brace of jetties.

“Benjirou: ryaiseru the Flag.”

“Kashikomarima–“

The Captain glared and Benjirou stopped himsef.

“Yes, sir,” Benjirou muttered.

Another sailor, who also wore his Imperial standard issue thick round coke-bottle glasses with pride, raised the Flag pole, which, to the Captain’s relief, successfully bypassed the little submarine that was resting on their big submarine. He was confident his Flag was plainly visible to the guardians of the harbor.

Onshore, in the light of a clear blue day, two men in U.S. Army uniforms stumbled out of a guardhouse at the end of the jetty outside the port of Colon, Panama, and stared as a monster rose from the deep.

“Tennessee,” drawled the first.

“Yeah, Kansas?” drawled the second.

“What did you say was in that bottle last night?”

“Forty proof Panamanian Tequila, Kansas.”

“Did the label say anything about seeing double-decker submarines after you drink the stuff?”

“Nary a whisper, Kansas.”

“Did I say to charge the booze?”

"After the second bottle, partner."

"Tennessee, next time I say charge the booze–do me a favor and kick my ass! If I know anything atall, I know there ain't no London double-decker bus service in the waters off Panama!" Kansas cranked the emergency phone.

"Wait, Kansas!" Tennessee put a hand on the other guard's arm. "Lookit at what flag that double-decker bus is flyin!"

They both stared hard. Kansas reached into the guard hut and brought out binoculars. He adjusted them.

"Well I'll be fubared!"

"Me makes two, Kansas. Damn if that ain't no lost London bus–that there's one of those new Panamanian national registries! Lots of ships are doin it."

Kansas whistled. "How do ya like that? Panama has its own submarines!"

"Nobody tells us a *god damn* thing around here... Well, let her in."

Kansas spoke into the phone. "Stand down HQ. It must be one of them new double-decker Panamanian water buses."

Inside the Japanese Emperor's sacred submarine, activity reached a crescendo as the sailors prepared to dock. "Ryaiseru the Emperor's sacredu submarineu!" shouted the Captain. "Kashikomarimashitzu!" yelled the sailors all together as water poured off the vessel, exposing the piggybacked German submarine stuck behind the conning tower.

The Captain looked in triumph through the viewscope. "Steadyeru as she goes! Straight aheadu iz Coco

Soro!"

"Coco Soro!" echoed the crew happily. "Los Bolos," yelled some, smiles breaking out. Several danced little jigs till the Captain peered their way.

"Loweru the ladderu! It iz time for this Kyaputen of the Emperor's sacredu boatu to see what the helleru is going on outside." He clambered up the ladder. Popping the hatch, he emerged on the deck and with a single glance verified that the submarine was indeed on track to berthing in Coco Solo, the chief American submarine facility in Colon, Panama.

He turned.

"Hand it to your Kapitan, you schweinhund! Zat is an order!"

Twenty feet behind the Japanese conning tower rose a second conning tower, on top of which two figures argued, the first figure towering over the other. The latter was dressed in a yellow and red stained jacket and was attempting to wrestle a coat from the taller one, who resisted fiercely.

"You are ze Kapitan of zis boat, Herr French! But not ze Kapitan of my jacket!"

"If Kapitan French vants your jacket, Herr Huntz, zen you vill hand over your jacket–like it or not!"

"NOT!"

French succeeded in pulling the jacket off Huntz, and Huntz raised it ready to throw it in the ocean rather than relinquish it–both stumbled as the Japanese submarine halted in its berth with a shudder. They stared about them.

"Vere are ve, Kapitan French?"

French looked at Huntz. "Panama!" With a sucker punch to the giblets French sent Huntz stumbling from the tower into the harbor, while he kept Huntz's jacket in a weasel-like grip. With a majestic sweep French sent his own tiny yellow stained blazer flying after Huntz and proceeded to don Huntz's jacket. Enraged to find it ten sizes too big, he tossed it too overboard.

"Iz disu how you sayeru Herro to your friends?"

Looking down from the German submarine's conning tower, Captain French was shocked to see the Japanese Captain Girusu on the conning ladder, removing the tiny yellow-stained jacket and Huntz's bulky German officer's jacket from his head and shoulders.

"Kapitan *Greasy*... So ve is mit ze meeting once again...." Captain French squinted downward at the climbing ladder with suspicion.

"Ah so, Kyupaten *Fukyunchu*. So our sacredu duties have brought us-ichee togetheru again... I am, how you say... over-joyudu." He stopped smiling.

"Velcome, Kapitan Greasy, to our superior German secret base in ze beautiful Panama..."

"Ah yeseru. Welcomichee, Kyupaten Fukyunchu, to the *Emperor's* secretu sacredu basu in the *Emperor's* beautiful Panama..."

Both glowered at each other.

"Los Bolos?" ventured Captain Girusu.

"Ya! Ve shall zee who iz ze most secret!"

"Los Bolos," cried the German sailors pouring out of the conning tower, followed by cries of "Ros Boros!" from the Japanese sailors who poured from their own.

They collected on the wharf and quickly exchanged

military uniforms for loose-fitting brightly-colored cotton shirts and tan shorts with rope belts. Only Heinz held back, helping Kommandant Huntz from the water, and refusing to change out of his lederhosen and suspenders.

"Please to give me ze dry clothes, Heinz!"

No answer. After assisting Huntz to the wharf, Heinz looked away and thrust his hands in his pockets.

Sighting a spare set of tropical clothes under Captain French's arm, Huntz snatched it. For one moment, French wrestled, then lost the struggle as Huntz was too far from the edge of the dock and too big to risk another sucker punch.

"Wha do you think of disu smalleru submarineu," said Captain Girusu to his crew with a smile, "could it be possiberu that its Kyaputenu no can find girrfriendu so he tryeru to stick its johnson-ichee in the Emperor's sacredu boatu?"

A dozen bespectacled cross-eyed crewmen broke out in laughter. They were delighted to find a German shorter than they and Captain French fit the bill. To French's annoyance, each of the Japanese was taller than him by at least half a foot.

Captain French squinted, popping his knuckles like walnuts.

"Heinz…" said Huntz.

The Nordic giant looked up, pouting.

"Ve are in ze beautiful Panama… Don you vant to relax unt have ze fun unt ze good times?"

Heinz's lower lip stuck out.

Huntz grinned and raised his arms above his head and

turned about. "Da da da daaa!"

Closing his eyes, Heinz said quietly, "I don vant Panama."

"Oh, but you do, my goot boy Heinz. Don forget Los Bolos!"

Heinz opened his eyes. He thought in silence.

"Unt *Mrs. Climax…*"

Heinz cracked the beginning of a smile.

"Unt you may have ze first turn…."

The smile became a grin.

Captain Girusu stopped adjusting his flowery shirt and stepped close. "Ah *no*…youseru had the firstu turnu last time-ichee we visit disu secretu basu! Dis-u time-ichee Kyaputen Girusu go firsturu!"

"Nein! Nein!" exploded a deep voice, the force of Heinz's voice sending the Japanese scurrying. "No fair ist! You vas first last time!"

When they calmed, Judge Crater spoke, having finally learned how to tie his rope belt. "Gentlemen, gentlemen! Why not take turns?"

Heinz looked shocked. "Our superior German strength iz being ze goot reason for vy ve don take turns," he said, his nose raised. "Ve don take turns like sorry little sister Amerikanischers. Unt ve don do ze circus clown moving about of ze hineys. Unt ve don fuck ze Amerikanischers in ze backside! Ya, Kommandant Huntz?"

Captain Girusu looked at them strangely.

Huntz looked uncomfortable. "Uh, ya Heinz…back to Los Bolos."

A German sailor yelled and pointed. "Ze Amerikanischer *stop-em-quick* ist coming!"

"Now iz ze making mit ze secret code!" screeched Captain French.

Crater cringed.

"Yavvol, Kapitan!" The German sailors saluted.

"Hai! Noweru is time-ichee for speekuru *Emperor's* secretu codu!"

"Hai, Kyaputen!" answered the Japanese.

Heinz leaned over Judge Crater and put one giant Nordic arm on his shoulder while he frowned–not one word from the little sister Americanischer.

Two brown-uniformed American soldiers with pistols on their hips strolled down the dock, puzzlement writ large on their faces. They approached the double-stacked submarines and halted. They looked at the Japanese dressed in tropical shirts, the sun glinting off multiple sets of spectacles and crossed eyes. Glancing at the discarded white uniforms with black trim lying on the ground, they looked at the Germans in their identical colorful shirts and tan pants. They took in the rope belts, the conning towers, the Japanese language insignia next to a big picture of a red rising sun on the side of the larger submarine, and they stared at the huge black German cross painted on the side of the smaller vessel.

"Who *are* you?" asked one.

The other stood at attention with a hand on his pistol.

Captain Girusu stepped forward and bowed deeply. "Ah so, Amerikanhito. Please accept my humbre aporogies." He glanced slyly at Huntz and French. "Nosotros soromente ros hombres de disu wonderfur pais de Panama! Nosotros comeru homu after long long tripu flying ouru beautifulu Panamaru flagu!" He pointed to the Panamanian flag waving over the submarines.

The two soldiers looked at the flag. The second glanced at the Germans.

Captain French stepped forward. "Ya!" came the high voice. "Ve vant to completely assure you, you beink ze goot Amerikanischer soldaten, zat ve ist only ze goot Panamanian sailors home from ze long long voyage flying ze goot Panamanian flag." He thought a moment. "Nosotros solamente los hombres de esto grand pais de Panama!" He too bowed.

One of the American sailors scratched his head. They exchanged glances. The other shrugged. "Must be that new double-decker Panamanian water bus I've been hearin about."

Captain Greasy and Captain French exchanged looks. "Ya! Dat ist us!" "Hai! We-uru are-yu new-ichee Panama-ru wada-ru bus-u!"

"Come on, Joe, let's get back to the card game. There's nothin to see here."

After they left, the submarine sailors–with broad grins–collected themselves and rushed to several waiting taxis. Throwing wads of yen and deutschmarks at the taxi drivers, they hit the road.

"Fort-eru Gulick-u!" yelled Captain Greasy. The Japanese sailors piled into two cabs and took off, well ahead of the Germans.

"Beink so nice as to follow ze hind end of zat taxi to Fort Gulick!" called Huntz, Heinz squeezing behind him, while the rest of the Germans filled two more cabs. Captain French tried to enter the cab beside Huntz, but Heinz stiff-armed him with a grin into the dirt till the cab sped away. At the last moment, French managed to dive through the back window of another cab just before it accelerated.

Heinz grinned at Huntz. "Da da da…daa!" Heinz moved his hips in time with imagined music. "LOS BOLOS!" he shouted in his deep voice, Huntz cramming a finger into his offended ear to protect his eardrum.

At the end of a long straight boulevard the cabs came to a set of gates where more brown-uniformed armed Americans sat in another guard shack.

One leaned out of the shack and peered carefully. "Vessel?"

Captain Greasy blurted "The sacredu Emperor's…I mean the sacred Panamaru doubleru deckeru wadaaru busu." He flashed a decal of a Panamanian flag that he had pinned to his tropical shirt.

"Destination?"

Herr Huntz said "Uh…ve are goink for to enjoy *ze fun unt ze goot times*." He looked around and glimpsed Captain French's face glowering from the back of the last vehicle crammed between two German sailors, his mouth jabbering silently behind the glass. "Unt ve are definitely not beink ze German unt Japanese spies. But ve are beink ze goot Panamanian citizens who are very much liking ze Amerikanischer soldaten!"

"Oh." The American nodded. "Well, have a good time!" The gate opened and he waved them through.

Crossing town, the cabs entered the main road to the south. In another fifteen minutes they arrived at another gate with yet more American guards. The train of cabs pulled up.

"Destination?"

"Fun-eru and-o good-u time-ichee!"

Another flash of the Panamanian decal and the gate lifted. Soon they arrived at a nondescript gravel parking lot.

The sailors piled out.

Before them was an inexpensive but well-maintained recreational facility with large signs across the front. One read "Los Bolos." Another proclaimed "Reserved for Panamanians." Below the signs were two giant white bowling pins flanking wide entry steps covered with green outdoor carpet.

"Meyuru firstu!" yelled Captain Greasy and raced up the steps.

"Not beink so fast, Herr Greasy!" called Captain French racing on his little legs to catch up. He ran into one of Heinz's well-placed tree-trunk legs and fell back stunned.

"Nein!" called a deep voice. "Heinz no vant grease!"

At the doors, Captain Girusu knocked shave and a haircut–two bits. And he was in. Then the sailors crammed through the single door, leaving Heinz and Huntz behind brushing dust from their faces. Heinz and Huntz tried to enter together and got stuck until Heinz sucker punched Huntz in the giblets, laying him low. As Huntz limped in, his giblets suffering inordinately, he slammed the door behind him, catching Captain

French in the face. Judge Crater caught him on the flip-slide.

"Bout time, boys. Long time *yo no veo*."

Episode 7

The sailors lined up in front of the hostess of Los Bolos, Crater's gaze, as he brought up the rear, settling on a small short woman of girth so wondrously round that she resembled the bowling balls lined up waiting for the first customers of the day.

"Who's gonna get the first ride, eh boys?" She wiggled her balloon hips and winked. Huntz glanced at the empty bowling palace, where a phalanx of pins and bowling balls stood at the ready.

"Meyuru firstu!" yelled Captain Greasy, snatching a pair of small rolling shoes dispensed by a waitress in red hair and purple dress from behind a counter.

Heinz was close behind, Huntz too distracted wondering about the cost of a gibletectomy to intervene.

"My freends, my freends. Oh it is so nice to be among my good freends again!" Mrs. Climax swayed from side to side as a wide grin spread across her chinless face. "How haf you boys been?"

Captain French sidled up, more than happy to finally encounter someone shorter than himself. He batted his eyelashes at her. "Mein beautiful beautiful butterball." He sighed. "Can ze fats be so cruel as to separate us again?"

Heinz sniggered. "*Fates*, Kapitan French. Not fats."

"Fates to you–fats to me!" The Captain's most severe glare had no effect on Heinz who continued to smirk.

Captain Greasy elbowed his way to Mrs. Climax's other side like a spacecraft seeking a landing on the moon. "Stayeru with meyuru, my sweederu rovry barr of beaudy! This humbre servanturu of the sacredu Emperoru will do-ichee anythingeru to make-ichee his rovry, uh…Mrs Climaxa, happyuru!" He too batted his eyes at her, the three–Mrs Climax, Captain French, and Captain Girusu–radiating more colorful smiles and batting more eyelashes than a migration of butterflies.

Girusu frowned. "You don need anythingeru from disu Kapitan *Fukyunchu!*"

"Bite ze big von, Greasy!"

"Boys! Boys! There is no need to fight over leetle mee!" She smiled like Mae West when the fleet came home. "Beleeve me, there is pleenty of me to go round!"

Captains Fukyunchu and Greasy nodded eagerly at what was truly a wondrous consolidation of feminine curves.

Growing dissatisfied, Heinz stepped forward. Both French and Girusu suddenly howled in pain and grabbed their toes as Heinz grinned down at Mrs. Climax as from a mountain peak.

"Oh, and here is my good boy Heinz," she smiled up at him seductively, the moon orbiting towards the giant pillar like the Hindenburg seeking the Empire State Building.

"Ya…ya! I am your goot boy Heinz." He paused to wipe a tear from his eye and drool from his chin. "I vill vin zis time–I know it, mein Frau! Just vatch me sving…" He glanced at Huntz guiltily. "I mean 'bowl'."

"And you bowl a meen one, I know, my dear boy Heinz." Reaching up on her tiptoes she touched his elbow, then she shook her ample hips and waved her arms as the two troops of sailors collected around two bowling lanes, the Bowling Palace empty of traffic except for the Panamanian Double-Decker crew, the red-headed woman behind the counter, and a young Panamanian man polishing bowling balls. At a signal, the waitress in red hair wobbled on high heels. She locked the doors and pulled the shades, while the young Panamanian man took up a position at the far end of the lanes next to several sets of gleaming white bowling pins.

"You must pay the *keety* first, boys! Before you can pet it!" She smiled, exuding the pleasure of one used to pleasing lonely sailors.

Eagerly the men threw piles of yen and deutschmarks into a big straw Panamanian hat on a table in front of the lanes. They formed two semi-circles around Mrs Climax.

"Are the doors locked, geentlemen?"

Twenty faces nodded.

"And the shades pulled down?"

Smiles responded Yes.

"Did everybody pay the *keety?*"

Everyone showed empty pockets by pulling white pocket cloths inside-out. Someone pointed. "Kyaputen Fukyunchu must pay too!" yelled sailoreru Benjirou, focusing crossed-eyes through his thick glasses.

"Nein!" screeched Captain French and stepped back. Before he could flee, Heinz and Huntz grabbed him and shook him upside down till all the change spilled out of his pockets. They let him go. "Nein! Zis is ze bad bad thing! You no can be doink zis to your Kapitan!"

Too late. It disappeared into the *keety*.

Mrs. Climax stroked Captain French on one cheek and he calmed and began to chuckle. "Of course, ve iz beink ze goot boys if it pleaz ze Mrs. Climax!" He squirmed and grinned.

"Are we all ready then, boys?"

"Yavvol!"…"Hai!"…"Yep and howdy!"

Everyone looked with surprise at Judge Crater, who had been quite forgotten, but was beside himself with curiosity.

Climax smiled her best Mae West smile. "Gather round, boys… And get ready to bowl." Taking her blouse in both little hands, she pulled it up and off, tossing it aside. Then she removed her spandex tights and threw it on top of the blouse, leaving her curvaceous form entirely nude. She folded her arms over her breasts. Sitting cross-legged on the floor, she pulled in her tiny legs so they lay flat with her derriere. Finally she rolled over to present her bottom, bare as a baby on a backslider. Crater did a double-take, barely able to distinguish her from the bowling balls lined up beside her, except for size.

"My good leetle boy Heinz goes first!"

Insane cackles escaped the Nordic giant's throat, and,

to the dismay of Captain Greasy and Kapitan Fukyunchu, he extended thumb and finger to grasp Mrs. Climax via two orifices barely detectable in her orb of flesh, which promptly grasped Heinz's digits with such surprising tenacity that he lifted her globular form upside-down from the floor.

The crewmen parted as Heinz carried Climax to the bowling lane. With a step-step-swoosh, he let loose his cargo sending the fleshy sphere spinning down the lane.

"Ay caramba pendejo besa mi culo!"

The sphere edged left.

"Tu madre es una puta!"

The sphere edged right.

"Coge los jotos y maricones!"

With a dull crash Mrs Climax sent the bowling pins flying–a strike!

"Hurrah!…Banzai!" The crewmen jumped for joy. "Los Bolos!…Ros boros!" They hugged each other, for the moment entirely forgetting their treasured ethnic feud.

The young Panamanian attendant sped back with Mrs. Climax in a wheelbarrow and rolled her out. Briefly she stood and brushed herself off. She smiled, none the worse.

"Me-uru next!" grinned Captain Greasy.

"Yeah, boys," Mae West grinned. "My leetle Asian freend goes next." Rolling over, she presented her behind to Captain Girusu, and he quickly clutched her, thumb and middle finger finding their grip.

"Banzai!" yelled the Japanese crew, brandishing

paper cups filled with punch and sake.

Exhibiting a little more difficulty than Heinz, not having his vast oversupply of strength, Captain Girusu approached and let loose down the second lane.

"Quiero ver el menu, por favor!"

The ball curved left, then right.

"Tu hermano no tiene la ingle!"

Spinning like a demented top, the sphere entered the gutter, then bounced back into the lane. Smashing into the pins, several in the middle fell leaving one standing at either end–a split.

The wheelbarrow returned. She brushed herself off.

"Oh, my cute leetle Capitan Greasy…"

"Girusu…"

"Girusy…Greasuru…" She smiled and pinched his cheek. "Don't worry, my leetle cutey, whatever your name. You may have a second chance." Again she rolled into herself and presented her bottom.

Step-step-swoosh. Captain Girusu paused, leg crossed behind, as the ball of flesh spun, aiming directly at one of the still standing pins.

"Coge el joto hijo de puta!"

Everyone held their breath.

"Yo cago en la leche!"

With a thump, she knocked over one of the two pins and stopped spinning. As they watched, a tiny arm quietly extended and, reaching across the lane, knocked over the other pin.

"Banzai!" yelled the Japanese. "Kyaputen Girusu! Mrs. Climaxeru!" Punch and sake splashed over Captain French who glowered at his rival's success.

When she returned, Mrs. Climax sidled up to French and rubbed her naked roundness against him, evoking simpering chuckles. "Don look so triste, my leetle Capitan. You know that your leetle butterball likes you just as much as los otros!"

Captain French grinned, hands in pockets.

"You may go neext."

While the crew were distracted by Captain French's attempts to bowl, which were even more feeble than Captain Girusu's, requiring the assistance of Huntz and another crewman, Heinz with his ever-present smirk teetered overhead.

Judge Crater held back.

"Pssst!"

Crater looked around.

"Pssst! Over here!"

To his left behind the counter stood the red-headed woman stumbling uncertainly on her high-heels.

Crater whispered back. "What do you want?" He looked back at Mrs. Climax, about to propel down the lane. "I don't bowl. And I don't think I want to start!"

"Who gives a crap about bowling?" hissed the woman in a surprisingly low voice under a roar of approval from the crewmen as Mrs. Climax crashed into the pins. "It's you I want!"

Crater stepped back and looked about in alarm. "You can't mean me. I don't do *that* either!"

"Not that, you idiot! Look at me, Judge! Don't you recognize me?"

He stared hard. Crater's eyes grew big. "Director J. Edgar Hoover! Of the Federal Bureau of Investigation!"

"Yeah," the woman whispered. "It's me! I've been undercover here in Panama for months." Hoover adjusted his purple dress and red wig. "Where the hell have you been, Crater? You walked out of my office seven years ago and disappeared. Your country needs you. The U.S. is crawling with German agents and you're the guy supposed to be catching them!"

More roars of approval as the ball of flesh spun.

"It's a long story, Director. I just got back to New York when Herr King Kong over there grabbed me." Crater glanced at Heinz. "Hey! You've got to get me out of here! I need to get back to the States!"

"You and me both, Judge." Hoover leaned closer. "Listen. There's something in the works. You–" The bowling palace suddenly grew quiet as the game ended, and Hoover returned to cleaning the counter, whistling Dixie.

Mrs. Climax stepped near. "Now, boys, it is time for you to get your leetle reward…"

The crew grinned and exchanged glances and gathered around their *beaudiful budderball*. Captain French and Heinz fumbled with their belts.

A whistle blew. The crew turned round and saw Captain Greasy speaking on a walkie-talkie. "Hai!" He listened. "Hai!" Another pause. He resumed speaking into the device. "We are-yu waiting-eru here at the Emperor's secredu basu now. Permission-uru to land is granted."

At the entrance to Fort Gulick several US soldiers hunched over a radar screen and scratched their heads as an enormous blip approached. "Must be that spare parts plane that General Drone told us to expect today. There's nothin to see here. Let's get back to our card game."

Within a minute a roar penetrated the Recreation Center from outside and above. Mrs. Climax threw on her clothes and rushed to unlock the doors. French and Heinz groaned with disappointment.

Moments later, a bomber aircraft with a giant red sun blazoned on its side glided in to land beside the Los Bolos Recreation Center and taxied toward the front door. A side door in the bomber popped open and a dozen Japanese soldiers jumped out, fully armed, followed by a half-dozen young Anglo men in black formal slacks, shiny dress shoes, short-sleeved white shirts, with narrow ties and short haircuts. Descending the portable stairs that Greasy's sailors pushed to the aircraft, the white-shirts fell in behind their leader, another white-shirt with a rosy chubby face. They walked arrogantly, glaring about them with hidebound books under their arms, the Japanese forming two parallel lines as if on parade, rifles at the ready.

Two more Japanese soldiers exited the plane, half-dragging, half-carrying a silent slender figure down the steps. The figure was dressed in a brown pilot's jacket, grey jodhpurs, and goggles, hands tied behind with a white cloth wrapped around the eyes.

"Hurry! You movuru now, Amerikanhito spy! You can no escape from disu secretu sacredu Japanese basu!" The Japanese rushed their captive across the dirt lot and into the Recreation Center where Mrs. Climax re-locked the doors and pulled down the shades.

"Can it be possibre," yelled Captain Greasy, "that you don unnerstanderu that you have offended the majestico dignity of the sacredu Emperoru?" At a signal from him, the Japanese crewmen seized the captive, who was escorted past the Germans and Judge Crater to the back of the Recreation Center and ushered into a small room. Moments later Judge Crater–finally remembered–was also pushed into the room. The door shut behind them and a lock slammed in place.

Outraged at his sudden change in treatment, Crater banged on the door. "Hey! I never got lunch! Don't you know your goddam Geneva Conventions? Articles 1, 2, 3 and… and I forgot the rest?" He banged. "And I never got my turn to bowl…"

A feminine voice sounded. "If we're alone, how about getting this damn rag off my head. And see if there's some way to cut these ropes from my wrists."

Crater's face puckered. He knew that voice. He turned, stepped forward… It couldn't be! Not here–not now! He snatched the rag away.

Music swelled in time with the welling of tears of joy in Crater's eyes.

"Amelia!"

She sucked a breath, shock on her face. "My Joseph!" Tears burst, the wet drops glistening on her freckled face. "What are you doing here, my love? I gave you up for dead years ago! I waited inside the Belasco Theater all evening. And half the night. Even after they closed the doors, I stayed there waiting for you until they finished mopping and finally turned out the lights.

When I came out, the street was empty."

"Oh, my love! I never meant to leave you, but… things happened. I've been away for a long, long time through no fault of my own–seven years in 'stick-walker' time, to be exact." He stepped back. "Then I saw the newspaper reports…they said you died at sea! Planes and ships looked for you for days, weeks even, and finally they all gave up." He gently brushed back her dark hair and planted a kiss on her full lips. "Oh my love. I'll never leave you again, I promise."

"Oh, Joseph, my dear! When you never came back I lost interest in life. I got married briefly because I didn't know what else to do, then I decided to lose myself by flying around the world. I trained for years, then I finally set out. And I almost made it–except I was asked to take some photos over some Japanese islands, and they shot me down and took me prisoner. Now they say I'm a spy!" She cried while Crater cut at her bonds with a metal shiv.

"Asked by who?"

"Some guy in a purple dress with red earrings. Do you know him?"

"Uh…maybe."

Just as Crater succeeded in removing Amelia's bonds, the door flung open. Two Japanese guards thrust coke-bottle eyes into the room. "You two get out! Weyuru must discuss what weyuru shall do with you Amerikan-hito spies!"

Several folding tables had been set up between the bowling lanes and the front doors and the half-dozen young men in white short-sleeves sat behind the tables in folding wooden chairs while the Japanese soldiers collected on either side in two lines, rifles blocking escape. Captain Greasy stood behind the crew-cutted white-sleeves as if waiting for instructions. Captain French rubber-necked from behind their seated figures, trying to peek over their shoulders. Heinz and Huntz stood guard at the windows and the rest of the Germans surrounded Mrs. Climax with admiring stares, or quietly ordered drinks from the surprisingly clumsy and deep-voiced waitress.

'You standuru heryu! No slouching lika you some lazyru kitty cat!" The Japanese soldier shook his rifle in their faces as if about to engage in calisthenics. "Now you two Amerikanhito spies bow down and showeru respecturu to disu honorable Leaderusu!" He kicked at Crater and he and Amelia hastily bent over in deference to the honorable 'white-sleeves.'

"Say herro to Most Honorable *Gary*."

One of them, the one with the chubbiest face–though all seemed young and thin compared to most in the room–took out a toothpick and probed between his teeth, his gaze directed up at the ceiling. He made no move as Crater and Amelia finished kow-towing and stood straight.

After a full minute of silence, Gary finally spoke, while staring at the ceiling. "They tell me you two have been *very naughty*." His voice seemed to have barely reached puberty.

Crater looked harder at Gary's rosy baby face. "Why…you're just a kid!"

Gary frowned. Taking out his toothpick, he pointed

it at Crater and Amelia. "If I were in your position, I don't think I would be in such a rush to insult people, *Judge Crater!*" Gary snapped his fingers and the Rec Center's male attendant approached with a drink menu. Gary pointed to an item and handed the menu back to the attendant.

"I.D.?" asked the Panamanian.

Gary fumbled in his wallet for his ID and handed it over. The attendant shook his head and handed it back. The other white-sleeves went for their wallets, but the attendant shook his head at each in turn.

"Don't worry. I've got it." Crater flashed his ID and the attendant rushed to get Gary's drink.

Gary cleared his throat and re-shifted in his seat.

"Now as I was saying," he said in his adolescent voice, "you and Miss Earhart here have been very very naughty. Our missionary work has been much inconvenienced by your spying."

Captain French interrupted, "Yavvol! You are making great trouble for our goot friends, ze Morons!"

"Hai!" added Captain Greasy, "you no make-uru no more trouble for the honorable Morons!"

The white-sleeves looked upset. "That's Mor-mons, you morons!" yelled Gary.

"Ya, Herr Crater! That's Morons, you moroni!"

"You mean our *angel* Moroni–" said Gary.

"Ya, zat beink zeir lovely Moronic angel!"

Captain Greasy pointed at the captives. "Hai! Don let us catch you-ru again insulting our Moron friends endo their Moronic angel, you Amerikanhito spies!"

Gary stared briefly at the ceiling. He cut the comments short with a curt wave of his baby-flesh hand. He stared at Crater and Amelia. The Germans and Japanese grew silent.

"I think you don't quite understand who you're dealing with." Standing up, Gary slid the chair back from the table. He strutted a few steps, flexing a thin adolescent arm as if there were biceps to show off. He walked slowly and calmly. "Take this Fort Gulick, for instance. Things can happen, you know. What if your American soldiers were to wake up one morning and find that all their *guns* were missing. Or their buildings had disappeared. Or their planes and tanks. How do you think they would *feel?*" He picked his teeth nonchalantly.

Crater looked at Amelia and shrugged.

"You think that's funny, Mr. Crater?" Gary rocked on his heels. "It's amazing what people can do these days in the middle of the night...with a few *bicycles!*" He stared hard as his harsh threat slowly sank in.

Again Crater shrugged. Amelia stared ahead blankly.

"Oh, that doesn't bother you either, I see, Miss Earhart. Then how about this?" Gary pushed the table aside and stepped closer to Crater, the other white-sleeves also rising from their seats. "Present Bibles!" As if on cue, the young short-sleeved missionaries presented their Holy Books. "Open to Verse *You-Know-Which...*" They followed suit, several with worried looks on their faces.

Gary stood in front of Crater and began to read in his high nasally voice. "Wherefore it came to pass that I, Nephi, did take my family, and also Zoram and his family, and Sam, my elder brother and his family, and

Jacob and Joseph my younger brethren, and also my sisters, and all who would go with me… ”

“No, no, no! I can’t take it! No more, I beg you!”

“Ah-ha!” Gary held up his Holy Book triumphantly, snapping it shut. He sidled closer to Crater and breathed on the side of his face, whispering in his ear. “Do you really want to see us going door to door in your wonderful U.S. of A…”

“No!”

“Opening up our Books…”

“No!”

“Sitting down next to innocent unsuspecting home-owners…”

“You can’t!”

“And telling them about Joseph Smith’s brass plates that no one has ever seen…”

“You wouldn’t!”

“And the Lost Tribes of Israel crossing the Atlantic in shallow rafts and turning into Red Indians…”

“No, no, you can’t be so cruel!”

“Yes,” hissed Gary, “Yes, I would! And so would the rest of us–if you don’t do as we say!”

The other Mormon missionaries lounged menacingly, hands in pockets, toothpicks in teeth, unsmiling, unsympathetic, their Latter-Day Bibles clutched like so many lethal weapons. The Japanese and Germans stepped back in horror, unable to comprehend such inhumanity.

“Or maybe your little lady here would like a taste!”

“No! Not her!”

Gary stepped in front of Amelia. He glared and

opened his book. The nasally voice resumed. "Now the Zoramites had gathered themselves together in a land which they called Antionum, which was east of the land of Zarahemla, which lay nearly bordering on the seashore, which was south of the land of Jershon, which also bordered upon the wilderness south…"

"Enough!" she cried. "Damn your soul!" Burying her face in her hands, she burst into tears. "I'm sorry, Joseph," she murmured, "I'm not strong. I can't take the boredom."

"You monster!" yelled Crater, only Japanese bayonets stopping him from tearing Gary to pieces.

"Oh, yes…I am a monster." Gary smiled. "Now you know what we are capable of. And you know as well as I do that you and your little lady here are both going to cooperate with us as much as you are able." He opened his Book. "Or *else*…"

"No more! No more, I beg you. I'll cooperate. I'll do what you want. Just don't read any more."

The Rec Center phone rang. Kyaputen Girusu picked it up.

"Secret sacredu Japanese bas-u speaking… Ah soo!… Hai, yessir-uru… I unnerstand-eru… Nossir-uru, the bad spies will not escapichee from Japanese soldieruru who love-uru sacrificing themselves for their sacredu Emperor… Hai!… No!… I unnerstand-uru… Hai!"

He gave the phone to Captain French.

"Achtung!" All the German sailors leapt to attention. "Yavvol, mein Kommandant!" French clicked his heels listening to the telephone. "No, mein Kommandant!

Herr Crater vill not be escapink from zis secret *German* base in Panama!" He cast a reproachful sidelong glance at Captain Greasy. "Unt neither vill Frau Earhart!... Vat iz zat?... Are you beink sure of zis, mein Kommandant?..." The voice at the other end blared like a horn through the phone. "Yavvol! Nein, mein Kommandant, I vill not beink questioning of your orders!... Of course I am beink ze goot German Kapitan, unt I shall obey... Yavvol!"

Captain French handed the phone to Gary.

"Oh, yessir!... No, of course I would not do anything without your instructions..." He looked at Crater and Earhart. "Are you sure, sir?" The phone blared. "As you say, sir... If you say so, sir.... Yessir, I understand they are a threat to our plans.... Yessir, he is in charge of hunting German agents... Yessir, she is in charge of photographing Japanese islands... But maybe you should check first with Adolf..." The blaring increased. "Oh, you did... And what about Benito. And Emperor Hirohito?" Even louder. "Oh you did that too... You even went over *their* heads?... But *He* would not answer?... Well, I guess there's nothing more we can do, then, sir... Right, then that's what you've decided... Okay, so that's that, then... Yessir... Okay... No, sir, it's not yet time for the Germans and Japanese to occupy the U.S... You're right, sir, we will invite them in later... I agree, sir... We must bide our time till Adolf and Benny and Hirohito give us the go-ahead. Right, sir.... Very good, sir... Okay, then. Goodbye, Uncle Franklin. See you at the Lodge. And please give my regards to Aunt Lucy and Aunt Eleanor. And no, I didn't forget Aunt Daisy."

Gary hung up the phone. Turning his back to the two captives, he stared at the ceiling as if he wished to forget what he had just heard, forget this life, forget his duty. The toothpick penetrated the ivory jungle once more. Then fractured. In annoyance he tossed it aside.

"Orangello! Lemongello!"

"Yes sir!" replied two white-sleeve assistants.

"Please escort our guests to the front porch. And into the yard."

The white-sleeves exchanged worried glances. They hesitated.

"Gary, isn't there anything…?" Orangello blinked.

"No! There is nothing we can do!" Gary slapped the side of his leg with his Latter-Day Book. He looked at the Japanese surrounding him, rifles at the ready, and hoarsely whispered, "Sometimes, gentlemen, duty weighs more than a mountain." The Japanese exchanged hard knowing glances. "We have our orders."

Captain French looked at Huntz, then Girusu. Girusu looked to sailor Benjirou.

"March, you lazy-ru Amerikanhito spies!" The soldiers pushed Judge Crater and Amelia Earhart forward toward the doors of the Recreation Center, crowding them to eliminate any possibility of escape despite the lack of bonds on their wrists. The others began to shuffle in their wake, some reluctantly, others brimming with schadenfreude.

The phone rang again.

"Hai ! Disu iz secret *Japanese* sacredu basu…" Captain Girusu smirked a gotcha-back at Captain French, whose tiny beard twitched in anger. "Hai. You have the correctu numberu. What-o iz zat-uru? You say I should look out of the window-ru?"

The others glanced at the windows flanking the front doors, while the ever-helpful Mrs. Climax raised the shades. Seeing nothing, the Germans and Japanese looked at each other in confusion.

"*FREEZE GOOFBALLS!*"

Everyone turned to the counter where the squat red-haired waitress in the purple dress stood, brandishing a pistol. The waitress tore her wig off and tossed it away. "Don't nobody move! This is the FBI! You're all under arrest!"

A loud voice boomed on everyone's eardrums, "Ya Egger Hooper of ze Fuck in ze Backside Institute! Nein! I don vant ze Fuck in ze Backside Institute!"

Huntz slapped him. "Stop it, Heinz!"

The windows burst. With a crash, booted legs clumped to the floor sending shards flying, arms clinging to swing-ropes. FBI-issue pistols fired warning shots in the air which had the peculiar effect of stripping away a portion of the Los Bolos roof, leaving a large section without a ceiling and the sun shining through. Through this section dropped two uniformed U.S. army soldiers who dropped into the midst of the bowling lanes, strangely unimpeded by swing-ropes.

Not waiting to see what the U.S. soldiers might do, or what odd personal interests that agents of a Fuck in the Backside Institute may have, being led as they were by a man in a purple dress and red wig, the Japanese opened up with their rifles at the FBI agents. A line of

German sailors promptly fell, leveled by the Japanese bullets. Captain French pulled his service revolver and emptied it at Captain Greasy, dispatching two Mormons to their heavenly reward.

Hoover clutched Mrs Climax, grabbed her between her legs and shouted over the gunfire: "Turn your head and cough!" She struggled to break free, but was unable to escape his grip. Hoover yelled triumphantly, "Aha!" He turned to the FBI agents, more of whom were piling in through the windows, "This 'woman' has two vaginas–and a *penis!*"

As one, the Japanese, Captain Greasy, and the Germans including Huntz and Heinz reeled back in shock.

Batting her eyes at Hoover, Mrs. Climax squeaked, "Yees, now you know my leetle seecret, my freends. I knew you would not accept me if I revealed myself *fully* to you."

"Datu no iz possibiru! Our butterball Mrs. Crimax with the two vaginas is…how you say… *all woman!* She no can have penis!"

"I zink ze Amerikanisher hot dogs are comink back," groaned Heinz and dropped to his knees.

"I'm mit chou," cried Huntz, jamming a finger down his throat.

Strange guttural sounds came from one of the American soldiers. "It is the *tibbet* we are looking for. Is this the tibbet we are looking for?"

The other U.S. soldier replied, "The Round One is the tibbet we are looking for. Is this a tibbet making trouble for ribbets?"

"The Round One is a tibbet making trouble for ribbets. Shall we take tibbet to Bogland?"

"We shall take tibbet to Bogland. Shall we take purple dress to Bogland?"

A deep rumble sounded and the soldier put his hand to his lips to suppress it. "We shall take purple dress to Bogland. Is purple dress another one making trouble for ribbets?"

"Purple dress is another one making trouble for ribbets. Should we–"

"Wait just a minute!" yelled Hoover, finally releasing Mrs. Climax. He thrust a finger at the two strange U.S. soldiers. "Just who the hell *are* you? And what the hell are you talking about? This 'Round One'–I mean this *woman-man*–is under the jurisdiction of the F.B.I!"

The first brown-uniformed American soldier pointed a shiny device at Hoover and the Director stopped speaking or moving as if frozen. "Korplash prefers purple dress be seen, not heard."

Korplash aimed his freeze gun at Mrs Climax. Like a turtle withdrawing into its shell, Mrs. Climax reverted to bowling ball.

The deep rumble returned, echoing through the Rec Center. The first soldier looked blankly at the second soldier. "Korplash make rumble. Korplash croak?"

"Korplash no croak. Xplak ears okay?" Quick as thunder and just as loud, Korplash croaked. Everyone in Los Bolos involuntarily covered their ears at the crashing reverberations while the pair of U.S. soldiers stood and stared at each other in silence. Their eyes grew big.

"Korplash croak," said Xplak matter-of-factly.

Through the hole in the ceiling a pie-shaped craft appeared, ripping the remainder of the roof away, dog heads thrusting out of a series of open portals. "Arf, arf! Woof, woof, woof!" Pink tongues lolling, the craft hovered over the lanes. "Get em, Windinface! Those Croaks won't get away from us this time! Woof, ruff, ruff, arooo!"

Crater recognized Bigtooth's grin, showing off every one of his canines.

Hoover came back to life and again grabbed Mrs. Climax, whose limbs reappeared. "Oh, my leetle freend! You no tell me you like me that way…" Looking at Crater, Hoover shouted, "Crater, help me!" He struggled as Mrs. Climax's stubby legs locked around his midriff. "Help!" His gaze flicked back and forth. "Dickless Joe!"

Crater grabbed Amelia, wondering how the hell Hoover knew that nickname. "Come on, Amelia, let's get the hell out of here!"

The two American soldiers had vanished–in their place squatted two bulbous toads with expressionless faces. "Korplash croak," repeated Xplak. "U.S. Army disguise gone?"

"U.S. Army disguise gone. Siridogs remove ribbet disguise?"

"Siridogs remove ribbet disguise. We take tibbet and purple dress to Bogland?"

"We take tibbet and purple dress to Bogland…*urk*."

While Heinz stacked Fuck in the Backside Institute agents on the ground like logs, sitting on them to prevent their escape, and Captain Fukyunchu hid under one of the tables jabbering fierce instructions in soprano that no one could hear, and Huntz marched and sieg-heiled as the Japanese soldiers sent volleys into German and Japanese sailors, and the Mormon missionaries rubbed baby finger fists in their eyes crying waah, waah, waah, the Croaks bounced in prodigious efforts to evade the siridogs as their piecraft oscillated in pursuit. Korplash aimed his freeze gun in the middle of a leap. The next leap took him into a blue dumpster that had suddenly appeared. Xplak joined him, followed by two figures who floated in supine and helpless under the influence of the freeze gun, and, without further ado, the blue dumpster launched into the stratosphere where white stars and black night enveloped them.

Episode 8

Xplak spun dials and pulled levers while his ample suctioned feet clung to the sides of the interior of the blue dumpster protecting him from gyrations as they evaded Bigtooth's gang. He pulled a switch and instantly the apertures around the exterior of the dumpster sealed shut. Korplash, similarly glued to one side of the dumpster's interior, opened a small cupboard. Inside were a language translation device, standard equipment on all dumpsters of this make and model, and a device consisting of concentric light-emitting bands like flexible neon bulbs. He attached the neon device to his forehead. A bright flash of white light and the dumpster reappeared in the depths of space far from any sun, the stars assuming the forms of unrecognizable constellations. Korplash flicked the switch and the constellations changed again. A third flick and they appeared by a planet of smeared grey and olive-green, a dense atmosphere hiding most of the surface.

A webbed foot pressed hard on a lever set in the floor and the dumpster slowed its descent. Xplak tripped the side switch. Pungent emanations filled the cabin as the dumpster came to rest.

"Tibbets look for good time, but find bad time. Did tibbets find bad time?"

"Tibbets find bad time. Tibbets cause trouble for ribbets?"

"Tibbets cause trouble for ribbets, blow cover, call siridogs. What ribbets do with tibbets?"

"Ribbets like purple dress. Korplash like purple dress?"

"Korplash like purple dress. Xplak like one called Mrs. Climax?"

"Xplak want see tibbet called Mrs. Climax…"

Xplak reached over to where the two figures lay in the back of the dumpster covered by a thick tarpaulin and who were now beginning to stir. A wide webbed hand reached forth and pulled the tarp aside.

Korplash and Xplak dropped their jaws. They exchanged silent bug-eyed stares.

Judge Crater sat up and rubbed his eyes and looked about. "So that's what happened to my shirt." He touched a cloth beside him.

Amelia Earhart sat up next to him. "Where are we,

Joseph? Who turned the lights out?"

He exhaled. "Better get a grip, Amelia… You know that little world tour you wanted to take? Well, you just did one better."

The ribbets popped the top off the dumpster. They all stood. Amelia and Crater stared at each other, then around.

"Eat your heart out, Lindbergh." Amelia saw a landscape of islands shaggy with green overgrowth–islands entirely surrounded by water. Except for a network of narrow bridges that connected them. Crater stared, puzzled. The bridges seemed impossibly narrow for the bulky toads. Korplash and Xplak cleared the sides of the dumpster with a single hop and stood on all fours beside it. With some difficulty, Crater managed to crawl over and helped Amelia join him. With a start, he noticed what looked like multiple bug-eyes observing him from the water, only to sink beneath the surface when he turned to look.

The island on which they had landed was barely wide enough to accommodate the four of them and the dumpster, most of its space taken by the moorings of two bridges, one spanning a stretch of water to connect with the next island, the other arching in the opposite direction where it fed into a network of more islands with more bridges, all underlay by an expanse of fetid marsh-laden water.

No one had to tell Crater where he was.

Bogland.

Korplash and Xplak shoved the dumpster onto the bridge mooring and to Crater's surprise it promptly floated in air. He noticed a steel beam that looked like a pipe set in the bridge and with a quiet look brought it to the attention of Amelia.

For a moment, Xplak stood looking from Crater to Amelia then at the dumpster. At them. At the dumpster. Finally they got the message and climbed back inside. At the last moment Crater grabbed two translation devices. Xplak and Korplash threw themselves into the water and with a sudden jerk the dumpster followed them seemingly of its own volition, Xplak and Korplash propelling themselves through the green-encrusted water and the dumpster floating after them to slide frictionlessly on bridge after bridge till they arrived at a wide low dark hexagonal building streaked with algae on a much larger island, itself overgrown with algae and ringed by trees whose roots seemed reluctant to remain below the water line. A lowering sky sent sheets of rain into their faces, Xplak and Korplash eagerly pausing to upend their faces and take the rain into their gullets.

The dumpster banged to a halt beside the low building in a queue of similar dumpsters, like grocery carts in a parking lot. From the distance loud reverberations echoed sounding very much like the loud burps Korplash had released on Earth, and, for a moment, Crater gazed overhead, half-expecting Bigtooth to re-appear. But no siridogs arrived.

The toads' kung-fu was better than that of the siridogs, Crater decided, and their planet too far away to be bothered by them. He sighed. Placing an arm around Amelia, Crater gave her a big sloppy kiss.

"Oh, Joe!" She melted into his arms. "I never realized how much I missed you." She looked into his eyes. "Please never leave me again."

He hugged her close. "I won't, my dear. I promise." He placed the translation devices on his head and Amelia's. "Here. I have a feeling we'll need these."

Twin doors pulled away from each other disappearing into their respective walls to reveal a wide low aperture, steam and gurgling emanating from inside and obscuring their view.

Low rumbles purred in the background and as they walked cautiously through the doorway, with Xplak and Korplash waddling in front, Crater thought he glimpsed other toads slipping away just out of sight, piled one atop another. Inside the building a large mist-covered pool rippled before them. The mist seemed to clear, and Crater noticed more bug-eyes breaking the surface and staring briefly at him and Amelia. Most sank immediately out of sight. But two eyes grew larger and in a moment an immense frog, much larger than either Korplash or Xplak, waddled from the lake to pause in shallows a few meters from the newcomers. Beneath the giant toad, Crater suddenly realized with a shock that the shallows were not the bottom of the pool, but were in fact the backs of more enormous toads, even larger than the one that had emerged and now observed them. Thinking of the endless marsh outside, he began to wonder where water ended and toad began.

While Amelia and Crater stood almost hidden behind the fat green bodies of Xplak and Korplash, Xplak addressed the large ribbet in the pool. "Xplak visit Dryland. Gork make ribbets?"

A cavernous voice came from the huge toad in the water. "Gork make ribbets. Xplak make ribbets?"

"Xplak make ribbets," said Xplak. One eye focused on Korplash. "Korplash make ribbets?"

"Korplash make ribbets," said Korplash. "Gork make ribbets?"

"Gork make ribbets." With the polite formalities done, Gork focused both of his chameleon eyes on Korplash. "Korplash scout Dryland. What result Korplash scout Dryland?"

"Dryland bad, must change for ribbets. Gork like Dryland?"

"Gork no like Dryland, must change for ribbets. Xplak like Dryland?"

"Xplak no like Dryland, must change for ribbets. Gork like Xplak and Korplash?"

"Gork like Xplak and Korplash. Xplak splash?"

"Xplak no splash," said Xplak. "Korplash splash?"

"Korplash no splash," said Korplash. "Xplak like splash shumans?"

"Xplak like splash shumans. Korplash like splash shumans?"

"Korplash like splash shumans. Gork like splash shumans?"

Gork rumbled, "Much talk about shumans… Ribbets find tibbet as Gork instructed?"

"Ribbets find tibbet," said Xplak, one eye directed hesitantly again to Korplash. "Ribbets find tibbet?"

"Korplash find tibbet," added Korplash. "Xplak find

tibbet?"

"Xplak find tibbet. Korplash find tibbet?"

"Korplash find tibbet. Gork find tibbet?" A hint of hopefulness crept into Korplash's voice.

Gork paused. "Gork no see tibbet…"

One of Korplash's chameleon eyes turned nervously to Xplak. "Siridogs come. Siridogs chase Xplak?"

"Siridogs chase Xplak," agreed Xplak. "Siridogs chase Korplash?"

"Siridogs chase Korplash. Ribbets lose tibbet?"

"Ribbets lose tibbet. Ribbets like shumans?"

"Ribbets like shumans. Shumans like splash?"

"Shumans like splash. Gork like splash…shumans?" Korplash sounded hopeful again, his webbed thumbs twiddling.

Gork extended one webbed hand and softly but firmly pushed Xplak and Korplash to either side, exposing Amelia and Crater, who had been standing silently behind them. Gork's frowning toad face frowned more deeply. "Gork no see tibbet. Gork see shumans…" Gork took a deep breath, both of his chameleon eyes swiveling to look at the ceiling. "Korplash croak? Korplash bring siridogs?"

Korplash turned his eyes nervously to Xplak. "Korplash croak. Korplash bring siridogs…" He looked at Amelia and Crater. "Shumans fat and brightly colored! Gork like shumans?"

Gork's eyes settled on Amelia and Crater, inspecting their smooth skin devoid of warts, their ghostly palor without any shade of green, and thin limbs lacking any hint of obesity. "Gork sooner splash with cacti from

Planet Dead-Cat." Gork put one webbed finger to the side of his face. "But Gork has idea..."

At this Gork went silent. With no warning, he turned and sloshed away into the misty depths of the pool. Xplak and Korplash stood in silence twiddling their webbed thumbs until Gork had vanished.

Crater looked to Amelia. "What in the hell was *that* about?"

She shrugged her shoulders.

Two smaller toads appeared on either side and pushed against Joseph and Amelia until they realized they would not be able to resist and they soon found themselves skirting the vast indoor pool, which was now squirming with the pulsating bodies of frogs of all sizes which seemed intent on some physical activity that constantly churned the water. Their de-briefing over, Korplash and Xplak disappeared through the entrance.

At length a series of further doors opened and Crater and Amelia found themselves ushered into a series of square rooms separated by deep canals filled with flowing streams of water. The only entrance to the complex was locked behind them, while below the water line they glimpsed metal bars. As they watched, their two guards belly-flopped into the stream and exited, locking the metal bars behind them as they left.

Crater looked around. Only one wide space remained dry and that seemed to be more of a medical examination room than a residence, with stainless steel table, glass cabinets filled with syringes and bottles, and sockets that glowed with different shades of light, which Crater concluded was the ribbets' usual power source, as electricity would be impractical on a planet awash with swamps and marshes. Someone had laid out two beds. To Crater's surprise, the beds were clean and soft and not damp in the least.

"Joe! How enticing!" Amelia rushed to one of the beds and flopped down. "I can't wait any longer. I've got to get some sleep–I'm still not sure I'm not asleep and dreaming even now."

"I understand, Amelia." He sat on the bed next to hers. "I'm exhausted, too." Without warning, the lights dimmed as they lay down, and within moments, before Crater and Amelia could focus on how such a mechanism might work, their minds shut down and both fell into a deep dreamless sleep.

A minute after Gork vanished beneath the pool's surface, Korplash and Xplak turned and waddled out of the building. Leaping into the nearest algae-covered pool, they swam until they arrived at a narrow canal bordering a series of modest root-enclosed thresholds, the apertures between the roots blocked by sedge leaving only a single entrance for each ribbet residence.

Korplash bypassed the block of root-homes and exited the canal only when he came adjacent to a solidly constructed building with a wide low entrance much like the edifice that he and Xplak had just visited, but smaller. Noises drifted from inside. Splashes. Buzzing. Loud croaking amidst crunching as of the happy munching of breakfast cereals.

Korplash waddled inside exuding happiness, with Xplak close behind. A shallow pool lay indoors with several low tables lining the circumference. They slid into the warm water and claimed an empty table. A small ribbet waddled over from a long wooden bar. It paused, pencil in hand.

Korplash watched as another ribbet pulled down a sign. "No more dragonfly special?" Korplash asked.

The small ribbet shook its bullet head. "Out. Someone left the wings on."

Korplash picked up a small plastic sheet and perused it. He focused his two eyes on the waiter. "Bowl of jacks and green goo."

"Urk," the frog scribbled on the pad and waddled away. Soon it returned with a bucket of insects that looked like a cross between locusts and crickets, and two tall glasses filled with green liquid. The frog started to leave.

"Straws!"

It paused and threw down two straws, then hopped away before they could demand more service.

Korplash sucked loudly and began slowly to crunch the squirming insects.

"Korplash no go roothouse," said Xplak. "Korplash home ok?"

"Korplash like bar, no go roothouse. Drink good to Xplak?"

"Green goo good to Xplak." He crunched some insects. "Jacks good tonight."

A commotion erupted across the pool.

"Ribbets splash. Ribbets make ribbets?"

Korplash looked and sighed. "Ribbets splash. Ribbets make ribbets."

Xplak waited for the response. "Korplash make splash?"

He lowered his stubby head. "Korplash no splash."

"Korplash no splash? Korplash no go roothouse? Korplash home ok?"

"Korplash no go roothouse. Korplash no splash. No make ribbets." He leaned his warty head against one webbed hand sadly, elbow on the table.

"Why Korplash no make splash?"

He shook his head. "Korplash seal bond with one ribbet. Korplash no more splash." He sighed. "Korplash no go roothouse. When Korplash see Korplash roothouse, Korplash sad."

"Korplash in siridog house?"

Korplash paused a moment, his eyes staring into the distance. Then he looked into his glass of green goo. "Korplash always in siridog house. Korplash never do anything right. Bond-ribbet never happy, always croak at Korplash. Little ribbets want much. Korplash avoid roothouse. Go bar instead. Drink much green goo."

"Green goo bad for Korplash." Xplak's face brightened. "Xplak have no bond-ribbet. Xplak make splash everywhere with young ribbets…on Bogland…on Lowland…in cosmodrones…on cosmodrones. Xplak make splash with young ribbets whenever Xplak wants."

Korplash's head sank further onto the tabletop. "Korplash never get make splash. Korplash sometimes think better die than life of Korplash."

"Maybe Korplash should bring jar of lily pads to roothouse. Maybe no more yelling from bond-ribbet."

"Korplash no think that will help." He sighed again. He took out a picture of his bond-ribbet, who was frowning deeply. Xplak looked at the picture and involuntarily shuddered. "My, isn't Korplash's bond-ribbet beautifully green and warty." Xplak looked quickly away.

Xplak's words seemed not to cheer up Korplash.

"Xplak sorry to hear Korplash sad. Korplash Xplak's friend." Xplak sucked his green goo and crunched his jacks, deep in thought.

A loud croaking suddenly reverberated from the back of the bar.

"K…O…R…P…L…A…S…H! KOR-*PLASH?! KOR*-PLASH!"

Korplash and Xplak exchanged fearful bug-eyes, their jaws dropping.

Korplash caught his breath. "Bond-ribbet find Korplash! Korplash swim!" Without another word he let loose a prodigious hop in the opposite direction, towards the front entrance. Xplak caught only a glimpse of his friend's olive back as he vanished out the door.

Several moments passed.

Two toads appeared at the entrance: one was Korplash; the other an enormous toad twice his size with pink curlers on its head and a rolling pin in one giant webbed hand. The huge toad's other hand gripped Korplash by one vestigial ear. Mercilessly, the bond-ribbet dragged Korplash back into the bar not releasing its vise-like grip until Korplash was deposited in front of Xplak.

The bond-ribbet shook the rolling pin threateningly.

"Korplash make *splash?!* Speak truth now or Korplash knows what will happen!"

"No, my little lily pad. Korplash no make splash with any ribbet but his beautiful green and warty bond-ribbet! Korplash swear!"

The rolling pin fell and caught Korplash on his bullet head.

"Korplash *LIE!* Bond-ribbet know Korplash make splash! Bond-ribbet next door say Korplash make splash with bond-ribbet next door!"

Korplash's eyes bugged out even further. "No, my little lotus leaf! Korplash leave Bogland in cosmodrone and go Dryland with Xplak! Korplash never make splash with bond-ribbet next door!"

All the neighborhood ribbets in the bar began to look, their bug-eyes staring.

The rolling pin landed again.

Xplak watched, mouth open.

"Korplash *lie* again! Korplash no lie to bond-ribbet!" The bond-ribbet looked around, its bug-eyes revolving independently of each other, taking in the activities of the den of iniquity.

"Ribbets splashing in back of pool! If Korplash think Korplash join in splashing, Korplash has another think coming! Korplash only splash with Korplash bond-ribbet!" The rolling pin swung, barely missing as Korplash ducked.

"Korplash drink *green goo?!*" The bug-eyes inspected the two tall glasses, each still half full. "How many times bond-ribbet tell Korplash no drink green goo! Korplash embarrass bond-ribbet in front of all

Bogland, make bad example for Korplash little ribbets!"

Behind Korplash's bond-ribbet a formation of little ribbets waddled in–ten, twenty, thirty, finally stopping at one hundred and thirty-two. But who was counting?

Xplak's jaw hung open further. He whispered to himself, "Korplash make much splash somewhere."

The huge bond-ribbet with the pink curlers pointed to the entrance. "Korplash go roothouse! No embarrass Korplash bond-ribbet anymore, no drink green goo and eat jacks! And no make splash with other ribbets! Or Korplash knows what will happen!" The pin rose.

"Yes, my warty lotus," Korplash finally muttered, eyes on the floor. He shuffled toward the door, dragging his long webbed feet.

With rolling pin at the ready, the bond-ribbet escorted a humbled Korplash out, the vast herd of croaking and waddling little ribbets swarming after, many of the older ones pausing to make splash with strange ribbets on the way, one eye watching out for the enormous bond-ribbet who, as always, was wholly preoccupied with Korplash and never paid any attention to what they were up to.

Xplak shook his bullet head. Consuming the last of the jacks, he tossed some metal fragments on the table for the service-toad, then turned and joined the splashing in the back of the pool, happily engaging in making more ribbets. Once done making splash he had several more appointments to make splash, including, last but not least, with the pleasingly green and plump and warty Gork himself in the imperial pond.

Gork was not there. As Xplak arrived at midnight and flopped into the imperial pond, instead engaging with several pleasingly huge amphibians that were so dedicated to the making of new generations of ribbets that they never left the pond, Gork emerged from the canal within the prison complex where the two shumans were housed.

Water spilled on the floor. Gork took a fluffy towel from a stack of towels next to the entrance, and, verifying that the grating at the bottom of the canal was indeed locked, he dried himself off in order to prevent contamination of the research facility. True, it had been designed for experimentation on tibbets and not shumans, but since those bumbling stooges Korplash and Xplak had brought back the wrong species by mistake, and it might be inconvenient to take the shumans back now that Korplash by his negligent croaking had alerted those pesky siridogs to the ribbets' interest in planet Dryland, he decided to make a virtue of necessity.

Gork had once had a plan–and a guest. Here was his chance to try again.

Movement in the soft bed next to him indicated that the male shuman called Crater was finally coming out of sleep. Having visited Dryland once himself, Gork knew that a shuman could go into shock should he awake in a sterile environment, and uninclined to ease the shock by engaging in immediate splashing with others of its kind, as ribbets would instinctively do, Gork quickly set about decorating Crater's cell pad–

which is indeed what it was–with paint and carpet and a kitchenette (operating on light power instead of electricity), even a picture of someone called Whistler's Mother, whom Gork decided to refrain from pointing out was really Gork memorialized in his previous clandestine infiltration of Planet Dryland.

Passing a webbed paw over a red and green light device, he called, "Zira. Bring roothouse cleaning crew. I need change shumans' habitat quick as a parallax leap." Immediately a small army of assistant ribbets appeared and in minutes, with a torrent of hopping and waddling, completed the transition.

Crater sat up.

He yawned and stretched his arms, his eyes fluttering. He took in Amelia sleeping gently in the bed next to his, some two meters away; he took in the picture of Whistler's Mother; he glimpsed the kitchenette which at first comforted him till he recalled where he was, and what had and what had not been there when he had gone to sleep.

Glimpsing the floor, he was puzzled to see that it was now blue-green where before it had been off-white. He recoiled from the new olive-green walls studded with staccatos of lumps like warts, and the wide but narrow oblongs that he at first thought were windows opening onto Bogland's swamps, but then realized were just pictures of the same–a swampy marsh topped with thick-grown isles of sedges and exposed roots surrounded by mist, all frozen on canvas. A scene only a ribbet could love.

"Joe...where are we?"

He looked over to Amelia. She was propped on one elbow, as confused as he, and almost as alarmed. Both stared with mouths open.

"I'm not sure. I think we're still on Bogland. But I don't know if we've been moved, or if they moved the building around us."

A guttural croaking sounded from a wide squat aperture, an open doorway. Crater and Amelia put their translation devices back on their heads.

"Nothing has been moved," came a deep croak. "I altered your current environment to be more in accord with your native habitat." Waddling inside, the toad swiveled his eyes around the chamber, taking in the several criss-crossing canals of water, the kitchenette, the wide low ceiling with gentle dim lights, and the carpet with giant images of bug-eyed hermaphrodite green frogs mounting each other by the dozen.

"Gee," said Crater. "I'm not sure whether I should thank you or not."

"Your habitat is pleasing. Your habitat is pleasing?"

"Uh, if I were a ribbet, I suppose this habitat would be pleasing."

"Then this habitat is pleasing. Crater now happy, ready to splash?"

Crater stood and took refuge behind the bed. "Oh, Crater happy but no splashing over here, no, no, no! We shumans really aren't so thrilled by all this splashing. In fact we really don't like to splash that much! Besides," Crater glanced at Amelia, "me and Amelia are…bond-shumans!"

Amelia quickly nodded.

"Gork happy if Crater happy. Gork happy if Melia happy." Gork looked to one picture that suddenly transformed from a picture into a window, the images of Bogland coming to life amid multiple pairs of swiveling eyes that stared with ardent curiosity at the captive shumans that strangely did not engage in splashing every few minutes.

" 'Gork'…that's quite a name," said Crater. "Where did you get that name from?"

"Gork old name in Bogland. Named Gork by our leader Klaatu who taught us ribbets not to enslave other races in his First Commandment: Klaatu barada nikto."

"Yes?"

"And we ribbets have barada'ed nikto ever since."

Crater looked serious. "Except me and Amelia!"

"You, Crater? And your bond-shuman Melia?"

"Yeah, you fat warty toad!"

"Gork thanks the shuman Crater for his wonderfully kind compliment."

"You do barada!"

"We barada no one–*nikto*–shuman Crater. There are no slaves on Bogland."

"Don't you get it? You barada'ed us!"

"No, shuman Crater. We ribbets of Bogland do not barada other races. We *liberate* them."

He rolled his eyes. "Oh, that's a good one!" Crater strutted about the room. "Ha ha! That's just great! There's that innocent phrase! As if we haven't heard that line on Earth for the past thousand years! So you fat buggers deceive yourselves just as badly as the awful politicians and conquerors on Earth! All you've done is 'liberate' me and Amelia into a padded cell!"

Amelia stood and approached Crater. "Joe is right! How dare you kidnap us and bring us here! You have no right to keep us." She looked outraged. "We've been barada'ed!" She cupped her hands and yelled out the window, "Help! We've been barada'ed! Help get us out of here and away from this big fat green toad!"

A chorus of chirping and croaking drifted in through the window in approval of her kind compliment, followed by happy splashing in the further reaches behind their audience as the back ranks of toads got it on, which did not necessarily signal approval of her speech, but just that the ribbets were alive and breathing.

"You are very kind, bond-shuman Melia. Of course, ribbets do not hate shumans or other species–except for those evil tibbets, of course–but ribbets make ribbets. Ribbets splash and make more ribbets. Bogland has more ribbets than water. Dryland will be better when Dryland become like Bogland and all Drylanders become like ribbets."

"What?" Crater looked alarmed. "You…you can't mean that you buggers plan to transport hordes of fat toads from Bogland to Earth?"

"No, Crater. Bogland perfect. No ribbets want leave Bogland." Gork waddled to the kitchenette where a series of light devices, syringes, and flasks with liquids were spread out. "But ribbets make ribbets. Ribbets want make more ribbets. On Bogland…"

He took up a syringe.

"On Highland…"

He squirted some serum.

"On Lowland..."

He turned toward Crater.

"Or on Dryland... Wherever life exists or can exist, there we ribbets want make ribbets the main species. On Dryland–your Earth–ribbets want warm up climate until oceans rise to cover all Dryland and there is only Bogland left." Gork stepped close. Out came a freeze ray gun.

"Beginning with you, shuman Crater. Maybe serum will work. All ribbets need is ribbet-agents on Dryland to promote process of raising Dryland's oceans. Then Gork will show agents how to make ribbets who will make more ribbets until Dryland becomes just like Bogland."

Crater retreated behind the bed, joined by a terrified Amelia. "You can't mean it! That's–that's impossible! You can't change us into ribbets!"

"Not ribbets. But Crater and bond-shuman want return to Earth, yes?" Gork aimed the freeze gun. "No other way. Besides, don't worry, shumans. Serum experimental. Maybe you not survive; then you be lucky...and *die*." Behind Gork in the back door appeared Zira, Gork's assistant, no expression on its bullet head and toad face. The gun zapped and Crater froze in place, with Amelia frozen next to him, but both still hearing and seeing and feeling. Gork took Crater's arm and injected him. Backing up, he flicked lights on his device and an invisible barrier warped into existence imprisoning both inside the apartment, while Gork hopped out of the room, Zira following.

As soon as they had left, Crater and Amelia both came unfrozen.

"Oh, Joe!" Amelia buried her face in her hands again. "I can't believe this is happening to us!"

He rubbed his arm. "What the hell was that that he injected me with?"

She inspected his arm. "I don't see anything except a small red mark. Maybe it's nothing."

"And maybe it's the worst thing that could ever happen!" Crater strode about the room excitedly. The window had reverted to an unchanging picture, no more swiveling eyes staring in at them. "Why do you think they chose us? Can that be true about us…about us becoming their agents on Earth? Did I understand that Gork right?"

"Oh, that can't be true," Amelia said. "It's impossible! It's ridiculous!"

"As impossible and ridiculous as us sitting in a zoo on a planet of toads light-years from Earth. Yet here we are." His gaze passed around the room looking for some way out, or some way to awaken from what increasingly seemed like an evil dream. "And what's all this talk about 'splashing'? They seem to be obsessed with…you know."

"Yes, I understood that, Joe. But I don't see what all that has to do with us. Why, we're just a couple of lovesick humans who don't want any more out of life except to be with each other."

Joe embraced Amelia. "Thank you, my dear." He kissed her upturned face. "At least we have that." He laughed. "And it looks like you outdid Lindbergh after all."

She chuckled. "Eat your heart out, Lindie!" She stared at the window, which, to her relief, remained merely a window. "No Spirit of St. Louis will ever cross this expanse."

Stepping back, Joe turned toward the bed. "I'm feeling a bit tired, dear. Going to lie down a bit." As he spread out on the bed, he added, "It might be a prison, but no one can argue with the amenities. No prisoner ever had it so good. Regular meals. Air-conditioning. No bills to pay. Our every physical need taken care of. And each other for companionship. What more could a guy and a gal ask for?"

Another moment and he was out. Snores echoed across the chamber. "Well, I guess it can't all be perfect," reflected Amelia, drifting into sleep next to him.

A day passed.

Amelia awoke, Joe still sleeping beside her. She was not certain exactly what prompted her but something about Joe's slightly labored breathing seemed out of place, and something about his position on the bed triggered some elemental alert within her.

She reached out to touch him.

He stirred. The snoring momentarily increased, resounding through the room, then abated. Sleepily his eyes opened.

"Hi honey. Did I sleep long?"

Amelia smiled, looking at a clock on the wall. "Only an entire day. I thought you would never wake up!"

He awoke. "An entire day!" He sat up, the lower half

of his body covered by blankets. "Well, how do you account for that?" He moved his arm. "Ouch." He rubbed the spot of the injection.

"Does it still hurt? Here, let me look at that."

"Not much actually; no more than any vaccination would a day later."

He twisted to show her the arm–the blankets fell off his nude body. "Honey… Honey, what's wrong?"

Amelia was staring, her mouth open.

"Baby, honey, what's the matter? What are you looking at?" Crater looked down at the lower half of his body.

With one hand, she pointed. With the other, she covered her open mouth.

Two penises.

Where the day before, Joe's body had been completely normal in every respect, this strange morning on this warped planet after Gork's bizarre injection for an unknown purpose, he now possessed not one, but two–perfectly formed and to all appearances functional in every respect–human penises. Each was huge. And erect.

Amelia continued to stare. As if again frozen by Gork's freeze gun, she sat and pointed, speechless.

"Omigod," said Joe. "What the hell has happened? What did that fat green toad do to me?" He stood and strode about the room, gesticulating wildly. "Why I'll kill that bastard! How dare he do such a thing? If he waddles his fat butt in here at this moment, I swear I would strangle his warty neck!" While he paced, both his members remained hard and upright.

"Joe, sit down." Amelia's hand still covered her mouth.

"Yes, dear?" Calming, he paused his wild pacing and stood in front of her. "What do we do? How do we get him to reverse this monstrous thing? We've got to get him to put me back the way I was!"

Finally dropping her hand from her mouth, Amelia continued to stare at Joe's new members. As she stared, they seemed to grow even larger. Her eyes grew big. She patted the bed. "Sit down, dear."

Puzzled, he sat beside her. He glanced at himself. "It's outrageous! If Gork thinks he can turn me into a ribbet, then I'm going to set him straight!"

"Maybe we should not be in such a rush, Joe dear."

"What's that?"

"Maybe we should think about this a bit before we make any…uh, sudden demands on the nice Gork." She continued to stare downward. "Here we are on this far off alien planet completely under this Gork's control. I mean, he hasn't really done anything really bad–except make just one itty-bitty little change–just a minor little alteration. I mean, how is this really different from the kind of thing that we do on Earth all the time, like circumcisions? Is this really so bad?" She leaned closer.

He glanced below at his new members that again seemed to grow and become harder as he watched. "Amelia…what are you trying to say? Do you realize what you are saying? What you are thinking?"

She reached out and hugged him. "Oh, my love! I'm just saying that maybe we should not be in such a hurry to condemn Mr. Gork. He has protected us so far. He has not harmed us in any way…just made one itsy bitsy change…" She kissed him quickly and looked down again. "I mean…maybe we should give this thing a chance…see how well things work–that is, just see if everything works out before we become hasty and start making accusations and demands on our nice host. Maybe this little change is just their version of a simple circumcision and nothing at all to get…*excited* about."

Joe's mouth dropped open. "A simple circumcision! Are you kidding me, Amelia? Just look!"

"I *am* looking…"

"That Gork has made me into a freak! How do I live with this?"

Amelia pushed Joe backwards onto the bed. Without taking her eyes off his new members, she tossed her clothes aside and sat on top of him. "One day at a time, Joe. One day at a time." She took his blankets and threw them across the room. "Right now–I want to climb your Twin Pokes!"

Joe kissed her. While his new members launched as if with a mind of their own, he panted, "If only the Chartreuse Gang could see me now–I would never hear 'Dickless Joe' again."

"What was that?" Amelia asked in between breaths.

"Never mind."

A day later an exhausted and happy Joe and Amelia lay snoring together, Joe's appendages finally–but only temporarily–at ease, after repeated launchings and re-launchings.

The apartment's electron barrier dissolved and Gork entered the room. Translation devices in hand, he approached the beds and sleepily Joe awoke and donned one of the devices.

"Shuman Joe and shuman Melia."

Gork was happy. By now, they had learned to perceive the subtle movements around Gork's arcing jawline that signified satisfaction.

"My liberated shumans enjoy splashing more than before. Not so bad to be like ribbets, I am right, yes?"

Joe glared. "Yes, we've had fun splashing, but that does not mean that I'm not still mad at you."

"Shuman Joe mad?"

"You had no right to interfere with our natural order."

"What is 'natural order'? Is it not natural order for ribbets to make things that change natural order?"

"You have to reverse this! I won't help you on Earth if you leave me this way."

By now Amelia was alert. She drew blankets over her nude form and put on her translation device.

"Maybe you should ask bond-shuman Melia before asking to reverse."

Amelia was shaking her head. "Joe, dear, let's not be so hasty."

Joe sat upright. He leveled an accusatory stare at Gork. "You must reverse this."

"No reverse possible, shuman Joe. More changes coming."

"But you said this is only an experiment."

"Yes, but final result known. Only question is if you survive to end."

Joe sucked a breath of alarm. "Wait a minute…you can't mean that you're turning me into a fat green toad? I won't have it! All you toads do is bugger each other. What are you trying to do, start your own Fuck in the Backside Institute?"

"No toad for shuman Joe. But changes. Other changes."

"I don't want more changes!"

Amelia sidled close to him. "Joe, honey, slow down. Let's wait and see what kind of changes the nice Mr. Gork is talking about." She smiled. Her gaze wandered below again. As if in response, Joe's new members began to grow and Amelia's eyes grew big as her smile broadened.

Turning, Gork waddled out the door and reactivated the invisible barrier.

Joe's members harder and larger than ever, he found himself thrust backwards once more as Amelia jumped on him with the alacrity of an ape, and began to pound and thrust with abandon. No result seemed to satisfy her as she ravished him, when one member momentarily weakened she switched to the other with a happy laugh, shaking the bed with her repeated shudders, her arms holding his shoulders down in a tight grip, his supine form, having escaped his conscious control, thrusting up to meet her.

"Melia, honey. My dear…"

"Yes, Joe my love," she panted.

"Slow down, I can't catch my breath…"

"I'll breathe for both of us."

"I have to take a break…"

"I won't let you."

"Getting tired…"

"I'll do the work for both of us, baby, just keep going."

"I'm trying but I can't…"

"You're hard as a rock, baby, don't stop."

"I'm too stressed. My heart…"

"No, you can't stop now! Just lie still."

"I– , I–" Joe clutched his chest.

Amelia climbed off. "Joe! Joe! What's wrong, Joe?"

He stopped breathing. As she put her head to his chest, he gave a gasp and his eyes closed. There was no sound from his heart.

"Oh no, Joe! Joe, no, you can't die! Not now! What will I do without you?" Amelia pounded his chest, and alternately listened for a heart beat and pounded some more. "Come back, Joe! Come back to me!" She pounded again. Getting no result, she finally sat on the edge of the bed. She put her face in her hands and cried.

For a long minute she sat, the corpse of New York Supreme Court Justice Joseph Force Crater still and silent, his eyes closed, no longer breathing, Amelia staring. Her efforts to bring him back had failed and there remained no chance of his returning to her alive.

"Gork!" she shouted. "Mr. Gork!"

No answer.

Looking up at the wide picture, only inanimate images stared back. Visiting hours at the zoo were over.

Finally, the tears stopped. Nothing more could be done. Her dear Joe was gone and there was nothing that she or anyone else could do about it, and, as she thought ahead to her fate on this desolate alien waste with no one to share it with and no one to satisfy her needs for perhaps years to come, her eyes settled once more on the Twin Pokes that continued to aim high, rubbery stiff and hard as reeds, and she wondered: *will this ever come my way again? This might be my last chance...*

Wiping her tears aside, she hopped on and resumed thrusting and pounding. No breath was forthcoming from Joe's corpse, but none was needed, as the members continued to function on their own according to their own nature, satisfying her as if their deceased owner was every bit as alive as formerly.

Lost in pleasure, Amelia's eyes shut as she worked and thrust, switching from one hard member to the other, then back again, determined not to waste a moment of what may be the last orgasmic pleasure she would ever experience, surprised but elated that no weakening in Joe's members was detectable. She took no notice as the room's lights slowly grew and the bedsheets and blankets dropped to the floor. An hour seemed to pass before–exhausted–she slackened, rivulets of sweat streaming down her breasts and back, and she finally began to entertain the thought of pausing to rest–but not yet, still not yet.

Something tugged at her mind. Eyes closed, she could not shake the feeling that she was no longer alone, and she slowed to catch her breath, her glistening breasts heaving. As she sucked a deep breath and blew it out, her eyes opened.

She screamed.

Beneath her legs outspread over his supine form with his members thrusting up inside her, was Joe, his eyes open, his mouth smiling–on his face a thick mask of white greasepaint. In perfect silence, he motioned with a grin that she continue thrusting.

"No! Oh, no!" With a shriek, she clambered off.

Slowly sitting up, Joe continued grinning, and, as his members shrank to normal size, he rose and walked to one corner of the room where he opened a drawer. From inside he extracted a pair of black pants, and a shirt with horizontal black and white stripes, and black suspenders. Donning them, he walked to a blank space on one wall. With thumbs and forefingers, he outlined a rectangle and peered into a nonexistent mirror and admired his greasepaint. Turning to Amelia, he danced a jig to nonexistent music. Again the evil grin.

Amelia covered herself with the blanket. "No, this can't be! These ribbets–that Gork–no one can be so cruel!" Sinking into her bed, Amelia Earhart, having far outdone Lucky Lindie and every other flier on Earth, unleashed a torrent of tears. "My Joseph–a *mime!*"

Episode 9

J. Edgar Hoover stood and held his head with both hands. "Oooh, my leg," he moaned.

A high voice sounded. "Don't make a move, Mr. Hoover." Gary stepped from behind the folding tables where he had taken refuge during the chaos. He held a

German Luger pistol in his hand. “We wouldn’t want anything *naughty* to happen to America’s chief spymaster, now, would we?”

Edgar smoothed his purple dress. One hand reached to straighten his red wig, till he remembered he had tossed it aside. As he watched, Heinz got off the sprawled stack of FBI agents and let them stand, guarded by a line of Japanese rifles. Herr Huntz, Captain Girusu and Captain French eyed the double line of executed German and Japanese sailors and shrugged their shoulders. All in a good cause. French in particular seemed to wear a smirk. Those sailors at least need not be forced to walk back to Germany and go on report. Sighting Karl and his party favor among the bodies, French smiled in anticipation of returning to his dark little room under the bridge where he could wait in ambush of passersby without encountering hoots and laughter.

“Ha!” said Gary, as the two surviving Mormons joined him. “So you thought you could just put on a tutu, Mr. J. Edgar, waltz in here–in our secret base!–and infiltrate our spy missions, did you?” He stooped to pick up his Latter Day Saints Bible. “Well, I hate to tell you this, Mr. Rumpled Dress–” With a frown, Hoover glanced down and again smoothed his gown. “–but we’ve been onto you from the beginning.” He aimed his Bible at Hoover as if it were more lethal than the gun. As indeed it was.

Hoover’s eyes grew wide.

“Oh, yes!” Gary turned to his two Mormon buddies. “Orangello!”

"Yeah, Gary?" came the adolescent voice, Orangello brightening in response.

"How's your brother Lemongello?" Gary asked without taking his eyes off Hoover.

"I'm fine, too, Gary." Both adolescents finished brushing the dust off their white short-sleeved shirts and ties, and stepped closer.

Gary continued, his eyes on Hoover. "Uncle Franklin told us of you before you even arrived."

A look of consternation came over Edgar. In nervous reaction, he unconsciously adjusted his bra. His eye wandered to the red wig on the floor.

"Go ahead. Pick it up." Gary smiled. "You look better with it on anyway."

"I know."

Hoover's eye wandered to his FBI agents being herded together in a bowling lane.

"But don't bother your pretty little head with them, Mr. Hoover." Gary turned and motioned to the two Captains. "They're going where they'll be well taken care of. Way out of the jurisdiction of your *U.S.A!*" Heinz and Huntz collided and, after exchanging elbow gaffs, finally succeeded in opening the twin front doors. The Japanese soldiers herded the agents toward the plane with the giant red sun emblazoned on the fuselage.

Hoover took a step.

"Not so fast, Miss Purple Dress!"

Edgar paused, his face twisted.

"Yes, I know about that too, my little pretty. You see, my Uncle Franklin tells me quite a lot. A lot about that spycatcher Mr. Crater, and a lot about that little camera snapper Miss Earhart–yes, and a lot about you, Mr. Hoover, running around using your cute little fetching disguise to interfere with our plans to occupy your country, stopping us from our plans to go door to door and spread our message among your people." Gary smirked. "Oh, and one more thing–that eyeliner really doesn't go with purple."

Hoover choked and bit his knuckle.

"Yes, we knew you were coming and now our trap has been sprung. You will now be so kind as to come with me." Jabbing him with the barrel of his Luger, Gary followed Edgar to the yard in front of Los Bolos where they watched the rest of the FBI agents file onto the Japanese plane. In another moment, the plane taxied to one end of the short runway and took off.

Behind the Japanese bomber rested a second aircraft, smaller and nondescript, no Japanese red sun or German black cross or swastika on it. Orangello opened the side door and Gary motioned that Hoover should board. Gary and Lemongello followed him while the rest of the Japanese and Germans stood at attention, saluting and heiling.

At the front sat another callow youth in white short-sleeves. He revved the motor. As they strapped themselves into seats, the craft barreled down the runway and was soon aloft.

Hours passed. A quarter day. A half day. Clouds came and went, covering and uncovering the sun, uncaring in its supervision of the raw harsh existence below. The day died. At length lights appeared in the midst of a blanket of blackness that stretched in all directions. All Edgar knew was that they headed north.

Their journey was over. The plane declined for a landing on a sparsely-lit rectangle somewhat removed from a tangle of lights that denoted a small city. Tires screeched on concrete and the plane rumbled to a halt.

As the door opened, a dry dusty breeze encompassed the plane's cabin.

"Look what the cat dragged in, youse guys. Oh, she's cute, ain't she?" Three brutes in overcoats stared as Edgar exited the aircraft and climbed down a short flight of pushcart stairs. "And that eyeliner. It goes poifect with the purple dress and red wig."

"Ya think so, Fat Tone?" Standing next to Fat Tony, the smaller Paulie straightened his tie in the bright lights of a small reception building.

"Coitainly. You know what, Bugs?" Fat Tone elbowed the third and most hulking brute. "I'm gonna call Radio City and see if they's missin a dancer!"

Bugs and Paulie guffawed in perfect octaves till Bugs leaned over and felt his nose, making sure the bridge was still there.

"Still thinkin of that beatin the nun gave ya seven years ago?"

"I told ya, Paulie, she sucker-punched me," Bugs said in his cavernous voice.

"Bugs, I hate to be the one to tell ya this…"

Hoover paused on the runway between them while Bugs and Fat Tony looked at Paulie.

"But wit you–every punch is a sucker punch." Fat Tony elbowed Bugs and he and Paulie laughed.

Bugs didn't see the humor and stared away, his lip out.

Gary emerged from the plane and the laughter suddenly stopped. He surveyed the scene as one used to being in command and having his commands obeyed. As he descended the short wheeled steps, Orangello and Lemongello followed, equally sure of their authority. The three gangsters backed away in respect, leaving a disheveled Edgar standing uncertainly among the lot.

Gary snapped his fingers.

A Stutz Limousine, its hood repaired after a collision with a mannequin truck years earlier in Hackensack, pulled up with a second Stutz close behind and Hoover was ushered into the back seat of the first where he was squeezed between Fat Tone and Bugs almost to the point of vanishing. Paulie sat in front beside the driver, another crewcut youth in white short-sleeve shirt. Gary and the Jello brothers occupied the second car, driven by yet another white shirt, whose eye similarly reflected unrestrained arrogance.

The deadly caravan plunged into the depths of the night, swaying with the rise and fall of an unlit road, its potholes and crevasses bringing wild imaginings to Edgar's mind, plunging deeper and deeper with ever diminishing chances of rescue into uncharted wilderness. How far had they flown? What fate awaited 'her' at the end of the road? Would the captors have the humanity to acknowledge him as her…or openly reject her as him? Edgar felt his ears and confirmed that his red ruby earrings were still attached and he felt comforted. He adjusted his wig. At least he had his dignity.

A sudden sign rushed from the darkness, announcing in frightful letters: "Salt Lake City."

Edgar's stomach wrenched. He thought he had seen the worst that could happen, that nothing worse could afflict him–now he knew he was wrong. Inwardly he shook. The Gates of Hell had opened and the Stutzes raced through as heedless as Lucifer in his terrible rebellion against Heaven.

His emotion burst forth. "No…no! You can't take me there! I won't let you!"

Two heavy hands gripped his shoulders, pressing him further into the expensive cloth of the back seat.

"Easy there, Betty Boop."

"Yeah, shaddup wit your whinin, Miss Harlow. You ain't goin nowhere nohow. Not when da Boss of da Chartreuse Gang gave us orders to bring youse to him."

"Chartreuse Gang?" exclaimed Edgar. "But that's in Chicago, in Cicero. This is Salt Lake City!"

"Cicero's just a branch office, Miss Purple Panty," replied Paulie. "We got orders to bring you to da Big Boss! Ain't no arguin wit dat. So youse comin wit us whether youse likes it or not."

The cars sped up and soon took a turn off the main road onto a lonely track, finally coming to a halt besides a modest two-story brick building. Behind the cars an electric gate topped with barbed wire slid shut and Edgar's gaze took in an occasional starlit glinting that signaled more fences with barbed wire running in either direction. More stars glinted off guns held by patrolling guards to the accompaniment of growling guard dogs.

The car doors opened and the occupants spilled out. With the Jello brothers behind, Gary approached Edgar, while the gangsters formed a tight ring to prevent any escape.

"It's time for you–" Gary cleared his throat to correct his high voice, and repeated himself striving for a deeper tone.

"It's time for you to meet some friends of mine, Mr. Hoover. In fact, it's long overdue. I think we'll have a lot to talk about. In fact, I think you will soon be begging to tell us all you know about your little…operations!" Gary rocked back on his heels, grinning, hands on hips.

Gary pointed. "Look!"

Edgar stared into the distance and thought he glimpsed more airplanes landing. The airfield was not so distant after all. The building was an adjunct to the field and he found himself wondering how America's anti-spy network, which he himself had set up and administered for the past decade, could have failed so completely, how such a vast organization could exist without his hearing a word about it. He shook his head, resignation and defeat taking hold. How much farther could this conspiracy extend? He had a feeling he was about to find out.

For a minute they stood and waited as more car headlights popped on and black cars brought more occupants to the building.

"Inside, Miss Hoover." Gary waved him inside at the point of a barrel.

The Gates of Hell opened. Pressed from behind,

Edgar was escorted through a long slickly polished hallway with bare walls, up a flight of stairs covered by musty carpet, then into a wide rectangular anteroom lined with chairs of polished wood with red velvet seats. Despite the apparent luxury of the furnishings and the opulent framed paintings on the walls, an aura of dust and age seemed to hang over all.

"Keep wit the walkin, Princess," rumbled Bugs. "You can powder your nose over dere."

Paulie and Fat Tone pointed to one corner where, once Edgar took up his appointed position, the three gangsters halted close beside. Paulie reached into a big square box and extracted a white apron. Wrapping the white cords twice around his waist, he flipped the top triangle down over the square bottom portion in 'Master' fashion. Edgar's eye was drawn to an image emblazoned across the front. He had heard of Masons and their rites; he had seen their aprons, been shown examples by friends of his, though he had never had the time to join any of their lodges. Now his eye settled on the most evil image he could imagine–the chiaroscuro outline of... *Joseph Smith*. Could this be the ultimate secret that the anti-Freemasons so railed against? Had he finally discovered their most guarded secret?

Behind the gangsters entered the fearsome Jello brothers. While Edgar watched in growing apprehension, they took up positions at the side of Bugs and stood with hands in pockets, toothpicks hanging threateningly from their thin lips, broad boyish grins on their freshly washed faces. One winked. Edgar stepped back, struggling to mask his horror. In another moment, the two brothers entered a small ante-anteroom and closed the door. When they returned, they had exchanged their white short-sleeves for Sicilian-style black silk shirts with white ties. Forever looking their evil parts, they donned their Joseph Smith Master's aprons.

Next entered two figures, strolling nonchalantly, and Edgar stared in shock as he recognized America's undisputed King of Crime. The figure strode directly to Edgar and held out a broad glad hand, a huge smile underlying round black rimmed spectacles. "Great to make your acquaintance, Mr. Hoover! I've heard so much about you!"

"Uh, pleased to meet you too, uh… Ambassador Joseph Kennedy, is it?"

"The one and only!" The Irish grin flashed. "Have you met my good friend, Brother Al?"

From behind Joe Kennedy stepped a solid portly figure in hat and coarse-striped suit, the remnant of a cigar stuck in his mouth.

Edgar extended a flaccid hand. With his mouth hanging open, he stammered, "I thought you were in jail… And don't–don't you belong in Cicero?"

"Dat's just a branch office. Didn't my guys tell ya? When da Big Boss calls, ain't nobody says no." He looked at the rest of the Chartreuse Gang. "And you didn't really think dat any jail could hold me when dat ain't part of da Big Boss' plans?" He winked. "Ain't dat right, boys?"

"Dat's da gospel truth, Mr. Capone. Ain't no arguin wit dat."

Edgar glanced at the pictures on the wall; one held

an image of Joe Kennedy wearing his Lodge apron. Edgar read aloud the writing underneath: " 'Past Master'?"

"Yes, sir, Mr. Hoover," Kennedy jumped in. He pointed at the wall. "Every picture tells a story, as they say!"

His gaze drawn to the pictures, Edgar suddenly noticed the familiarity of the other pictures stretched along the wall, including one that said "Past Master Big Al." Before he could comment, two more figures entered the anteroom while Al and Joe donned Joseph Smith aprons.

One, clothed in a plain dark suit, was engaged in a heated conversation with the other, who was clad in brown semi-military garb and tasseled veteran's cap, an open expression on the latter's outsized clean-shaven features, his eyebrows perpetually lifted well above his large receptive white-rimmed eyes. The former swept a long flap of black hair across his forehead where it seemed reluctant to remain, and a red swastika on a white armband. He constantly twitched a Charlie Chaplin mustache while his hands gestured wildly.

"I am tellink you ze captain of zat blimp must've been a Jew!"

"And I'm-a sayin if you hada put an Italiano in charge-a, that biga blimpa would have arrived on time-a and be safe at Lakehurst today-a." He joined his fingers together and kissed them with a loud noise.

They paused in front of Edgar.

"I–I don't believe it," he blurted.

The man in the dark suit swept his forelock over his

forehead. "Gooten morgen, mein Herr." He paused to pass his glance over Edgar's purple gown. He shook his finger. "I zink you should know–zat eyeliner no ist goink vell mit zose earrings."

"Nice-a ta meet-a you, amico mio," said the man in the military jacket, sticking out his chest, then the two walked away to resume their private conversation.

Edgar bit his knuckle again and suppressed another tear. He really must find time to check his mascara.

At the entrance another figure paused to exchange words with someone positioned in the hallway invisible around the corner.

"I can't tell you how great it is to see you again, Harry! And I must say you're looking great as usual!"

"Thank you, Franklin. You always have the kindest words. And we'll get your photo on the wall next to the others just as soon as the new Worshipful Master takes up his duties."

"Well, best to your wife, Harry. And don't worry about a thing. You're in the queue for 1944. Oh, and by the way, Hirohito called, and Uncle Joe from Moscow, to say they can't make it this time. They apologized profusely."

"Next time, Franklin." Harry ceased speaking to Franklin and entered the anteroom.

"Who's that?" Edgar asked Paulie.

Paulie shrugged. "One of da brudders. And a real good one. Harry Ass Somethin."

All except Hoover had donned their Joseph Smith aprons and stood or sat in anticipation of an event that remained a mystery to America's chief spycatcher, his self-confidence sinking faster than that big-a blimp-a that no arrive-a on time-a.

Shave-and-a-haircut–two-bits sounded from a large wooden door at the further end of the anteroom. A frumpy overweight man with glasses and a hangdog look opened the door from the inside and, as he held it open, all the guests excepting only Hoover and the Jello brothers filed through.

"Good evening, Earl," said Kennedy, as he passed by with a smile.

"Evening," he mumbled.

"Hi, Mr. Browder," added Paulie, "how's da old hammer and sickle?" Paulie paused. "Now, you let us know if you need to borry more muscle to smack around dat pesky John L. Lewis again. We's here ta help."

"Thank you, Paulie," came the hangdog reply. "But I don't think he'll cause my Communist Party USA any more trouble after you worked him over."

Everyone filed in and the door shut.

For what seemed an eon, Edgar remained in the anteroom which seemed to grow colder the longer he stood though not from any drop in temperature. The blackness of his thoughts reflected off the blackness of his captors' mafia-style black shirts to form a mirror of darkness, each image of doom more frightening than the last, replicating into the abyss of his mind. Stroking his ruby earrings and smoothing his purple dress, which always calmed him under other circumstances, this time provided no relief at all–not under the fierce gaze of the freshly scrubbed Jello brothers. One of them–Orangello–smiled and winked. The other–Lemongello–rocked back on his heels, hands in pockets, and began to whistle a merry tune. Edgar's stomach twisted with horror.

Finally, after the passage of an enormous span of time during which Edgar felt he could not hold up any longer–the door rang with a repeat of the fearsome secret code. And Edgar knew his time was almost up.

The portal slowly opened.

Browder announced himself. "Tiler for the Joseph Smith Chartreuse Lodge of the Latter-Day Masons of Lower Middle Utah and Fish Fry." He banged shave-and-a-haircut once more with the brass doorknocker.

"Tiler Browder," came a high voice from inside the lodge room, "What disturbs the peace of our sacred lodge?"

Earl turned his sorrowful expression to the lodge room. "Worshipful Master, it is a penitent who has offended the peaceful dignity of this lodge. The Brethren request that he be brought before the assembly."

"Escort the penitent before the lodge."

Orangello and Lemongello took Hoover by one arm each and followed as Earl led the way into the lodge room. Around Edgar appeared a surprising panorama of aged furnishings, dusty seats, pictures of Joseph Smith, and the same collection of personages that he had encountered in the anteroom, except here they were regaled in the august flower of their Latter-Day Saints Masonic aprons together with glorious purple sashes that draped diagonally across each man's chest.

Edgar noticed three small lecterns, set in the north, west, and south. Most surprisingly, however, was the presence behind the loftiest piece of furniture, an antique polished desk raised upon a dais, of a small chubby-faced boy propped under an outsized Western hat clearly intended for persons of much larger stature. Behind him a giant green letter G hung on the wall, ringed by outspread plastic rays.

Seated behind the other three stations were Big Al, Kennedy, and Benito, the whites of Benito's eyes framing his perpetual open amazed expression. Together with Harry 'Ass', the Chartreuse Gang sat in the interstices–far too few to fill the many empty seats–while Adolf frowned and sat by himself with his arms folded. He alone had no purple sash to match his Joseph Smith apron. Beside Gary but lower sat another figure–and Hoover again reeled in shock. The other figure wore golden robes and a split golden hat under his Masonic apron, in his left hand a golden staff.

"Bring–" began Gary. He struggled to lower his voice an octave. "Bring the penitent to the square and compass."

On an altar in the middle of the lodge room lay a book–and here Edgar strove to compose himself, guessing the gruesome nature of the fiendish portfolio, the only book that could reside in such a monstrous place. Try as he did to retain his composure, he could not help stumbling on his high heels as the Jello brothers shoved him forward. Not the Book of the Dead, or even the whispered nightmarish Necronomicon, could approach the depths of madness and despair of–*The Book.*

A candelabra burned lightly and the brothers brought

him to a halt directly before The Book, which lay open to what Edgar could only suppose was the most fiendish passage in that hellish composition. Half obscured by a Mason's square and compass, he could barely make out the passages underneath, and his mind reeled.

"Mr. Hoover, sir…uh, ma'am…uh, it has been determined by this august assemblage–" Gary looked to the south lectern for confirmation, "Did I say that right, Benny?" Benito solemnly nodded, his eyes half-closed. "–that you have offended this Master Chartreuse Lodge of the Latter-Day Masons and violated its bylaws in a most naughty manner." Gary looked to the others present. "All that remains is for us to vote on whether you are to be found guilty."

Gary picked up a small wooden judge's gavel and smacked the desk once.

"In the north, Brother Kennedy, do you find that Mr. Hoover is guilty of the most serious offense provided by our bylaws?"

Joe Kennedy stood and looked at Edgar without smiling. Producing his own gavel, he smacked his lectern. "I so find." He shifted in his chair and stared straight ahead.

"In the west, Brother Al, do you find that Mr. Hoover is guilty of the most serious offense provided by our bylaws?"

Al Capone stood. He stared at Edgar with a mixture of amusement and contempt, his cigar still thrust into his mouth. He growled, "Fuckin A."

Gary peered harder at Brother Al.

"I so find," said Al. He sat.

"In the south, Brother Benny, do you find that Mr. Hoover is guilty of the most serious offense provided by our bylaws?"

Mussolini had already stood. His gavel smacked his lectern louder than the rest. "You betcha I do-a."

Gary rolled his eyes. "Benny, you have to say the words."

"Alright-a." He puffed out his chest. Directing his gaze at the ceiling, he bellowed so that the entire lodge echoed, "I-a so find-a!"

"Thank you, Benny."

"And from the Treasurer, Brother Pius, do you find that Mr. Hoover is guilty of the most serious offense provided by our bylaws?"

Pius stood. Leaning on his staff with his left hand, he traced an elaborate cross with his right. "Ego concludam," he solemnly pronounced.

"Padre, you know we need it in English."

He shrugged. "I-a so finda." He sat.

"What does the Tiler say?"

"I so find," mumbled Earl Browder, standing by the door.

"Earl, you're mumbling again."

Raising his hangdog face, he repeated louder, "I so find!"

"And the Secretary?"

A voice familiar to Edgar drifted in from an open door behind Gary, the same voice which had resounded in the hall. "His act will live in infamy! I so find."

"Now, by the votes of all–"

A voice rose from behind the Chartreuse gangsters. "I don agree mit ze diktat of zis League! You are alvays leavink ze interests of Deutschland behind!"

"Adolf, Adolf, how many times do we have to tell you, you are only a provisional member of this Lodge. Hirohito and Stalin must vouch for you, so you will have to wait before you get to vote."

Hitler stood on a chair and gestured. "I haf only von more demand in zis lodge–I demand zat zis November criminal be tried unt shot!"

"Thank you, Adolf. As the Worshipful Master I shall take your opinion into account, but you know that the final decision is not up to us. Now please take your seat."

Adolf exhaled harshly and pursed his lips. He sat and folded his arms, glaring. "Yavvol, Mein Herr Gary," he muttered.

"Thank you. Now for my vote: in response to my own question, I hereby reply 'I so find.'"

The gavel came down once more.

Edgar looked around. No one smiled any longer.

Gary pointed his judge's gavel at Edgar. "You have been found guilty!" His voice, inevitably, had crept up to his usual pre-adolescent octave. "Do you have anything to say before your punishment is decided?"

Edgar's eye settled briefly on the nightmare text spread out before him.

> *For if this people had not fallen into transgression, the Lord would not have suffered this great evil come upon them.*

Yeah, thought Edgar: *it's all your fuckin fault.*

"The punishment for your crime is that you be silenced forever," continued Gary. "All that remains is for us to consult the Boss and see if he agrees."

Edgar's jaw dropped. "The 'Boss'? I thought *you* were the Boss."

Fat Tony and Paulie chuckled. "Lookit the genius."

Bugs rumbled. "Big Al's the Boss."

Joe Kennedy spoke up, his smile returning in a flash. "And Gary's the *Big* Boss."

"Then who–?"

Benito spread his arms wide. "We mean the Big-a *Big-a* Boss! And I betcha you cant-a guess who-a dat is-a!"

Do I really want to know? Edgar thought to himself.

Behind Gary a movie screen slowly descended. As Earl dowsed the lights, a new-fangled three-color projection device threw its images on the screen and Edgar realized he was looking at an amazing instance of futuristic technology that might one day grace the living room of every American. Did these Latter-Day Masons possess the power of magic as well?

"We call it 'Television'," called Gary. "*Two-way* television."

On the screen the inside of a small chamber appeared, the background nondescript but for a library of antique books flanked by pictures of rural still-scenes. What surprised Edgar more was the person whose visage occupied the bulk of the screen. An old-fashioned tweed jacket with white bow tie and upraised archaic white collar were mostly covered by an enormous bushy beard that accented an ancient faded face on a pear-shaped head, white fluffy sidelocks framing a giant white forelock, with no sign of creeping baldness even at what clearly was a very advanced age. The ancient eyes glinted with lack of moisture. Recognizing the Lodge through what was apparently a two-way visual and audio communications system, the mouth began to move in response to his efforts to speak.

Everyone in the Lodge stood and put their hands over their hearts, their mouths open in fawning adoration. Adolf and Benny stiffly arched their right arms.

"Hail Joseph!" they cried. Then several cried.

The ancient face cracked a brief smile. "My holy brethren," the aged voice rasped, "it behooves you to follow your hearts along the path that our Lord God has set for you. It is for you to resist the lamentations of lesbians and the deceptions of cross-dressers. Our followers can always be tested with water." The effort of his words seemed to tire him. Drawing another long breath, he asked, "What is the nature...of your inquiry?"

"O Elder Smith!" called Gary, taking care to speak loudly as if to a very old person with poor hearing, "We have in our lodge today an evil one who has violated the bylaws of our holy Chartreuse Lodge of Latter-Day Masons," Gary cast a reproachful glance at Edgar, "and a cross-dresser who cares not whether he offends the dignity of those around him," he glanced again, "and with little taste in eyeliner and whether purple gowns go with red earrings, or red wigs."

No change registered on the ancient face suspended

on the giant screen in the lodge. Finally the voice rasped.

"Cross-dressers are not to be humored. Their jokes are all reruns. They are an offense against the Big Green G." His eyes closed, seeming to fall asleep.

"*AND*," continued Gary in a loud voice that startled Joseph awake, "he keeps chasing our spies and making them sit in inconvenient seats in movie theaters and eat their hot dogs too fast, and with ketchup instead of mustard, and without pickles or onions."

"A most evil person, this."

"Our Lodge in a legal session has concluded that this evil Mr. Hoover should be silenced. What say you, O Most Holy Smith of the Invisible Brass Plates?"

Again a minute passed while the face struggled to respond.

"Yes, the evil one must be silenced." The face composed. "Is his name Joseph, by any chance?"

Edgar looked suddenly nervous.

"No, O Holy Smith. It is John."

"Then there is no appeal. Silence him without delay."

With that the screen went dark and the face disappeared. Earl turned the lights back up and after another sounding of the horrific secret code upon the door of the lodge, Hoover found himself ushered out. Within minutes he was back in the Stutz in the wee hours of the morning, escorted by the Chartreuse Gang and the Jello Brothers who had again donned their chilling white short-sleeves, on the same bumpy lane as before, wondering, while knowing he was being taken for one last ride, what the hell he had just witnessed.

Episode 10

The first chill October breeze of the coming winter of 1938 blew down 44th Street causing the flap of his greatcoat to lift, penetrating his tartan shirt, its icy fingers rising along his skin all the way to his collar where they met other fingers descending down his inadequately padded neck. The fingers made secret signs, merged, and shook hands–Joseph shivered. Although the season was still not far advanced, summer was long gone and autumn on the way out.

He paused to pass his glance over the building facades and the ephemeral gaudy signs that came and went. Not that he expected to find an answer. Seven years earlier he had burned some papers in a trash can, cashed a check for a huge amount, delivered the cash to his employer wrapped in a box, dropped him off by his home on Fifth Avenue, and then….then, at Judge Crater's own request, he had taken the remainder of the day off and gone home.

And the Judge had vanished.

His own life had since changed, but somehow he could not clear his mind of the mystery of what had happened to his former employer, Judge Joseph Force Crater, and for years now he had returned, despite himself, to the scene of the crime–if that is what it was… standing, walking, looking, thinking of what could have happened to his friend, and how, and why.

Usually starting with Billy Haas' Chop Shop on 45th,

then tracing the route which the Judge had followed two blocks down and one over until arriving at the Belasco Theater. As he had done yet again today.

His practiced eye wandered over the front of the Theater. No point in entering. A dozen inquiries with management and ushers over the years had led nowhere. Plainly Crater had not entered the place on that distant night so long ago, but had been waylaid–or worse–before he arrived at the Belasco.

Yet rumors abounded. Strange tales, such as that told by certain haberdashers who swore they had seen someone much like the Judge the next day and that he had briefly shopped but declined to buy anything and had voluntarily left their haberdashery, strangely choosing to exit by way of the back alley. And beggars and church-goers on their way to a midnight mass swore they had seen Judge Crater jogging down 44th in the middle of the night. *In the nude!*

Joseph smirked scornfully at their wild imaginings.

Then there was the report of the Judge being mugged at dawn by several huge crooks whose heads were covered by black habits trying to pass as nuns. And still more rumors of his trafficking with Al Capone's men, or with cross-dressers, or with huge foreigners, or even stranger involvements, none of which made any sense at all.

He shook his head. It was confusing. And there was no evidence to go on. Joseph rubbed his chin. He had been too efficient that distant day, burned everything that Crater had told him to burn, even the ashes, leaving no record of the serial numbers of the cash he had handed to Crater. Not even offering to pick up the Judge at the end of the night, leaving the Judge to the untender mercies of that most villainous of breeds: New York cabbies. He stifled a tear at this, the greatest indignity.

He slapped his thigh. If only he had thought…*if only.*

The tears fell.

Wandering down 44th, he passed again in front of the clothing shop, remodeled and enlarged since 1930, now serving women as well as men, but whose clerks continued to work their same positions as before. For a full minute Joseph stood in the growing cold and stared at the glass windows. He took in the changing fashions: the firm lines that had recently appeared on the shoulders, the wide bow ties that bespoke feminine innocence in contrast to the out-going flapper styles.

A face appeared at the window. For a moment nothing registered with Joseph and he turned to walk down the street. Then paused. He knew that face. Glancing back, he managed to glimpse it just as it was withdrawn. He nodded. Yes, it was the same clothier whom he had briefly interviewed those many years before. And the clothier had clearly recognized him.

Joseph entered the haberdashery.

Behind him, the large twin glass doors silently closed and he was met with a rush of warm air mingled with a hint of perfume. He stepped forward, inquiringly. The man had gone. Pushing forward through the growing customer traffic, this being the run-up to Christmas sales, he fixed his stare on one clerk after another, but failed to locate his quarry. Towards the back of the store, he paused. Could he have imagined the attempt to communicate? Could he have mistaken another person for the clerk he had met only once, long ago? Could he have read something into a brief stare that had not existed?

The back exit consisted of a smaller door not intended for customers, its upper half graced with its own glass window, and now, as Joseph gazed through that window, his eye passing through to view an alleyway and the backs of other stores that fronted another block–the same face pressed suddenly against the glass.

The clerk looked straight at him. Then backed out of sight.

There was no mistaking the meaning of this interchange. The man had something to say, and wanted to say it to Joseph. In private.

He swung the door wide. Stepping into the alley, now darkening swiftly and chilling even more rapidly than the light was dying, he strode forward, avoiding the detritus scattered about as he sought to view the alley that stretched in either direction.

Something scraped.

Rushing forward to a well-worn blue dumpster that sat some twenty feet from the store's back entrance, he stopped short. A man in hat and overcoat stood behind the dumpster, his back turned, oddly facing the wall as if reluctant to let his face be seen.

"Excuse me, sir," ventured Joseph. "But I could not help but suppose that you wished to speak with me." He stepped forward. The man continued to present his back. "I don't know if you remember me, but I am

Judge Crater's former law clerk and I once spoke with you many years ago about his disappearance..."

Still the man did not turn.

"Sir, I do not mean to disturb you, but if you could but turn for one moment so I could settle my curiosity..."

Joseph reached out his hand and touched the man's shoulder.

He turned.

Joseph choked. For a long moment he could not breathe; his heart raced in its efforts to supply blood to a brain that entirely failed to understand, despite its frantic efforts, what he now gazed upon, realizing that he viewed the utterly impossible.

He faced Judge Joseph Force Crater.

Crater spoke in a low rumbling voice. "We are recruiting Josephs. Do you volunteer?"

Before he could answer, Judge Crater reached into his pocket, pulled out a small shiny device, aimed it at his former law clerk and squeezed a trigger. Instantly, Joseph could no longer move. He thought; he felt; he dreamed. But his feet and arms were stilled as if encased in solid ice.

Behind Joseph sounded squishy footsteps as of webbed feet on unfamiliar ground. Before Joseph's uncomprehending eyes, Judge Crater melted and was replaced by a green bulbous toad riddled with lumps, its eyes swiveling on either side of its warty head like a chameleon, its hands and feet transformed into frog-like appendages. A second toad joined it.

Another squeeze of the trigger caused the front of the

dumpster to open. Each toad grabbed him by an arm and carried him easily inside, then the front raised up and resumed its connection with the sides, the toads taking up what were apparently familiar positions inside the container, their webbed hands and feet cranking dials and pulling levers.

With a rush, the container bolted skyward.

Before Joseph's glazed eyes peering through slats between the dumpster's roof and its sides, he glimpsed stars sprinkled in blackness and a blue globe that shrank to the size of a marble. A bright flash like a camera light-bulb in his face, and the constellations abruptly changed. Another bright flash, then a third, and a new globe filled his vision–olive green in parts, but mostly obscured by a permanent grey cover of cloud. The dumpster shot straight ahead until it penetrated the clouds like a shot.

A sudden deceleration, which had no perceptible pull on Joseph, and the dumpster landed gently on a small expanse of moss-covered island–another island entirely surrounded by water. Joseph regained control of his limbs.

"Koringa deridu, Xplak."

"Pluribus unum e, Korplash. *Urk*."

The front of the dumpster fell flat allowing the ribbets to walk out without having to climb the walls. The dumpster upgrade that Xplak had long requested from central supply had finally come through.

Joseph still felt sluggish and, though he found he could put one foot in front of the other, before he could exit the dumpster, Xplak fiddled with a control on one of its outside walls. Nothing happened.

"Eternal tibbetdom," murmured Xplak, though Joseph could not understand him, as he was not wearing the translation device. A webbed foot kicked the wall of the dumpster. With a whine and creak, the front of the dumpster arighted itself, blocking Joseph inside. A second later the dumpster was pushed onto a magnetorail and, to the accompaniment of Korplash and Xplak who swam zestfully in the fetid green waters beneath, accelerated without friction from island to island until arriving at the line of carts where it finally jerked to a halt with a loud metallic bang.

The front panel fell flat, this time ejecting Joseph. He stretched his arms and legs. He had regained his limbs' use, and stood, stretching and rocking on his feet. But he soon stopped as his eyes took in the surrounding marsh and mist and he began to realize the full extent of what had just occurred.

"Wh-what the hell is this place? And who the hell are you?"

Korplash waddled inside the dumpster. Retrieving translation devices, he slipped one over his head, and the other over Xplak's.

"You are on Bogland, paradise of ribbets. Gork summon this shuman?"

Xplak gave the required response. "Gork summoned this shuman. Gork like shuman?"

A rapid-fire exchange followed…

"Gork like shuman. Korplash visit Dryland?"

"Korplash visit Dryland. Shuman named Joseph?"

"Shuman named Joseph. Gork like Joseph?"

"Gork like Joseph. Joseph like Gork?"

"Joseph like Gork. Xplak like Joseph?"

"Xplak like Joseph. Korplash like Joseph?"

"Korplash like Joseph. Gork like Xplak?"

"Gork like Xplak. Xplak like Korplash?"

"Korplash like Xplak. Xplak like Gork?"

"Xplak like–"

Joseph slapped Xplak hard across his olive-green chin, the slap echoing. Both ribbets went silent and stared at each other with their toad jaws open.

"Take shuman to Gork," said Xplak. "Shuman *his* problem."

Taking out his freeze device, Xplak zapped Joseph. Picking him up with ease, Korplash and Xplak carried frozen Joseph toward a low-slung edifice that he had not previously noticed due to the vines and algae that covered it. An entrance appeared and they carried him inside. Another moment passed to the accompaniment of a rushing sound and Korplash stretched out one webbed hand to feel thin air, as if to detect whether an invisible barrier had been removed. As his hand encountered no resistance, they carried Joseph into the room. Turning, they waddled out. A second rushing sounded and Joseph concluded that the barrier had returned behind them.

He felt back to normal–whatever normal might be in this strange corner of the universe where fate had decreed that he be confined. His eyes were met by a long rectangular picture that seemed to represent a nightmare scene of marsh and grey sky and more of the trees he had glimpsed outside which seemed as if a giant had reached down and pulled them up to expose their roots. Beside him was a nice little kitchenette, the kind that would command extraordinarily high rents in downtown Manhattan. Behind him lay two beds, one of which looked recently slept in. The walls were olive-green and studded with irregular bumps. On one was a large picture of Whistler's Mother. But the strangest was the rug on the floor. It seemed to represent an endless tangle of obese green-hued frogs mounting each other with furious abandon, while Joseph was unable to discern order of any kind, or gender.

After a time the outer door buzzed open and a new larger ribbet waddled into the room. Without hesitation, it approached him.

"Shuman jump from Dryland. Shuman jump from Dryland?"

He stepped back. Trying to compose himself, he replied. "I don't know what you are, but I assure you I have not jumped anywhere. But I certainly was kidnapped."

"Shuman jump from Dryland. Shuman want return Dryland?"

Brightening, Joseph stepped forward again.

"Now you're talkin, Mac! You're damn right this shuman wants to return to Dryland."

"Gork want shuman return Dryland. Shuman is Joseph?"

His eyebrows rose. "What the hell does my name have to do with it? Just take me back to Dryland, Mr. Gork…if that's your name."

"Shuman is Joseph. Shuman like splash?" One of

Gork's eyes swiveled toward the rug with its labyrinth of eternally mating frogs. The other eye swiveled at the rectangular picture on the wall which came suddenly alive. A multitude of toad eyes swiveled to look at Joseph inside the room.

"Uh…I'm not sure what exactly you're getting at, Mr. Gork, but, uh…according to the Intergalactic Treaty on Space Abductions, Articles 1, 2, and 3, and–and I forgot the rest–you have to take me back pronto!"

"Shuman Joseph no like trips?"

"Trips? Of course I like trips. But trips are for when you have a family and go on a picnic!"

"Ribbets like trips."

"Silly ribbet. Trips are for kids. This is an abduction!"

Gork reached behind him and picked up a small white object with one appendage. "Ribbets are for galaxy. Galaxy is for ribbets. Ribbets need no treaties." He lifted the syringe and tested the liquid.

"Wha–what is that?" Joseph suddenly realized that his abduction might be due to something more than whim or accident.

Approaching, Gork produced another freeze gun.

"Oh no, you freaking toad, you're not gonna do that to me again–"

Gork did it again. As Joseph froze solid, Gork half-waddled, half hopped to one side and injected Joseph with the contents of the syringe.

"Shuman Joseph will walk again soon. But electron shield will not allow Josephs to depart until Gork is ready."

Joseph heard; thought; comprehended; and–his body

still refusing to obey the commands of his brain–the activity of that organ suddenly froze as solidly as his body, as it focused on that one surprising slip of Gork's tongue–if he had a tongue–that slip being the little matter of plurals: 'Joseph-*s*'.

A suspicion crept over him. It could not be, he told himself, as his limbs thawed. Could it be? No, it was completely impossible. This destiny was his alone, it was beyond imagining that such an unlikely fate could have come to another in all the crazy things in this crazy universe. Much less to another of the same name. No, he shook his head clear, dismissing the thought.

Even as he slowly became aware that something was happening to his body, that his sex organ, which heretofore had been as normal, even undistinguished, an organ as ever graced the state of nature, had not only come alive as if every hormone ever ID'ed by science had flooded his system, but that a second organ had suddenly sprouted beside the first, growing with astounding rapidity until less than a day later, standing before the only mirror in the room, he could not but begin to fancy himself *king of em all ya'll.* He began to eye the rug of frogs with more interest, despite his scientific detachment. Somehow, returning to Dryland and his previous life seemed not so urgent as before.

The door swished open.

The enormous blob of green waddled into the room.

"Shuman happy with room. Shuman happy with room?" said Gork. A second ribbet appeared behind him, holding another electron barrier device.

Joseph had been lying on the bed. Now he stood, attempting with some embarrassment to cover his erect members with the blanket.

"I–I don't know what to say, Gork."

"Shuman happy with pokes. Shuman happy with pokes?"

"Would it make any difference if I were happy? Or weren't?"

Gork's rubber-necking eyes inspected Joseph. "Change working. Serum good. Almost time for next change."

"*Next* change?" Joseph could not decide whether to be apprehensive or enthusiastic. "What more can happen, Gork? I mean, this is quite a change, and may not be the worst thing that could happen to a guy. What else is there?"

"Look on wall. You will see."

Joseph walked across the room. Spared further embarrassment by the sudden shrinking of both his members to normal dimensions, he faced the mirror. At first he could see nothing, which surprised him, since it was, after all, a mirror. He was comforted a moment later when a face appeared. He stepped away.

Then halted.

Something was wrong.

Looking again, he noticed that it was indeed his face, but his skin had somehow become pale. Pale he had always been, but this was more than pale. Rather white–*very* white. Even as he stared he noticed a thick layer of whiteness with the density of greasepaint erupt seemingly from the skin and creep over his features.

"No…no!" Joseph turned and leveled an angry glare

at Gork. "This can't be. You can't do this to me!"

Another look in the mirror and Joseph realized that the fearsome realization was true, his eyes had not deceived him. The face of a circus clown entirely covered with white paint, black streaks accenting eyebrows and lips, with small vertical black marks above and below his eyes for comic relief, stared back at him.

Joseph turned. He pointed at Gork. "You can't do this! God won't allow it! This is the worst thing that any creature could do to another! How can you live with yourself, you fiend?" He took a step towards Gork, then, as Gork extended his freeze ray again, Joseph turned back toward the mirror and stared again. Somehow his features seemed suddenly different. Whereas before his lip gloss was thick and the line of paint along his jaw was in one location, now the black gloss was thinner and the line of paint had moved. And the vertical marks had gone, to be replaced by diamond-shaped squares around the eyes. There was something about those eyes, about the way they stared back at him…with an expression that suggested…*evil triumph.*

Jumping backward, he paused.

The image in the mirror grew larger. Filling the rectangle it grew forward and sideways, and a figure emerged from the wall into the room itself till it stood directly in front of Joseph, who stared uncomprehendingly at what could not possibly be, who could not possibly be.

"It *is* you!" he rasped. Something grabbed his throat from inside and laid its cold hands on his vocal chords.

With a gasp, he tried to speak, but failed. From somewhere a new feeling emerged, one of confidence and pride and arrogance, a powerful feeling of superiority over mere mortals, and Joseph found himself grinning with equal fervor at the greasepainted figure that stood before him in black pants, horizontal striped shirt, and black suspenders, grinning back at him from a faceful of evil whiteness around black-purplish lips.

Gork handed Joseph a spandex jumpsuit all in yellow, with a red star over the heart, and a bowler hat one size too small. With curiosity that soon blossomed into enthusiasm, Joseph dressed himself in his new attire and balanced the hat on his head.

He took a deep breath. The grin grew large. Standing alongside, the other Joseph linked arms with him, and the two Josephs in unison danced a little jig. Simultaneously, their mouths opened wide and together they shook hard with silent feigned laughter, their chests heaving together in triumph.

The door swished aside again. A young woman rushed into the room.

"Joe, dear, don't disappear, I have the whole afternoon to myself and I thought the two of us could–" Amelia halted, her eyes settling on the new clown on the block. "Well, hello to you…." she purred. A smile of ecstasy settled on her face.

Gork pressed the barrier button and she was suddenly blocked from approaching them.

"Shuman Melia coming along well?"

She nodded and felt her tummy which had grown. "Three months and counting." She smiled contentedly.

"That is good. But shuman Melia must entertain self. Gork has other plans for Josephs."

Arm in arm, the duo skipped out the door and disappeared from view, Gork waddling close behind.

Shouts followed. "But that's not fair! It's not fair, I tell you!" Amelia turned and leaned against the invisible electron wall, now extended to keep her in the room. Exhaling sharply, she kicked at it with the back of her heel in frustration and folded her arms.

Episode 11

"Move your Amerikanischer *keepemfromdroppin!*" rang out an incredibly loud voice that echoed among the bullet-ridden walls and smashed rafters of the Los Bolos Recreation Center. At the front of the Center, FBI agents with hands raised filed through the open front doors under the direction of Japanese rifles and shouting German soldiers, and behind the soldiers several fresh-faced kids guided a clumsy woman in a purple dress and bad haircut towards the same entrance, while a young Panamanian watched.

After everyone had filed out, the Panamanian sat at the shoe dispenser counter to help himself to a Coke and a hamburger.

At the back of the Center, one eye peered around a corner and watched. Satisfied that her absence had been overlooked in the chaos, and for once unconcerned that Miguel was again scarfing a meal without paying, the eye quietly withdrew.

Mrs. Climax turned and wobbled to the back corridor that provided access for servicing the bowling pins. Passing an elaborate low-slung door to a large room constructed in imitation of an Indian teepee with a sign above that read 'Back-to-Nature Wigwam,' her eyes settled on a smaller sign tacked above the threshold of a smaller room adjacent to the Wigwam. By some, this small room might have been mistaken for a restroom; by others, a supply room; by still others, their suspicions might well be aroused that something untoward, possibly subterranean–even subversive–was suggested. If they knew what she knew–that all bowling alleys everywhere had such supply rooms attached–and that all such rooms served the purpose for which it was now about to be used, Mrs. Climax knew all too well what the consequences would be, for her, and for her co-conspirators.

The sign read: 'Nun Such.' This was code. Smiling her leetle butterball smile, she turned the doorknob, which was of such unusual design that only persons with a certain bone in their wrist could turn it properly.

She entered.

She saw an assortment of white bowling pins arranged on the floor in a certain configuration surrounded by a complicated contrivance of bowling pin erective apparatus. She nodded–as far as her neckless head was capable of nodding, merging as it did seamlessly with the remainder of her freakishly round body. Christmas tinsel blew within the skeleton of the apparatus as if blown by a steady fan. Except there was no fan. And no breeze.

On the wall was another small sign above a soft hide-bound loungechair. It read: 'Nun Much.' Above it was a placard. The first part was permanent and read: 'This month's donation the compliments of:' The rest of the placard held individual mylan letters three inches in size where had recently been inserted: 'Unitarian Church of Panama City.' The temporary mylan letters could be removed in seconds in the event of future contributors–or unwelcome investigators.

But most odd, and what drew Mrs. Climax's gaze next, was the purple mannequin that reclined on the lounge chair, dressed in a nun's black skirt and white and brown habit. Approaching the inanimate thing, Mrs. Climax carefully descended on her little knobby knees, the movement lowering her globular form by no more than inches, and she pressed her hands together in supplication.

She addressed the mannequin. "Jail Maria, fool of geese, the Lord is weeth me; blessed are you para los mujeres, busted ees the fruit of thy loom, Jessie Christina. Holy Maria, Madre de Dea, pray for us folk-seengers, now and at the happy hour of los fun and good timez with the bowling pins of Fatima ameen."

With some difficulty she stood–not that any observer would have noticed much change in her elevation given the amazing brevity of her limbs–and she took hold of the purple nun. Lifting it overhead, she gently and respectfully placed it upside down in one corner of the room, taking no notice of the fact that the black skirt promptly reversed under gravity leaving its legs indecently upraised and exposed.

Climax sat in the seat. Inlaid in the right armrest of the loungechair was a nondescript white button. Settling back, she pressed it.

Immediately, the complicated contrivance of bowling pin setting equipment that apparently had been recycled in a fashion not originally intended by the original equipment manufacturer–though perhaps it was the resetting of bowling pins that was in fact incidental to the equipment's true purpose–began to crank and move. Pins were lifted, raised, and deposited in unexpected configurations, some, despite their apparent intention, ending upside down or sideways, or set to spinning in place.

Finally the engine stopped. Extracting a small device from the other armrest, she pressed another white button on the device.

A bright light flashed.

Mrs. Climax's balloon-like form suspended on a backdrop of white stars against a black curtain. The bright flash was not repeated, and she remained motionless floating in ether as it were for minutes, then hours, then days, thereafter the units of time merging interminably one into the next until finally the stars themselves changed into unfamiliar constellations. Mrs Climax said nothing, thought nothing, felt nothing at all; did not breathe, eat, or excrete; but floated still as a corpse that refused to decompose through the ethereal vastness as if time and space mattered nought, her little round ball gathering no mass but slowly rolling through the immense waste as if seeking its destined encounter with a nine set of pins at the end of time.

A second flash and she became encased in total darkness, gravity pulling her suddenly down, her mind jarring awake.

With some effort, Mrs. Climax pushed until a sliver of light appeared, the light of a normal sun, its orb entirely hidden by a dense layer of grey cloud. She emerged from under a blue metallic dumpster and stood in the midst of brush and sedge, the dumpster one of a long line of such containers, a magnetized metal rail running beneath them.

A ribbet squatted at the other end.

Cool drops pelted her. Quickly she pulled out a vinyl sheet to cover her head from damage by the polluting water. Some distance away a commotion in what seemed to be an endless lake briefly drew her attention. The backs of innumerable green objects seemed to launch into a mutual frenzy of annihilation and took no notice of her sudden black leotard-wrapped appearance.

Oh my my my, she reflected. As a number of bug eyes swiveled in her direction from the lake, her form changed. Where a moment before had stood a short round Panamanian woman, now stood a squat green toad. Nothing to attract anyone's notice.

The toad hopped to the main entrance of what passed for Bogland's main governmental building and continued through to the other side, ignoring yet another frenzy of splashing that erupted in the lake inside. *Preserve me Santa Lucia.*

Another building soon appeared, smaller, lower, but of the same design, cratered by the incessant rains, streaked by vines and algae, large wide windows set in one side for the amusement of passersby who may be curious about the activities of the new strange species that lived such short lives and had other interests besides constant reproduction and thus were in imminent danger of extinction. Not that the ribbets were upset over the prospect of the Earthlings' early extinction–they had their own plans for planet Dryland.

Outside the structure, Mrs. Climax waited till the sun went down. Darkness swiftly fell to encompass the city in a blanket of blackness edged with silver mist. She knew for whom it waited, for whom its bell tolled. At length, she was rewarded by the emergence from the darkness of another toad of remarkably similar size, color, and shape. A similarity that could not have been accidental.

Twenty feet from the entrance to the shelter, the toad stepped suddenly into her view. The other toad halted. No sign of concern or surprise emanated from the newcomer. Not even when Mrs. Climax produced an angular red device from under her vinyl cover.

A red ray briefly shined.

With a silent shudder, the newcomer melted into a pool of running olive-green liquid. As Mrs. Climax watched, the liquid soaked into the grass till nothing remained.

Two bug eyes swiveled once more, taking in the quiet silver mist, ensuring that no one had seen. Mrs. Climax turned again to face the shelter.

The doors to the secretive experimental shelter swished open and, folding the vinyl into an unobtrusive packet, she entered, waddling into the secret rooms where Gork kept his experimental subjects. One of them stood there now, her back to the entrance.

Amelia turned.

For a moment, the intruder stared expressionless, the soul of circumspection. Then she spoke. "Does the shuman need anything from Zira? I am here to serve."

The shuman smiled. "Nice to see you again, Zira. No, thank you. I don't need anything at all." Amelia rubbed her bloated belly, which could be only hours from giving birth. "But I'm sure I will need your help very soon. I just don't understand how I can be so far along so quickly."

"I am sure all is normal, shuman Melia. Please do not hesitate to call on Zira at any time. As always, I will continue to be within range of your shuman voice, small and weak though it is."

The door swished and Gork entered.

"Zira is prompt and responsive. Zira is prompt and responsive?" Gork halted, one of his chameleon eyes directed to his long-time toad assistant.

"Zira is prompt and responsive. Gork is satisfied with Zira?"

"Gork is satisfied with Zira. Zira likes ribbets in small shelter?"

"Zira likes ribbets in small shelter. Gork likes ribbets in large shelter?"

"Gork likes ribbets in large shelter…."

Both exited the room, their conversation–mostly obligatory statements with expected ritual responses–quieting into silence as they left.

Amelia Earhart looked down. She had little experience with children, and none with babies, not having had a child before, but she smiled confidently. If there was anything she knew about the ribbets, it was that they were technically unsurpassed and could accomplish anything they put their bloated olive-green minds to, if they could just pause in their constant preoccupation with poking each other. True, Bogland was not much of a place to raise a 'shuman' child. But in that she had no choice at all. And the enthusiasm which had led to her pregnancy had been beyond her powers to resist. But worst of all: her husband had lost interest, Joe having become strangely fixated on green balloons he had found in a cupboard.

Piling up blankets and pillows, which Zira had provided to her as if they were as plentiful as leaves on trees, Amelia organized her mind and prepared her belongings for the inevitable, which the increasing occurrence of contractions told her was imminent.

She sat on the edge of the bed and struggled to catch a breath.

"Zira!"

As if he had been waiting by the door, Gork entered, with Zira close behind.

"It's…it's coming…almost here," she blurted between pants.

"*Urk.* Have no concern, shuman Melia," said Gork. "Ribbets have reviewed libraries of Dryland reference materials. All theory is under our control. Is Melia calm and relaxed? Does Melia need warm towel across forehead?"

"Uh, no thank you, Gork. Just let me lie down here," she fidgeted in the midst of the landscape of pillows as Zira assisted, "and prepare to feed my little treasure."

"Melia looks prepared. Melia wishes to feed baby gold?"

"Gold?"

"Ribbets have much little treasure."

"No! That was just a figure of speech."

"Melia wishes to feed baby figure of speech? This may be difficult to find."

"No! I only mean my baby!"

"Gork think maybe not good Melia be mean to baby."

Melia shook her head and just smiled. "Thank you, Gork."

"Does Melia wish injection?"

For a moment she looked scared. "Injection! No–no, no injection, thank you, Gork." Then another contraction arrived and she thought again. "An injection for what?"

"For shuman pain. Ribbets make tadpoles size of small cute warts–painless and quick. Shumans make big blubber ball, much pain, long time–bad design. No wonder shumans reproduce so slowly and are in danger of extinction. Melia is ready?"

Gork prepared the syringe and injected Amelia, this time without any freeze ray. Instantly she relaxed. Her eyes closed like someone had flipped a light switch.

Gork turned to Zira. "Zira must watch and assist when baby comes. Zira will watch and assist when baby comes?"

"Zira will watch and assist when baby comes," assured Zira. "Zira will be good for baby?"

"Zira will be good for baby," replied Gork. "Zira will assist when Gork sees baby?"

"Zira will assist when Gork sees baby. *Urk*."

"Gork munch jacks now. With wingless dragonflies."

Exiting, he vanished down the hall.

For the next two days, Zira stood in place beside Amelia, waiting patiently as her contractions came faster and stronger. In the wee hours of the next morning events took their inevitable course and, with the lights turned low, as Zira and Gork had inferred from their theoretical inquiries was best for mother and infant, the baby came.

Conscious and happy, and mostly if not entirely free of the pain she had feared, Amelia accepted the little cooing bundle which Zira placed in her arms, wrapped from head to toe in white and yellow cloth. And she did not feed it gold or figures of speech, but shuman milk.

Breathing an exhausted smile, Amelia looked into the little sloe-eyes and whispered one word: "Maggie." Looking up at Zira, she repeated. "Maggie…for Magdalene."

"It is good name for shuman," said Zira. "Better than Joseph."

The two-way image and audio transmission device flicked off and the anciently aged Earthling with the fulsome grey beard and upright collar rose from his seat, his decrepit joints creaking. He turned and took several steps to the rear of the small chamber that had served as a backdrop for his interview and whose walls were covered with antique books and pictures of rural scenes such as might be found in 19th century Illinois or Missouri. Brief though it was, the interview had tired him immensely. Slowly he crept forward.

Exiting the chamber, he shuffled down the narrow hall bare of decoration or anything to relieve the eye, until he came to a larger room. Rain gently tapped at a window. Reaching into a pocket, he touched a small device and instantly the old man vanished to be replaced by a bulbous green warty toad.

Two eyes swiveled like a chameleon's toward the other occupant of the room.

Joseph spoke. "Joseph did well. Joseph did well?"

The other toad was larger and, for connoisseurs of ribbetdom, exhibited a healthier younger shade of olive-green and his eyes were entirely free of the cataracts that clouded the vision of the older decrepit toad.

"Joseph did well. For Gork's first experiment, Joseph did very well. Too bad the experiment failed and Joseph Smith cannot return to Dryland. But at least Joseph Smith breathes and can live out his days enjoying the privilege of being one hundred percent ribbet. Gork's first experiment is happy on Bogland?"

Joseph, who was already old when Gork had 'privileged' him with being his first experiment on Bogland when he once had paused to glance at a painting of Whistler's Mother in the year 1844 in Nauvoo, Illinois, looked through the wide rectangular window that opened onto a yard where rain trickled down and into another wide window of an adjoining low-built structure where he saw other ribbets in the company of strange figures with white faces cavorting in striped shirts and hats one size too small. He had had no idea the circus was in town.

Sounds of splashing drifted through the window from the lake behind the structure. In response, the two male organs between Joseph's legs came alive, and he also became conscious of the vagina beneath them, a fact that he could never quite get used to, despite the century that had passed since its appearance. Being a three-organed hermaphrodite toad that remained sexually active to the end of its long life had its rewards as well as drawbacks.

Heading for the lake, Joseph said, "Yes, Gork. Joseph Smith is very happy on Bogland."

Episode 12

"Mmmmaggie. Mmmmaggie."

"Look, Zira! Did you hear that? Maggie already knows her name! Isn't that marvelous? It's been such a short time." The shuman Melia held the baby close and adjusted the blanket. The temperature at times grew cold in the shelter. Amelia grinned in Maggie's face and the little round face grinned back and kicked. "Alright, alright. I'll let you down so you can run."

Unwrapping Maggie, she briefly held the little bauble of energy while the infant's legs kicked freely in the air, then, like a racecar that suddenly engaged, Amelia let the legs contact the ground and away Maggie went. Angling sideways, her little eyes settled on a sharp projection and, like all infants, immediately rushed directly towards it aiming with unerring accuracy, like a boat with a stuck rudder.

Zira's webbed hand quickly covered the angle with a soft cloth and Maggie narrowly missed colliding with the table, choosing instead to fall flat on her face in the only uncarpeted section of the room.

"Aaaaaaah, waah, waah, waaaaah!"

Amelia looked annoyed. After a moment she picked Maggie up and tried to comfort her.

"My information says this is not bad development."

"I agree, Zira. I am no expert on motherhood–in fact, I never wanted to have a child–but in my eyes little Maggie is completely normal."

"If you say so, shuman Melia."

The shelter's inner door swished open. As he often did after a morning of relaxed splashing in the lake casually making more ribbets, Gork the ribbet half-hopped, half-waddled into the private quarters of his only captive female shuman.

"Little shuman Maggie appears healthy. Is little shuman Maggie healthy?"

Amelia looked up and smiled, catching her infant as Maggie raced past. "Yes, Gork. The little rascal is already so energetic that I can barely keep up. She has very strong legs. You really must let her run around the outside of the shelter more often. She loves to play with the little ribbets who come hopping up to play with her." Amelia took a swig from a glass bottle filled with amber liquid by her bed. "And thank you for the little nightcaps."

"You are welcome, shuman Melia. I did not know all shumans must have large supply of Johnnie Walker to function properly during the day." He looked at Maggie again. "Her healthy development is good," replied Gork. For a long moment Gork stood in front of Amelia staring at Maggie in silence as if contemplating the best way to broach a difficult topic.

Amelia spoke first. "By the way, Gork…" She took another swig and smiled her nicest smile. "I know I've mentioned this before, and I don't want to become a pest about it, but…how can I put this?" She looked pensive. "Twice a day really isn't enough!"

"How is that?"

"I'm only shuman, you know, Gork!"

"I thought that shumans no like splashing so much. So Josephs told me."

"I need my husband more than twice a day…"

"He is busy, shuman Melia."

"Then what about that cute little number in yellow spandex with the bowler hat?" Her eyes half closed, smiling.

"He is busy also, shuman Melia."

"I'd like to get busy too! That's just what I'm talking about…"

Gork looked back at Maggie, who was again racing across the floor, already having corrected her rudder and now avoiding the table with confidence.

"Gork has plans, Melia. Plans that involve…everyone."

Puzzled, shuman Melia stared back. "Of course, Gork. I know. I have accepted that."

"Enough talk for now. Gork want shuman Melia be happy." He emitted a high-pitched whistle and in moments, Yellow Spandex appeared at the door, one finger in his ear, looking around in exaggerated fashion, eyes and mouth wide open as if in a strange place, though this was far from his first time to visit Melia's room.

Gork looked at him. "Joseph. You have duty to perform."

Happiness overcame Amelia like a starburst, to such an extent that she shoved Maggie to one side where for the first time she collided with the table.

"Aaaaaah! Waaaah, waah, waah!"

"You take her, Zira," said Amelia, annoyed. "I'm going to be busy for a while… Quite a while in fact." As the Joseph drew near, Amelia grabbed her bottle of Johnnie Walker and jumped from her bed like poultry at the County Line Chicken Ranch on Uncle's Day.

With what passed for a shrug among green bloated amphibians, Zira wrapped Maggie in her bundling, picked up Maggie's lunch, and exited.

"Do not kick, little one. You will be running again soon, very soon." Zira stared with one bug eye into the almond eyes of Maggie who could not resist poking the eye with a finger. "Ouch, Maggie. Not nice to jab your faithful nurse in the eye. Be nice and eat your motzah balls."

"Jabbbb…in eyeee…" Maggie cooed. Then kicked Zira in the face.

Draping the twitching bundle over one shoulder to

avoid further injury, Zira exited the low-slung building and waddled and hopped into a light drizzle, which was even worse than the previous occasional drops of water. Quickly she draped the waterproof sheet of vinyl over her head again to avoid any contact with the punishing chemical, and her twin eyes swiveled, each independently but carefully scanning the surrounding murky tangle of uprooted trees and marsh that extended as far as her eyes could see in every direction, there being no spot anywhere entirely free of commotion and rolling olive-green bodies as the ribbets engaged in their favorite pastime, not even pausing to avoid crushing the hordes of smaller ribbets striving to splash beneath them.

Her webbed hand touched something attached to her leg and, confident that splashing meant total preoccupation and therefore that no one was watching her, Zira's image suddenly changed from that of Zira the nurse ribbet to that of a young athletic ribbet.

Gripping one of the magneto-rails that transported the blue dumpsters, she clambered forward, her tibbet feet clinging with difficulty to the smooth metal, the webbing between her toes, which was characteristic of actual ribbets, merely an illusion. Finally she arrived at the line of magnetic rail dumpsters by the main governmental building and slid off the rail in relief.

She hid around a corner.

Within minutes what she waited for appeared. Another young athletic ribbet hopped into view. Zira blocked its path. Before it could react, the red ray shined from beneath the vinyl. The ribbet melted into another puddle of olive-green liquid. Instantly, Zira's features morphed into those of her victim.

At the far end of the line of dumpsters stood another guard toad. Even younger than the liquidated toad, the guard was preoccupied inspecting a centerfold of this hour's edition of Bond-Ribbets Gone Wild.

Stuffing a wad of lakeweed into Maggie's mouth to keep her quiet, Zira slung the infant over her back, hastily wiped the stinging water off her fingers, and, with a prodigious hop, soared over the guard toad to land just behind him at the head of the line by the next available dumpster.

The guard frog turned. "Derkal, you are early," it croaked. "Splashing with the boss is not enough for your ambition? You must make me look bad by also showing up early? Too bad for you that I, Ixtad, will stay at my post."

"I am sorry you think that, my good friend Ixtad," said Derkal. "Someone told you wrong about me. By the way, there is a young toad on the back island asking for you, whose green back is a sexy light shade of olive covered with many lovely warts. I rushed here to tell you, since you are my good friend, Ixtad."

Ixtad looked up and behind with barely concealed eagerness. One eye glanced back at the line of dumpsters that duty said could not be abandoned, the other eye still transfixed on the centerfold.

"Don't worry, Ixtad. Derkal will watch the cosmodrones until you return."

"You are truly Ixtad's friend." Stuffing the centerfold into a fanny pack, Ixtad bounded into the nearest water, narrowly missing several spinning green bodies, and was gone.

Derkal changed back into Zira. She unlocked the next dumpster with a muffled clack. Retrieving a control device from a box in the side of the building, she pressed it and the dumpster sprang free of the constraints and dropped its front panel. Briefly she waddled to the next dumpster where she popped off the license plate and switched it with the plate on the dumpster that she had released.

Zira hopped in. Squatting inside the dumpster, she carefully laid Maggie on a tangle of dry cloth. Zira pressed the button again to raise the panel back up. She spun a dial and pulled a lever, and hesitated. *Which is which? Only one way to find out.* Grabbing the lever, she yanked.

The dumpster launched through the grey drizzled clouds into the cold stratosphere. While Maggie kicked and cried, Zira struggled to maintain control and soon found her attention occupied with ensuring that they did not materialize in the middle of a sun or under the intense gravity of an undetected black hole. Close to a detected black hole is what she wanted and in moments she was awarded by the dumpster's reappearance in another part of space as attested by the unfamiliar constellations. Another yank and they jumped to another location; once more and the cosmodrone materialized in the vicinity of the recently discovered, but badly contaminated Wetland. *There is much work to be done to decontaminate this place*, she thought. *How unpleasant it is to reside here in the meantime. How hard this evil chemical has been on my tibbet toad body...*

With a last spin of a dial, the cosmodrone plummeted towards the surface, though the change in gravity inside the container was imperceptible. Maggie even stopped crying to play with a cloth that had the pleasing appearance of two widely separated eyes and a wide toothless jaw.

The dumpster slowed to a gentle stop in a field on a cool October day, the crisp breeze flowing across brown grassy stalks to encompass several farm houses and a copse of tall trees shielding a tall patchworked steel water tower.

Dropping the front of the dumpster to the ground, Zira took a chance and waddled out in broad daylight. Something was clearly not right. *Pleasingly dry and desolate, yes; but where are the convent's neon signs?* Waddling her green bulk toward a road that ran adjacent to the field, she halted.

An automobile was parked by the road. Beside the shiny new Packard stood a young man who had paused to obey the call of nature. Slightly heavy-set and portentously serious in expression, his gaze lit on Zira. His eyes drilled Zira and the dumpster without respite, striving to comprehend what he saw.

Zira took a chance and put on her best spy voice. "Oh Meester, can you tell me pleeze, ees thees the planet Earth? I have come a loong way to see thee place called Nevaada."

His jaw dropped. Stumbling, he fell back against the auto. In a flash he dove inside and, gunning the engine, belted down the road where he disappeared behind a small sign that read 'Rabbit Hill Road' beside another sign that read 'Welcome to Grovers Mill.' A calling card fluttered in his wake, 'Orson Welles, Director, Mercury Theater' printed on the front.

Zira looked down at her green toad body. Oops. She pressed the small device again and instantly morphed into a shorter figure with black leotard and tan skin almost completely round in appearance. *That job would have been better for the shuman Mrs. Climax,* she thought.

The little legs of Mrs. Climax transported her roly-poly figure back to the dumpster where Maggie had already kicked off her covers and was staring at the great big new world outside.

"Stay inside, my leeetle dung beetle. Weee are not home yet."

Maggie's legs kicked the side of the dumpster with a resounding thump as Mrs. Climax raised the front panel, and in another few moments the container was once more aloft, rushing westward at a cruising altitude of ten thousand feet. Swiftly passing the occasional biplanes and monoplanes barely visible far below, being little more than kites a short distance above the ground in comparison, the cosmodrone passed over the vast unknown of the Great American Desert of 1938 to arrive at last in the middle of an equally vast expanse of desolation by a dully placid lake surrounded by dusty plains whose edges slowly rose to dry ridges on several sides. Their peaks gleamed in the last rays of the sun as dusk settled on the wide outspread valley, no other lights visible as far as the eye could swivel.

A single-story building appeared below, blue and red sparks rapidly enlarging into sweeping neon signs that graced the front façade as the cosmodrone lowered. The dumpster alighted in the unpaved parking lot with a bump.

'Maxie Climax's Bowlarama Chicken Ranch & Casino for West Middle Nevada – Opus Dea Precinct 7' flashed the lights–the lights still lit at this late hour–casting their unlikely sprawling invitation into the uninhabited surrounding stretches of the Nevada desert.

Episode 13

The car rocked as the left front tire hit a pothole.

"Jesus, Mary, and Joseph," said Paulie. "Whatsa matta, Fat Tone? Ya forgit how to drive?"

"You try keepin this jalopy on the road. We ain't in Jersey any more in case you hadn't noticed." Fat Tony peered out the window into the darkness, cacti and spiny bushes sailing past. "They don't lay asphalt so good out here, ya know?" Tony accelerated to catch up with the black car in front.

"Just keep watchin the Bruddas up ahead and don't lose em. And watch dat road." Paulie looked at Edgar riding beside him. "We don't wanta upset the little lady here. No ma'am."

Bugs and Tony laughed deep laughs.

"But if youse hits another pothole, I'm gonna ask Bugs here to take de wheel before youse jalopies us into da ditch."

"Not me."

Paulie looked at Bugs. "Not you? And why da hell not?"

"Cause the case bein that I cain't drive," said Bugs.

"What…what was dat?"

"What I said, Paulie. I cain't drive."

"Now, why would dat be, Bugs… By the way, when I say Bugs, dat means I'm talkin to you, okay Bugs?"

"Yeah, Paulie. Okay. Youse talkin to me–Bugs."

"Glad we got dat straight." Paulie looked over Edgar to stare at Bugs. "Now Whadaya mean ya cain't drive? Ya broke ya little wrist, like maybe Miss Mary here?"

Bugs looked put out again. He shrugged. "Cause I ain't got no license."

Tony looked back at Paulie.

"Ya ain't got no license?" Paulie looked puzzled. He cocked his head and stared at Bugs. "What's a license got to do wit it? You plan on cuttin someone's hair before ya plug em?"

Tony and Paulie chuckled.

"My driver's license, Paulie. I never got it." He looked out the window into the darkness as if about to confess a deep dark secret. "I failed the drivin test. I was a kid and didn't know no betta."

Paulie dripped empathy. "Oh, youse was a kid and youse didn know no betta. Now dat explains *everythin.* Youse cain't turn a wheel cause youse was a kid and youse hit a plastic cone once. Yeah, dat explains *everythin.*"

"Wadn no plastic cone, Paulie. It was…"

"Yeah?"

"The writin part. I failed the writin part, cause I…"

"Yeah, well out wit it, ya moron. What was it?"

"Cause I cain't write nuttin."

Tony and Paulie looked at Bugs in surprise.

"Ya cain't write nuttin!"

"Yeah, that's what I said. I cain't write nuttin. So I ain't got no license. And that means I cain't drive no car."

Paulie smacked Bugs on the back of the head. "Youse knows what dat means? It means youse is a moron! Dat's what dat means–and nuttin else!" Paulie settled back in his seat, fuming. "Cain't drive…of all the stupid things…"

Paulie looked up again. "Ya got your piece, dontcha?"

Bugs patted his breast pocket. "Yeah, I got my piece."

"Ya got a license for dat?"

Bugs took out his pistol and looked at it. "No, Paulie."

"So what good is it, then? Why dontcha just shoot the car wit it, cause ya ain't got no license for either one! Ya see what I mean?"

Bugs aimed the pistol at the dashboard and pulled the trigger. A colossal explosion filled the car's interior as the massive bullet penetrated the dashboard and lodged in the engine. The Stutz spun 180 degrees spitting crushed limestone from the road's shoulder in all directions and came to a screeching halt in a parking lot.

The first light of dawn illuminated the gangsters as they spilled out of the mortally injured vehicle, smoke pouring over the roof of a roadside motel. The other

Stutz halted and backed up. Mormon missionaries exited to stare at the wreck.

Next to Bugs, Paulie stood with his hands pressed to the sides of his face, jaw open.

Fat Tony shoved Bugs. “What the hell didya do dat for, ya moron! Ya almost drilled me!”

Bugs looked confused. He looked at the still smoking gun barrel.

“Well, why dontcha say somethin?”

Orangello and Lemongello approached. They peered as Tony lifted the hood, though it was already clear that the auto was unsalvageable. Edgar slid out of the back seat and stepped away–no point in allowing soot to damage his wig, which he had repositioned on his head.

Bugs stepped next to Paulie. “Paulie…”

Paulie slapped a hand over Bugs’ mouth. “Don’t say it! Just don’t say it!”

He mumbled till Paulie removed his hand. “Ya told me to do that, Paulie. Ya told me…” His lip protruded again.

Tone and Paulie both let out long quiet sighs. Paulie patted Bugs on one shoulder. “Youse right, Bugs. Ain’t your fault. I told ya to do dat.”

Bugs risked a smile.

The sun edged the horizon and threw more light over the scene to reveal a dozen or so cars, new ones appearing steadily from the direction of Salt Lake City.

Edgar glanced at the motel’s sign. It read “Welcome Jehovah’s Witnesses–Utah Chapter.” Sensing trouble–as if more were possible–Edgar shot a glance at Lemon and Orange. They were staring at the sign transfixed, their faces fierce. One glanced behind as if scoping out a path of retreat.

Too late.

Even as they and Edgar watched, a car of young men in white button shirts and crewcuts pulled into the motel parking lot, another car of burly men in thick overcoats close behind. The Hudsons jerked to a stop. Bibles and bats appeared–they had been spotted.

Paulie tapped Bugs who stopped smiling. “Lookit! It’s No-Nose Knuckles!”

“Hey, yeah! And Pussy Louie, with Rat’s Ass Rudy! Howdaya like that?” They looked at each other. “What the hell is the Mauve Gang doin out here?”

Paulie elbowed Tony and motioned with his eyes for him to look to their Lodge brothers. Orangello and Lemongello were loosening the straps on their Latter-Day Bibles for quick access. Their hard look darkened as they saw the three Jehovah’s Witness youths similarly loosen straps on their Books. Neither side was prepared to back down.

The motel’s other visitors strolling across the parking lot sensed something was up and stepped back to seek cover, not sure what was about to happen but certain it spelled no good for anyone, for the town or its inhabitants.

No-Nose, Rat’s Ass, and Pussy Louie lined up behind the three Witnesses, who stood stiffly but casually, as if they cared not whether they lived or died. Tumbleweeds rolled over the freshly shined shoes of the Jello Brothers, who took a step forward, hands drifting down, seemingly uncaring, but their thumbs never far from the Books hanging in felt pockets on their belts. Paulie, Bugs, and Tony spread out behind them, hands perched in coat pockets, their loyalty to the Chartreuse Lodge of the Latter-Day Masons too deep to be removed short of death.

The leading JW produced a toothpick.

Orangello produced his own. For a long moment he dawdled, exploring crevasses in his gums, as the JW did the same. Unsmiling, Orangello squinted up at the rising sun, its heat already beginning to bake down on the mortals whom fate had decreed must play out the savage scene, come what may.

After several minutes of silence during which no one dared move, Orangello steeled himself. Slowly stretching out one hand, he offered his toothpick to the lead Witness.

"Cinnamon. Want some?"

The young man, every bit as determined and hardened to his fate as Orangello, said nothing but also squinted at the sun. At length he showed his own toothpick, careful to make no sudden moves.

"Red Hot. Got all I need."

Fat Tony cast a nervous glance at Orangello and dug in his heels. Pussy Louie and Rat's Ass Rudy did not have the massive weight of Fat Tony and Bugs, but their baseball bats made up the difference. No-Nose lived up to his name; his face was screwed but inscrutable, and he wore a set of high decibel ear protectors to reduce the chances of losing another appendage.

Like statues the opposing sides stood for what seemed an eon, no one risking any sudden moves that might trigger a lethal response from their rivals, but neither side willing to back down and abandon the field.

From somewhere a dog howled mournfully. Its echoes evoked Mexican trumpets as the rising sun glinted in their unblinking eyes squinting from the heat.

Edgar shivered. Unable to take the stress, he backed across the parking lot until he was out of reach of stray Bible passages; turning, his high heels slipped and he fell onto gravel–still none of the Bible-toting gladiators twitched a muscle. Crawling to his feet, Edgar took refuge behind the main entrance door where a dozen frightened pedestrians rubber-necked at the windows, too scared to risk full exposure to the showdown.

The sun rose higher. Still no one moved. The Mexican horn sounded louder.

Suddenly the Witness shut his babyface mouth and let his Red Hot toothpick drop. "You're the Jello Brothers…aintcha?" he said in his adolescent unbroken voice.

Lemongello glanced once at the highway, then back again.

"Yep."

Slowly nodding, the Witness risked a single sideways glance. His companions looked back. "I've heard of you." He continued to stand motionless. One hand reached for a second toothpick, and paused.

Orange spoke. "And you are…?"

The young man with the determined face glanced down at his new shoes, a layer of dust covering the just shined black saddles. He adjusted a pocket protector over his left breast. "Ben and Jerry. And *Little Joe*."

Even the Chartreuse Gang were taken aback by the menacing names of their adversaries, accentuating as they did the nightmarish button-down vacant white short-sleeves and the spotless black slacks. The Gang shifted their feet nervously.

Orangello rippled his lips. "No last name....?"

"Smith." The second Red Hot went in. "Just 'Smith'."

The Jello Brothers registered no response; they may as well have been told that the sky was blue, or that chickens lay eggs.

" 'Smith' sounds...familiar," Lemongello said at last, Orangello edging closer to his side.

Ben carefully nodded. "It do at that...in these here parts."

Orangello decided to make his move. "Then you know this is *Mormon country*. Ain't no room for JW's hereabouts." He slid a second Cinnamon toothpick into his mouth. "I suggest you boys climb back into your autos, back em up, and ride em to the next town." His hand moved closer to his Bible.

Ever so slightly, Ben's composure seemed to ease, as if that which he knew must happen, but which he had hoped could somehow be avoided, had been shown to be inevitable despite his efforts, leaving him steeled to his fate but relieved to be finally free of doubt.

As if reading his thoughts, Lemongello's and Orangello's faces similarly eased, their expressions as alike as mirrors.

Lemongello slowly crushed some limestone under his

shoe, change jingling in his pocket.

For a long tense minute silence reigned.

"Ha-ha-haa!" JW Jerry broke suddenly into loud laughter and rocked happily back and forth on his patent leather shoes for half a minute, then just as suddenly grew quiet, again deadly serious. He glanced at the statue beside him that was Ben.

Silence returned.

Despite the hammering sun, a darker shade seemed to cover the Jello Brothers' faces–Ben and Jerry darted their eyes rapidly between Lemon and Orange in response while Little Joe's hand moved closer to his Book…the Mexican horn reached a crescendo. The Jello Brothers did not miss the move.

Again the dog howled.

The horn stopped.

With a flash, JW Ben whipped out his Watchtower Bible–the dreaded Emphatic Diaglott with Alphabetical Appendix–and snapped it open.

Before his eyes could settle on a passage, Orangello had his Mormon Bible primed with First Nephi, 10. He shouted: "Lehi took the records which were engraven upon the plates of brass, and he did search them from the beginning, and he beheld that they did contain the five books of Moses, which gave an account of the creation of the world!"

Ben staggered back. One hand clutched Jerry's shoulder and he managed to steady himself, the blow not being mortal. With deadly accuracy he recited in reply: "And the whole city assembled at the door, and he cured many sick of various disorders, and expelled many demons, and permitted not the demons to speak…1:43."

Orangello fell to one knee. He gritted his jaw. Before he could rise again, Lemon aimed his Latter-Day Bible and unleashed One Nephi, 22: "And the angel said unto me: Behold, these shall dwindle in unbelief. And it came to pass that I beheld, after they had dwindled in unbelief they became a dark, and loathsome, and a filthy people, full of idleness and all manner of abominations."

Jerry doubled over. Little Joe unexpectedly jumped in, brave for his fifteen years: "Judge not, and you will not be judged; condemn not, and you will not be condemned; forgive, and you will be forgiven!"

It was Lemongello's turn to stagger. Almost dropping his Latter-Day Bible, he managed to catch it in his other hand, but he was winded and had to pause to recover his breath.

Before he could respond, Paulie stepped forward brandishing brass knuckles in his right hand.

Jerry recovered. He immediately aimed his Emphatic Diaglott at Paulie: "And he Jesus was about thirty years old when he began his work, being, as was allowed, a Son of Joseph, the son of Eli, the son of Matthat, the son of Levi, the son of Melchi–"

Unable to stomach any more, Paulie dropped his knuckles and fled. Bugs stepped up.

"–the son of Jannai, the son of Joseph–"

Bugs gasped and doubled over. Fat Tony stepped in front to protect his Lodge Brother.

"–the son of Mattathiah, the son of Amos, the son of

Nahum, the son of Esli–"

"Oh, God, I can't take it!" That was enough for Fat Tone and he and Bugs ran for the far side of the parking lot.

Jerry stood straight, a calm smile on his face, his Bible emitting dust like smoke.

Standing beside Ben, No-Nose Knuckles lifted his bat.

Little Joe yelled: "If thy right eye insnare thee, pluck it out, and throw it away; it is better for thee to lose one of thy members, than that thy whole body should be cast into Gehenna…5:33!"

Staggering back at the prospect of losing another organ, No-Nose turned and fled, leaving his bat clattering on the ground as Jerry and Ben stared in surprise at Little Joe. Friendly fire.

Rat's Ass Rudy and Pussy Louie looked at each other.

It was Lemongello's turn to unleash the big guns: "But behold, I give not the full account, but a part of the account I give, from the tower down until they were destroyed. And on this wise do I give the account. He that wrote this record was Ether, and he was a descendant of Coriantor. Coriantor was the son of Moron. And Moron was the son of Ethem. And Ethem was the son of Ahah–"

That was enough for Pussy Louie. He jumped in the JW's second car and took off, pausing only to pick up No-Nose who was thumbing a ride on the turnpike and desperately slapping himself to stay awake.

"–and Ahah was the son of Seth. And Seth was the son of Shiblon. And Shiblon was the son of Com. And

Com was the son of Coriantum…Ether 1!"

Rat's Ass Rudy was tough but he was wavering. A gesture from Orangello as he aimed his Latter-Day Bible, licking a thumb the better to flip pages, proved enough to send Rudy packing.

Ben still struggled to catch his breath. Finally he had recovered and with a swift move, he grabbed a woman who had naively attempted to walk past the scene of combat. He pressed his Emphatic Diaglott against her smooth exposed neck. The book was open to a verse whose lethality only he could know.

Lemon and Orange moved closer, hardened to hard deeds.

"Let her go, Ben." They directed fierce stares at the Jehovah's Witness, whose eyes stabbed left and right desperately searching for an exit while Jerry and Little Joe, alarmed at the escalation, stepped back, though they understood the logic that permitted no backing down without a final decision. "She ain't done you no harm. No need to drag a stranger into this. This is between you and me."

Sweat poured down Ben's neck. Dragging his hostage, he took a step backward. Maybe he still had time to leap in the remaining Hudson and make for the border. Would the Jello brothers allow him the time? Could he afford to wait for Jerry and Little Joe, or would he have to sacrifice his friends to save himself?

"Haaaalp me, Jesus!" cried the woman. "Don't let dis white cracker ass do dis to me! I got chilluns at home!"

Ben pressed the Watchtower Bible harder against her neck, shutting her up, then broke out in laughter–laughter of a desperation bordering on insanity. "Ha ha ha! I told you you can't win, Orangello! You'll never take me down–*never!* Jehovah's Witnesses can't be stopped. Not by you! Not by anyone!"

"Let her go, Ben. This won't help you at all."

Ben suddenly looked serious. He looked sorrowfully up at the sky. "You just had to push it, didn't you? You and Lemongello." He swallowed. "This is a big state they tell me…could have been big enough for the both of us." As Jerry and Little Joe watched in shock, with his free hand Ben pulled out another Red Hot and quietly savored it. He stared down the barrel of the Jello Brothers' twin Mormon Bibles aimed directly at him. *What will it be like on the other side*, he wondered? The sound of a plaintive slide guitar drew him toward the next world. *I never really liked horns.*

With a shove, he thrust the woman aside and snapped open his Bible: "The Lord of the promise is not slow, as some regard slowness! But is patient towards us, not wishing that any one should perish…John 3:16!"

Lemon and Orange were too fast for him: "The Lord suffereth the righteous to be slain that his justice and judgment may come upon the wicked! Therefore ye need not suppose that the righteous are lost because they are slain…Alma 60:13!"

They ceased reciting. Slowly folding their Books in the midst of a cloud of smoky dust, they saw Ben fall to the ground and stare at the sky without moving. His Watchtower Bible lay at his side, open but face-down in the dirt.

Little Joe stared in horror at a sprinkle of toothpicks

scattered over Ben's body. Little Joe shuddered–fifteen years was too young, after all. Jerry closed his Book and put it back in its felt holder. He stared away at the far horizon.

The patent leather shoes of the Jello Brothers neared, crunching gravel and shell. Their scripture kung fu was better.

"Yep," said Jerry. "I hear tell the next state is big and beautiful." He put his hands in his pockets. "Plenty people there never heard of Jehovah." Little Joe looked up at him in wonderment. From somewhere a gentle acoustic guitar picked up its beat as if a new life awaited. A little boy stared from behind a white picket fence, his dog yapping happily.

Sliding their instruments of destruction back into the felt pockets hanging on their belts, Lemongello and Orangello slowly strode toward the motel office, Fat Tone and Bugs venturing near again, with Paulie behind. Although they could see Jerry and Little Joe pick up Ben and help him brush the dirt off his shirt and slacks, they knew the JW's would not be so foolish as to repeat their challenge. The Jello Brothers safely turned their backs and walked. Their legend had increased by several more notches. Moments later the last Hudson was gone.

Unhurriedly, Orange pushed the double doors to the motel office wide open, keeping his distance, his Bible still unstrapped–old habits die hard. The other guests scrambled back from the windows and bunched themselves at the other end of the room.

"This town ain't safe with those Bible-slingers

around," mumbled an old woman, then quieted as her husband hushed her with a stare. He turned to the newcomers. "We don't want no trouble, now, misters. Just tell us what you want and you can be on your way."

Lemon and Orange looked at the guests, then exchanged glances. Edgar was not among them.

Episode 14

Which button is it again? A quick push and the front of the dumpster fell flat, sending Mrs. Climax rolling across the pitted asphalt of the parking lot. When she finally stopped rolling she unfolded her tiny legs and arms and stood. Was it disappointment she felt? Or envy? Had the sacred white pins risen up before her righteous onslaught, such a magnificent roll would have resulted in a strike. Momentarily she reflected that maybe she should drag the ribbet dumpster inside, the better to improve her score.

Night had fallen. Before her spherical form flashed the long row of huge letters: 'Maxie Climax's Bowlarama Chicken Ranch & Casino.' A lot to hang on the front of the building, but then she and her Sisters had a lot to say–to some people, that is. For the rest, the tangle of neon, and more that remained unlit, would serve just as well to invite visitors to lose their money.

"Mmmmmelia. Mmmmmelia."

Mrs. Climax's arms reached down to invite little Maggie into her embrace, not very far down given that Mrs Climax's height was more on a level with bowling pins and infants than the height of most adults anyway. "I am sorry my leeetle dung beetle, but you will not be seeing your Momma *Melia* for some time. Johnnie Walker is not the best medicine for leetle beetles like you. Now come kiss your new Momma *Maxie*."

Springing out of the dumpster like a jackrabbit, Maggie launched her tiny body directly at Mrs. Climax, the collision sending Climax rolling again, Climax withdrawing her limbs before the impetus could snap them off. Hitting the initial steps of the Bowlarama, she bounced and rolled up several steps before coming to a stop. *I really should set up some pins out here*, she thought.

Maggie stepped forward on her two strong little legs, surprisingly strong for an infant her age, at first walking hesitantly, then with more confidence. Then she ran. At the last moment, she attempted to brake, but failed, and again collided with Mrs Climax, who bounced up the remainder of the steps to spin on the highest like a top.

"Besa la puta, el pendejo!" Try as she might, Mrs Climax could not shake her Panamanian roots and the worst still came out when the worst came over her. Her momentum slowly dispersing, she finally steadied herself and stood holding her head.

"My jumping bean, I theenk I need to slow you down a leetle." Turning, she pushed the entrance doors wide and entered the lobby of a modestly furnished bowling palace with two pairs of one-armed bandits flanking the vestibule. Most of the back end was unfinished, and several dark-clothed bodies could be seen rising and falling as in heavy labor, amid clanks and clunks.

Climax walked to the shoe dispensary and reached behind the counter. Extracting a length of cord, she tied one end to a dog harness and clipped the harness around Maggie's body. "Now you will not be causing me eeny more trouble, will you my leetle dung beetle?"

Jumping up, Maggie let loose with a kick that sent Mrs Climax falling flat, for once not having time to roll into a ball. "Trou-ble!..." burbled Maggie with a sweet smile.

Recovering, Mrs. Climax reached behind the shoe dispensing counter and withdrew a pair of small roller skates that someone had abandoned in the Casino. She strapped them on Maggie's feet, stuffing newspaper to fill the gaps. "And this should keep your feet on the ground," she said, rubbing her globular midriff where Maggie had kicked it.

"Oh *my my my!* Maxie is here, Sisters!" One of the black-clad laborers dropped a sledgehammer and came to greet them. "And look at this cute little one!" They stared as Maggie wobbled on her new outsized skates like a skier trying on skis for the first time.

"Thees ees the leetle one, Magdalene. Or 'Maggie' for short."

Maria bent over, hands on knees, and flashed her best smile almost on Maggie's level. "My name is Maria! Are you glad to be here with us, little Maggie?"

A finger darted out and poked Maria in the eye. "Jab.... eye...." Maggie grinned and burped. "Momma Maria. Momma Maxie." One hand yanked Maria's habit and exposed her breasts. Maggie locked her mouth on a nipple and suckled, yanking the leash from Climax's hands, her infant but muscular legs holding the nun to the ground, her heavy skates serving as anchors.

So surprised that she had no time to react, Maria lay flat with her mouth open and one hand over her eye while Maggie sucked with terrific force, and they were soon joined by Marina, Marie, and Mary, who laid aside their hammers and crowbars. Together they tried to pull Maggie off, without success.

"Oh my my," they said in unison. "Maybe we should try to find some milk."

Behind the black and brown-clad nuns of the Nevada Chapter of Opus Dea, approached several more in decidedly less confining attire, their head-habits utterly at odds with the expanses of bare skin showing below, covered by nothing more than narrow two-piece swim suits as if parading the latest avant-garde combination of swimwear for the spiritually-minded.

"Marie," said Mrs Climax, "how is everytheeng coming along?"

One of the fully-clad nuns replied. "Oh my my. Right on schedule, Maxie! We are so proud of our work–sinfully proud."

"That ees good, my Seesters of the Sacred Precinct. But don't forget to say two Hail Mary's and two Our Mother's for every time you are seenful. And don worry. It is those seenful men who make us do theese seenful things."

"Oh yes yes, Sister Maxie. It is those sinful men for sure. That's why we have dug all the way to the third level underground to protect our Sacred Precinct from their sinful ways. Why at this rate, Sisters, we will finish the fourth underground level by early next year!"

"Won't that be nice!" said Mary.

"Oh yes!" added Marina. "Way ahead of schedule!"

"And you, Maryann?" asked Maxie. "Are wee about ready to open for beesiness?"

"Yes, Mother Maxie," said one of the scantily-clad nuns. "We are all ready for those sinful men–and anyone else who wants to gamble their money away. After all," she added, "if everyone else in Nevada is doing it, why can't the Opus Dea Sisterhood of Sacred Precinct 7 of West Middle Nevada?"

"Yes, indeed! And you, Mary?" continued Maxie, "is the Wigwam compleeted?"

"Yes, Sister Maxie," said Mary. "And look! Here comes our first customer!"

Mouth open in eager anticipation, Maxie Climax joined all the other nuns–supernal oriented and otherwise–in rushing to the broad clear windows where the flashing neon signs illuminated a single vehicle, a car with one occupant.

The door swung wide and out stepped a nondescript man of average height and average build, nothing to distinguish him from any of a hundred, or hundred thousand, other such unwashed men wandering the empty dusty plains of mid-twentieth century Nevada. As he hesitantly approached the front doors, his eyes fixed on the portion of the sign that said Casino, and the pearly gates parted to entice him in. It was quite out of the way and he would not have seen it at all had he not taken a wrong turn off I-95. But work was over and this time of the day was his. Placing one hand over his wallet to ensure it did not jump out and vanish, he walked in.

His eyes bulged. It was surprise enough to glimpse fully dressed nuns here in the middle of nowheresville where the word 'traffic' was irrelevant, but the sight of swimwear matching holy headcovers was more than unexpected. For a moment he glanced back at the sign, wondering where he may have gone wrong–while half hoping that he had gone wrong indeed–then the nuns closed around him with smiles and offered to bring him drinks while they fetched bowling shoes, and, like worker bees herding a drone, led him to the closest stained and varnished blond-wood bowling lane, the whole institution quite a surprise given its remote location next to all-but-forgotten Papoose Lake. Before long he was reeling under the influence of strong lemonade, subtlely cute smiles from the barely clad, and disingenuously accentuated hips and waists with long sleek legs from the younger nuns who were clearly enjoying themselves.

"What's your name, good-lookin?" One smiled.

He stopped to think. "Charlie." He commenced to grinnin.

"Maryann, Charlie looks like he might be hungry. Can you bring us some free sandwiches and lemonade, please?"

"Oh yes, yes." She jumped to it while Charlie broke out in a broad smile, unable to believe his luck after his wrong turn in the middle of the Nevada desert.

Behind the shoe counter Marie whispered, "That's enough for now, little Maggie," and with the assistance of two other nuns again attempted to pry her lips off her breast, but Maggie's lips refused to relinquish and stretched her teat like a balloon.

It popped.

"Eeyah!" Marie staggered to her feet, one hand over her eye, the other over her nipple.

A leg kicked and connected with Marina, flooring her as it had Maxie, the heavy skate barely restraining Maggie.

"Mmmmore!" cried Maggie, though there had been no milk to begin with, and not likely to be any from someone with the build of a lumberjack who had been pouring concrete and hauling dirt for months. Maggie stood and rolled in a circle, already adjusting to the skates.

On the lanes, the customer was carefully counting out hard-earned dollars when he paused to look behind the shoe counter for the source of the commotion. Mary and Maria hastily snatched up Maggie and carried her off–leash, skates, and all–to the complex of back rooms behind the bowling lanes. Not even Maggie could overcome the muscles of two hardhat construction nuns.

Maxie followed. As Mary and Maria deposited Maggie in the nuns' bivouac area–pausing to watch in alarm as she promptly began to skate into furniture like a locomotive, soon leaving much of it marred and marked–they locked the door and retreated back to the safety of the hallway, then to their holy official meeting room, holy living area, holy recreation room, and holy communal locale, otherwise known as the kitchen, thumps and grinding penetrating the walls to assure them of the continued vitality of their new little gift, though perhaps less so regarding the integrity of the furnishings.

The nuns looked at Maxie questioningly. It was not every day that an Opus Dea nun brought home a stray anything, especially the nominal head of the local Sacred Precinct, much less what seemed more like a missile of mass destruction.

Meanwhile, Charlie had scored his first strike, despite the increasing distraction of the youthful bare-midriffed nuns, one of whom had even let her habit drift backward to reveal a magnificent crown of long brunette hair, which caused him twice to roll into the gutter.

Charlie focused on his game. Two strikes later, the nuns clapped, "Yay, Charlie! Three strikes! You have won your *Special Reward!*"

" 'Ree-ward'?" He perked up as if his fortunes might be about to become better than he dared dream, surpassing even the turkey on rye.

"Here at Maxie Climax's Bowlarama Chicken Ranch & Casino, everyone who wins three strikes gets a Special Reward! To get your reward all you need do is visit our Back to Nature Wigwam and let us share our good fortune by learning about the teachings of our Sacred Precinct!"

"Teachings?" Charlie gulped more lemonade and felt the dizziness return. He reached for another bowling ball. Hands pressed him back.

"Yes! In fact, we are having a special presentation in the back room in just a few minutes which will instruct all of our Church's teachings. We want to present to you the Good News that has come into our lives. We're sure you will like it too!"

"Good News?" He took another drink. "I'm always for Good News."

"That's great! Then come this way…" The scantily-clad nuns gently but firmly drew Charlie to his feet and escorted him past the lanes and into the back, where they bypassed the holy kitchen, the holy bivouac which had finally calmed and was no longer emanating thumps through the walls, and the holy supply room with the small sign over the door that read 'Nun Such,' and finally to an irregularly-shaped aperture under a somewhat larger sign that displayed in large green letters: 'Back-to-Nature Wigwam.'

Inside darkness loomed.

Charlie pulled back.

"Don't worry, Charlie, we'll all go inside together." One of the nuns winked. "You won't complain if we all get cozy inside our wigwam, will you? Just you… and us?" More sexy smiles followed.

"Uh, no," he smiled. "I wouldn't mind at that, little lady." He bent and stepped through.

Inside was a paucity of furnishings, and he was directed to sit on the floor in the middle of the Wigwam, while smoke from several incense censers circled and rose toward a small hole at the top. On ersatz deer-hide walls, loosely hung wooden signs in Frontier font read: 'Peace & Justice,' 'Earth Day,' and 'Unleash your Fem.' He shrugged. *Nothing wrong with all that I guess*. There were pillows tossed around, and elaborately large Indian peace pipes and primitively surfaced drums, but the only actual furniture in the teepee was an old Western style rocking chair. In the chair sat a stiff purple mannequin with its dummy hands folded in its lap over a paisley dress with a blond wig on its head.

"First we must say our prayers, of course. This is a church, after all."

The nuns sidled close, collecting around him on the floor. Maryann led the prayer while each nun clasped her hands and closed her eyes.

"Our Mother, who bakes in heaven, Jessie be thy name, thy kitchen come, thy cook be done in baking as it is unleavened. Give us this day our daily bread, and forgive us our recipes as we forgive the recipes of others; and lead us not into conception; but deliver us from the sinfulness of men."

A little odd, thought Charlie. But he was reassured by the renewed smiles of the nuns surrounding him and he watched as they began to assume Buddhist lotus positions, legs folded. Glancing at the mannequin, Charlie thought it too was odd and a bit inconsistent with either prayer or meditation or even what he supposed should be the best teaching principles, but with another glance at his attractive companions, he shrugged his shoulders again. Whatever… Once the oddness was over, the one-armed bandits waited. And he still had his wallet.

"We do our teaching during meditation. To get your reward, you must join us."

A minute passed in silence as Charlie sniffed the incense and tried to keep his eyes closed and his mind clear despite the expanses of lustrous female skin surrounding him, such as no church casino that he had ever heard of indulged in. *This has bingo shot to hell*, he thought. He also thought of reaching out and touching while they had their eyes closed, but decided that that might be crossing a line, or–worse–might end the flow of free sandwiches and lemonade. *After all,* he thought, *gotta keep our priorities straight.*

Finally the lead nun opened her eyes.

"Now repeat after me."

"Okey-dokey," he mumbled.

"Momma knows best," came a quiet voice.

A tear ran over his cheek. "Momma! Hadn't thought of her in years… Momma did know best!" He bit his knuckle, then lowered his hand and closed his eyes again.

"Don't mess with Mother Earth," continued the speaker.

Charlie felt dizzy. Not sure whether it was still the powerful lemonade or the effect of the incense or perhaps just the late hour, before he knew it he found himself mouthing: "Don't mess with Mother Earth."

The nun passed a hand over her face. "Zero children is best for the planet."

He nodded, his chin on his chest. "Zero children is best for the planet.'"

"Smoking is a crime against Nature."

"Smoking is a crime against Nature."

"Except for marijuana peace pipes."

"Except for marijuana…" Charlie ceased speaking.

"Peace pipes," repeated Maryann.

"Peace…" Charlie began again.

"Pipes," suggested the nun.

"Tits," replied Charlie.

"Peace pipes!"

"Perky tits."

A frustrated sigh came from Maryann. She continued.

"Ibsen's Doll House was a great book."

"That doll has a great look."

"Doll House!"

"Brick-house."

"Ibsen's Doll–"

"Bras on dolls…"

"Was a great book!"

"Fucked a great nook."

Maryann shook her head, her hand on her forehead. *As sinful as a sinful man could be*. Finally the hand lowered again.

"I must stop global warming," intoned Maryann. The tones were deep and rich and resonated.

Charlie's interior universe crumbled and his resistance evaporated. Eyes closed, he dully repeated, "I must stop global warming." No thought of lever games of chance remained. His head lowered with his chin resting on his chest and he breathed more deeply, unaware of the lights that had begun to gleam in the pupils of formerly inanimate eyes staring a few feet away. The deeper his slumber, the more animated the glowing eyes became. At length they were open and shining, as open and shining as had been Charlie's eyes in the minutes preceding his entrance into the Wigwam. From somewhere a Drum Circle sounded and Charlie realized that the drums had been thumping for some time.

The drums thumped louder…and louder…and louder…

They abruptly stopped.

Slowly the nuns stood and stepped to one side, all eyes on the purple mannequin, whose hands moved ever so slightly, followed by its arms, then its head. The jaw opened and closed. One hand rose and felt the blond wig, adjusting it. Slowly it rose from the chair, unconcerned as to whether the circling incense affected its mousse. Standing over Charlie, the eyes looked down through the darkened interior of the teepee and stared unsympathetically. Even as it watched, the purple hue of its skin changed to a sun-tanned shade–the precise shade of Charlie, whose own skin now grew pale and chalky, more gypsum than human. One of the nuns offered a stick of lip gloss. Extending a hand that mirrored Charlie's own hand as it was when he had first walked in, the mannequin's hand applied the gloss to lips on a face that was now indistinguishable from Charlie's face, complete down to his five o'clock shadow.

The mannequin smiled and took a brisk step. "Dang, I feel funny, ya'll. I suddenly have an urge to shave my legs and check whether my earrings match this nice summer dress!"

"You look beautiful, Charlene! You can go home now."

Charlene put one hand on 'her' hip and flipped her hair behind one ear. "I think I'll go stop those bastards who want to rape the Earth with their global warming."

"Oh, don't forget this!" They handed her a book. The cover read: 'Walden'. "Be sure to read it every day!"

"Thank you, girls. I'm one of *you* now." Stepping over the body on the floor, which had ceased to draw breath and crumbled to dust even as he watched, Charlene adjusted her empty bra under her paisley dress, made sure her high-heels were on properly, and prissily walked out.

As Charlene passed the front counter, heading for her car and having entirely forgotten about the games of chance, Maxie Climax cast a serious look at Mary and Maria. They returned her look.

"So eet beegins, my holy Seesters. Let us hope that wee are in time."

At the shoe counter, Maxie motioned for the nuns to draw close. Standing on the counter, she crossed herself, or, more accurately, traced the sacred Opus Dea triangle over her globular midriff, the topmost angle over her navel.

"Wee must prepare for the future, my Seesters. Evil Gork ees laying hees plans on Bogland. So far, Gork's seerum only works on Josephs, but hee is trying to improve his seerum so it will work on names that start with 'M', and the rest of the alphabet weell follow. Wee must protect leetle Maggie and keep her away from Gork and hees seenful ribbets, or hee will take her back to Bogland and expeeriment on her–then wee will all be in beeg, beeg trouble!" Maxie attempted to put her hands on her hips, though in truth she had none. "Beesides, Maggie's momma will not say her Hail Mary's and Our Mother's, and forgets to say the Rosary after doing the bad theeng. So I rescued leetle Maggie."

The nuns caught their breath in horror. No one forgets to say the Rosary after doing the *bad theeng*. "You are forgiven, dear Sister!" they mumbled in unison.

Maxie's gaze was drawn to a truck that pulled into the dusty parking lot beneath the flashing neon sign at the same time that Charlene drove away into the darkness. It backed to the front door and halted. An unshaven man in blue overalls strolled to the back of the truck. Opening the back panel, which had suffered damage some years earlier where a Stutz had collided with its back bumper in Hackensack, he commenced to unload his latest shipment of purple mannequins that he had picked up from a warehouse in New Jersey for delivery to bowling alleys across the country, mannequins both male and female in their form, complete with sundry-colored wigs and varied styles of dresses, along with boxes of brassieres and a selection of high heels to warm the heart of Imelda Marcos.

Picking up the first mannequin, he approached the nuns. "Where ya want em?"

"Oh my my my," answered Marie. "They go in the Nun Such supply room, of course. Except for one, which you can put in the Wigwam for our next...meditation."

"Whatever you say, Sir...uh, sorry, I mean Ma'am." He hauled it in and soon reappeared with a flat loader on wheels, which enabled him to haul the rest inside in a short time.

Dollars changed hands.

The delivery man looked around as if noticing the

bright neon sign for the first time, lighting up the darkness in every direction. "Nice place. I can roll a few dice here, can I?"

"Oh yes yes yes, you dear man! We're always open–for you!"

He smiled. "I'll have to tell the other guys about this place. Especially my pals down at that new Air Force Base off Highway 95. You know, the one by Indian Springs." He touched two fingers to his temple in salute. "I'll be back." Climbing back into his cab, he drove off to the sound of Hail Mary's and Our Mother's reverberating across the bowling lanes.

Episode 15

At the first light of dawn, the black autos moved in. Two turned south onto Rabbit Hill Road from the north, matched by two more that entered the road from the south, converging by an open field bordering a modest farm house in the sleepy burg of Grover's Mill. Several suit-clad men leapt out and bent over the hoods of the cars brandishing Chicago typewriters.

One, shorter than the rest, directed them with silent hand signals. There must be no screw-ups this time. An agent pointed in alarm at a looming figure that towered amidst a cluster of trees, still shrouded in the night's darkness.

Their leader motioned.

A hail of bullets unleashed, the lead sending a cloud of greenery snapping in the air, but with no discernible effect on the menacing alien. Several agents cautiously approached and soon signaled back–a private water tower.

The leader thrust out his lips in frustration. Flicking on the radio, he listened to the impassioned voice.

"–and here they come again out of Grover's Mill, ladies and gentlemen, monstrous tripods with tentacles twisting underneath like snakes, grabbing victims too slow to escape–"

"Sonofabitch!" He threw the radio on the ground, smashing it. Paused. On the road was a rectangular slip of paper–a business card. He picked it up and read aloud: 'Mercury Theater, Madison Avenue, New York.' To his agents he growled: "New York City. Quick!"

Two hours later, an armada of black autos sailed past 44th Street in Manhattan, briefly reminding Hoover of a clandestine meeting years earlier with his special agent who afterwards had disappeared a second time in the strangest of circumstances after an all-too-brief rendezvous. 44th passed by and the cars entered Madison Avenue. They pulled up in front of a seven-story building. Jerking to a halt, the agents jumped out and flashed their badges to ward off interference. A dozen men hoofed the stairs and occupied the elevators.

"CBS recording studio!" Hoover barked to the elevator operator. He snapped open his badge.

"Sure thing, ma'am–I mean, sir." The young lady popped gum while she cranked the handle.

Edgar glared. He wore his business suit today, but had forgotten to remove his earrings. Ruby. Red. Surreptitiously he removed them from his ear lobes and slipped them into a pocket. This was not the time.

The operator cranked open the elevator door. Bursting out, Edgar and his agents swept into the recording studios of the Columbia Broadcasting System, flashed their badges at the many shocked faces of young suited men (note to self: get to know that cute young man in the corner) and various women, a vast conglomeration apparently required to work the magic of broadcasting, many more than Edgar would have supposed.

Several men without jackets strode laughing out of a sound-proofed studio looking self-satisfied. A neon sign flashed overhead: Off the Air.

Hoover pointed and two of his agents cornered one of the men–the one in black tie, long white sleeves rolled up past his elbows. The laughter vanished and the young man's smile faded into a serious look, which was actually more becoming than laughter on his heavy wide face.

"Mr. Welles?"

The man looked alarmed. A deep rich voice echoed back and Hoover immediately understood why he was in radio. "Yes, sir. And what can I do for you?"

Hoover stopped directly in front of him. "I'm Director J. Edgar Hoover of the Federal Bureau of Investigation." He thrust a finger in Orson Welle's face. "You can start by telling me about *the Martians!*"

For a moment, Welles stared in silence without comprehension at the diminutive Hoover. Amusement crossed Orson's versatile face. He chuckled. Then laughed. "The Martians? don't tell me my little Halloween joke took you in, Mr. Hoover. It's just my way of saying 'Boo'!"

The pointing finger came closer. "Don't toy with me, Mr. Welles!" He drew closer and whispered in Welles' ear. "I've seen their agents… I know they're real…"

Orson stopped laughing. Passing a quiet clandestine look about him, he nodded his head in the direction of a sound-proofed room not in use and entered, followed by Hoover and one of his agents. They grabbed several hard-backed chairs and sat.

"Take notes, Clyde."

Clyde produced a slim notebook and poised, pen over paper.

Orson glanced through the room's thick glass windows. Mentally he closed non-existent drapes. "Okay. So you know it's no joke after all. This was just an elaborate way–my way–of alerting people to their existence." Orson rubber-necked again. "They're here. I know it. I *saw* one…"

"Where?" Hoover leaned forward.

"At Grover's Mill in New Jersey."

Hoover produced Orson's business card that he had just retrieved from the shoulder of Rabbit Hill Road and waved it in the air, a triumphant look of 'as if I didn't know' on his face.

Welles ignored him and continued, "I was touring the countryside as part of Mercury Theater's research efforts to identify scenery for an upcoming production, when I…paused by the side of the road."

Hoover was all eyes and ears. "And…?"

"And that's when it happened. This…thing rushed upon me. I was frozen in place, I don't know how I managed to keep from losing my sanity, I struggled desperately to control my thoughts, but it was strange, bizarre, monstrous! It landed in a machine, just like in the tale by my cogno-nomenclatured Herbert G. Wells, whose name my own is forever linked with through an accident of Providence, which is of course what drew me to the story in the first place–"

"Mr. Welles. The machine..."

He turned his deep eyes on Hoover. "Yes. As I was saying, I was drawn to this thing–or it was drawn to me–in the most melodious and dramatic fashion and I instantly recognized the dramatic power of the situation, and I began thinking how I could transfer the moment to celluloid or harness it to this 'newfangled' medium of radio and share it with the world." Orson paused, a complex series of emotions rippling across his elastic face, amazement, profundity, fear, amusement. "Yes, the machine. It was stupendous, immemorial in its fixity in my memory. It shook, it vibrated, steel tentacles flew about me as in a twister, its maw opening and closing like the Gates of Moloch, eager for sacrifice, and indeed there was a poor creature already entangled in its gullet, its little legs and arms waving wildly for succor, for some brave soul to fend off the monster and rescue it from its dire fate–"

"Mr. Welles, please tell me about the *thing*." Hoover frowned. Clyde, who had not yet written anything, frowned too.

"Oh yes, the monster." Welles peered through the window where the FBI agents lounged, several exchanging quiet smiles with young ladies in the CBS office. "The monster was ungodly in its appearance, such a construction of nature as to inflict a stamp of terror on any mind that beheld it, innocent minds that we fragile humans have, unprepared for such nightmarish images that the Outer Gulfs may throw at us from the unpredictable infinitudes…"

"The thing, Mr. Welles! Can you get to *the thing?*" The frowns deepened.

"Yes, *the thing*. It rushed upon me out of the darkness, wild flashes of lightning forming a halo around its head, as thunderclouds gathered over us, its mouth screaming like a banshee to wake the dead, and I daresay the neighboring cemetery was prepared to disgorge its dead in reaction to the creature." Orson stood for effect and swung his arms. "It leaped! Seeking to gather me in its unholy embrace, its two green-complected legs framed two tentacles with the strength of steel, and that's when it looked straight at me with its two pyramidal eyes, focusing like a predator focuses on its prey just before it takes the measure for a strike–"

"Mr. Welles, can you PLEASE get to the point…"

"Yes. *The Thing*. Indeed, the thing! It came at me! It stood as close to me as I stand now before you, and its eyes glazed upon mine, which is when it spoke…"

"It spoke?" Edgar leaned closer with eyes like Mussolini's, "Yes? Yes? And what did it say?"

Orson sat again and leaned forward, his face expanding. "It said: I have come to seize Nevada."

Confusion took hold. Hoover leaned back. " *'To seize Nevahda'?*"

Orson solemnly nodded. "*Nevaada*. As in 'vat'. " He

raised three fingers. "Scout's honor."

Hoover passed a hand over his forehead while he thought. "Nevada…is right next to Utah," he muttered. Hoover stood while Clyde pocketed his notebook, having written only Orson's last three words.

"That's all it said? Nothing more?"

"Well, there is one more thing, if it means anything."

"Yes?" Hoover looked up again, hesitant.

"Just before the incident I was alerted by an astronomer friend that he had witnessed an explosion on a planet, like a meteor being launched, and that he believed he knew the exact location where the meteor would land."

"That location was…?"

"Grover's Mill."

"And the planet was Mars, I assume…"

He shook his head. "No, Director Hoover. The planet that my friend Richard Pierson sighted using a special telescope donated to him by an anonymous private donor… That planet was…"

"Yes, Mr. Welles? Yes?" Both Hoover and Clyde leaned forward.

"Pluto."

"Pluto! Not Mars?" Hoover contemplated the information in silence. Clyde wrote down the word, carefully drawing a giant P across the page of his notebook.

"And that telescope, Mr. Hoover, is located in the state of…"

The Director looked up. They both said it together.

"*Nevaada.*"

Hoover directed a hard stare out the window.

Welles continued. "Now you know why I was so shocked and why I fled in such surprise when I encountered the *thing*, and learned to my great surprise that all that Richard Pierson had told me was true. The machine and presumably its inhabitant came from Pluto… and were heading for Nevada."

Hoover stood and took a few steps, deep in thought. He turned to look at Orson again and put his hands on his hips. "Mr. Welles, I'm sorry I bothered you. You've been very helpful to your country–more than you know." He turned to go as Clyde elaborately dotted a period next to the giant P and put his notebook in his pocket.

One hand on the door handle, Hoover paused.

"Oh, Mr. Welles, one more thing."

"Yes?"

Hoover suddenly grabbed Welles between his legs. "Turn your head and cough."

"What?!" For once Welles was caught entirely by surprise and tried to jump back but Clyde held him fast.

After groping a moment, Hoover released him. "He's okay. He's not one of *them*."

"One of *who*, Director?"

It was Hoover's turn to stare clandestinely through the sound-proof windows to make certain no one was listening. He whispered, "The *ribbets*, you fool. The toad invasion!" He passed one hand over his mouth. "You didn't hear this from me. We did not talk. I was not here."

Orson's eyebrows crawled across his forehead. He crossed his heart. "Hope to die."

"And…uh, you didn't by any chance happen to see any two-legged dogs in the vicinity of the device, by any chance?"

Welles looked puzzled. He shook his head.

"Forget it. Just a stray thought."

As a crowd of excited reporters pushed into the offices of the Columbia Broadcasting System, causing the overworked elevator operator to swallow her gum, the FBI filed out, led by Hoover, leaving Orson standing and thinking, plots and subplots of a possible sequel to his October radio broadcast formulating and reformulating in his mind as fast as he could think.

Six years later…

"Pulled rank? What the hell for? Don't you know what you're getting yourself into?" The tanned clean-built young man in U.S. Naval aviator's uniform turned an earnest face to his colleague.

"Yep. And I wouldn't have it any other way." Lieutenant Willy avoided his friend's stare. "Well, it's done and that's that. Like it or not, you have a new co-pilot. I suggest we strap in and get launched."

"Oh, I like it fine, John. Nothing personal. Just so you know what's up and what's down."

"No problem, brother." John stood straighter and delivered an unnecessary salute. "Just to keep it official: Lieutenant Kennedy, sir…I'm Lieutenant John Willy reporting for duty."

Lieutenant Kennedy returned the salute with a smile. "Off into the wild blue yonder, then."

The two lieutenants checked their goggles, their boots, ensured no change was on their persons–just in case the unimaginable happened and they found themselves on the ground in France fighting Germans. They clambered up the push-cart portable steps onto the massive Liberator that occupied a considerable portion of the airfield in Suffolk, England. Minutes passed and they were strapped in, soldiers wheeled the tarmac step ladder to one side, and the Liberator taxied down the runway.

Kennedy looked at John. "How about we light up a Havana?" The other looked alarmed. "Relax! Just my little joke." Kennedy looked back to the jam-packed interior of the aircraft. "Two thousand tons of high explosive would not get along too well with a spark."

"You got that right," said Willy.

Pulling back on the throttle, Kennedy sailed the heavily burdened aircraft into the firmament. After they circled the airfield, they sighted a second aircraft.

"There she is. I never thought I'd be happy to see a Mosquito."

Behind them trailed a British bomber, a glint in the cockpit signaling the presence of a movie camera already running, intent on capturing the result of the latest American radio-controlled pilotless flying bomb. Pilotless, that is, after its pilots parachuted out. He raised his voice over the engines.

"Ten miles is ground zero, John. The plan is to pull the trigger then bail eight miles out."

"Roger, lieutenant."

"Time to lean back and let the plane do the driving."

The minutes rolled past as the bomber made a wide slow turn by remote radio control. While they made their final adjustments to their parachutes and goggles, the eight-mile boundary approached.

"Time to arm that sucker."

John stepped back to where a device displayed a menacing looking single pin. Carefully he withdrew the pin from its lock. He returned to his seat as the bomber completed its turn.

Eight miles.

"Send the code."

Willy leaned over and signaled 'spade flush.'

"We're done, podner. Let's head for the exit. This thing is set to fly itself all the way to the target and I sure don't want to be near when it hits."

"Me three," added John.

Evacuating their seats, they turned–and froze.

Blocking their path squatted an olive-green amphibian with webbed feet and prodigious legs, a pair of eyes on either side of its head busily swiveling in all directions. The toad put a device on its head, where it clung to vestigial ears. A deep rough voice croaked and, to the lieutenants' surprise, made intelligible sounds.

"Your appellation is desired. What is your appellation?"

Kennedy and Willy exchanged stunned looks. They rubbed their eyes.

One chameleon eye settled on an insignia sewed on Willy's shirt. "This is appellation. Does this name apply to you?"

"Uh…it says I'm a Lieutenant."

"You have name. Is your name 'Lieutenant'?"

"No, it's John."

"We don't want Johns." The toad looked at Kennedy. "Is your name 'Lieutenant' also?"

"I am a lieutenant but my actual name is Joseph. Joseph P. Kennedy, Jr., to be precise. My father was Ambassador to this country." He pushed out his chest pridefully. Then shook his head in disbelief. "Why am I talking to a giant frog inside a bomber over England? Especially when it's time to bail!"

"You are the one we seek. We are recruiting Josephs. Do you volunteer?"

Kennedy looked at Willy again, and settled on a silvery object in the toad's webbed hand, which looked uncomfortably like a weapon. "Volunteer? What the hell for?" He had to raise his voice to be heard over the plane's engines, which were picking up speed.

"Volunteer job like what you are doing now. After transformation, you will do secret work on Dryland. You will live long. When you accomplish your task you will enjoy nice retirement on beachfront property and splash with hundreds of young ribbets. Better than seventy-two virgins."

"And what if I don't want to 'splash' with hundreds of...ribbets?"

"I know nice bond-ribbet with pink curlers named Big Bertha. Hot-to-trot, lots of fun, every ribbet's dream. This ribbet will be glad to hook you up."

"I think I'll–"

A flash of light emanated from the silvery hand weapon. Joseph Kennedy and the ribbet vanished. As they disappeared, Kennedy's parachute and clothing, no longer occupied, dropped to the floor, the metal clasps on the harness emitting a spark.

"Oh hell," said Willy.

A second later, just over the eight mile mark, the plane exploded.

Episode 16

"Korplash like new model. Gork like new model?" Korplash turned one respectful eye on the Great Toad Leader, the other eye observing Xplak who stood hesitantly behind him.

Gork waddled his enormous legs in a circle around the silver pie-shaped craft showing off his latest project, and admiring its tasteful construction. The pilots nodded their bulbous heads in approval. It beat the heck out of Art Deco.

"No more will siridogs chase ribbets like galactic mailmen when we visit Dryland. Finally our great toad race will be able to come and go on Dryland in peace." Gork turned a flexible eye to his two most experienced dumpster pilots. "Same as dumpster cosmodrone, but designed to look like siridog craft. Those mutts will see this and believe it is one of theirs so they will finally leave us alone."

"When do we launch, Great Gork?"

"You don't. The interior is same as dumpster version, therefore…" the other eye fixed temporarily on Korplash "if a certain pilot–who shall remain unnamed–

croaks again…he will still be heard by evil siridogs."

Korplash's eye which stared at Xplak acquired a guilty look.

"So this is not for ribbets, but for Josephs. They shall go to Dryland as soon as possible to begin the Great Work. The sooner, the better." Gork's eyes focused separately on Korplash and Xplak. "Have you two heard of Three Stooges?"

They shook their bulbous heads.

"Look mirror and add one."

They shrugged uncomprehendingly.

"In other words… All you two Stooges need to do is…"

"Yes, Great Leader?" They looked up eagerly.

"–stay out of the way!"

Gork pressed controls at his side and the front of the piecraft opened wide, wide enough to admit several toads. Xplak and Korplash stared with envy at the luxurious interior with bucket seats and seat belts and cup holders–one already holding a cup of green goo. They, especially Korplash, looked crestfallen as crests, heretofore hidden, suddenly appeared on their bullet heads only to promptly fall.

Gork whistled. The note was too high for toads to hear but a moment later the door swished aside and a shuman entered. Clad in single yellow spandex outfit with red star over his heart, he paused at the threshold to wobble his one-size-too-small bowler hat, bumping it repeatedly against his skull. A smile broke out, dark lips accentuating the corpse-white paint on his face. His smile turned into a look of terror. Raising his hands he marched into the room, eyes wide.

Behind him stepped another silent actor, pressing an umbrella into the back of the first like a gun barrel. Wearing green pants, a stretch shirt with black and white horizontal stripes, red suspenders, and a bow tie, his white painted face distorted into an image of Edward G. Robinson, silently mouthing "This is how it's gonna be, see."

A third corpse face appeared behind the second. Striding carelessly into the room, he failed to see the leg that Green Pants thrust out, and tumbled to the ground.

Yellow Spandex and Green Pants broke into gales of silent laughter, while the third one, in black and white horizontal stripes with purple lips, looked up, his face distorted in exaggerated outrage. He pretended to swim. He rose slowly from the floor in defiance of gravity, while the others stared in wonder and admiration. Finally his feet touched the ground and the three mimes together let loose silent but uproarious laughs.

"Attention, Josephs. Clearly your talents qualify you for this serious new assignment. It is time to listen to your Leader."

The three lined up in front of Gork, Yellow Spandex unable to resist posing rabbit ears behind the heads of Green Pants and Purple Lips. All three leaned forward, mouths open, listening as if their lives depended on it–that is, they inspected their nails.

"Time to get serious."

The three suddenly looked like George Raft, each flipping a coin repeatedly.

"*More* serious."

They each closed one eye and thrust cupped ears directly in Gork's face.

"Korplash and Xplak will train you how to run the new cosmodrone. Between your talents and their dedication–" He passed an eye over his two toadying toad pilots and his other eye over the three grease-painted Josephs as if hoping to reassure himself. "–I am sure you will learn quickly and, when you arrive on Dryland, you will send this new–*and incredibly expensive*–cosmodrone, back to me on autopilot in one piece."

All three mimes nodded, upturned thumbs and silent exaggerated expressions of assurance passing between them. Piece of cake.

"Don't worry about the siridogs. This cosmodrone is designed to look like their own spacecraft so you should not attract any interest from them. But if they do chase you, just remember," Gork pointed to a large red button inside the craft. "This is the *Return to Bogland* button. If you get into trouble you can press this big red button and the craft will instantly launch its autopilot sequence and automatically fly back to Bogland."

The three mimes compressed their lips and nodded in complete assurance–they got the Bogland button.

"Now this one." Gork pointed to a second button, also big and red, two inches from the first button, "our ribbet engineers cleverly located this button within easy reach of the first so after you drink your green goo you won't have to stretch your hand very far to press it. It is of course the cosmodrone's *Self-Destruct* button."

They exchanged looks of open-mouthed wonder.

"Do not under any circumstances press this second big red button. There is no scenario that I can think of that would ever require you to press this other big red button. So of course it is located directly *next* to the first big red button, which you absolutely *must* press after you arrive on Dryland. Our ribbet engineers are in complete agreement that this is an excellent design that will serve us very well whenever we use our new *very* expensive cosmodrone."

The three Josephs nodded in agreement. It made perfect sense.

"Now get in. And good luck."

They piled in, only twice tripping over each other's legs to silent mirth.

"And, oh, welcome aboard, new Joseph. Thank you for volunteering." Green Pants dropped his jaw and demonstrably grabbed his crotch in way of thanks.

Five minutes later Xplak and Korplash finished their lesson and exited the craft. Together with the assistance of a crowd of younger and smaller ribbets, and with only a half-dozen pauses to splash with several, they pulled aside the huge double sliding metal doors to the hangar.

Inside, Purple Lips assumed command, surreptitiously rubbing recently consulted cheat notes from his palm. He pulled a crank and pushed a lever. With a rush, the piecraft sped out of the hangar into the perpetual mist of Bogland and after a few more moments, had penetrated the stratosphere of the planet, empty blackness replacing the grey mist.

One pale hand pulled another crank and the craft vanished to reappear momentarily in a location marked by entirely different constellations. Another yank on the crank and the craft jumped many parallaxes again. A third crank and they arrived in the stratosphere above Earth, the bright light of a new day streaming down on them.

They stared out the front plexiglass window in open-eyed wonder as a snow-capped chain of mountains passed on either side, the craft flying along a wide valley between two ranges. As they progressed down the valley, they silently ooh'ed and aah'ed at the natural beauty of Dryland, and pointed and laughed at the unidentified crawling objects stuck far below on the ground.

Green Pants picked up the bottle of green goo and took a deep draft. Pulling rank, Purple Lips assumed his leadership privileges and snatched the bottle with a look of exaggerated scolding. Then downed several deep drafts himself.

Not to be outdone, Yellow Spandex grabbed it and managed to drink a swig before Purple Lips took it back again. Wiping the mouth of the bottle with his palm–the other palm–he took another drink, glaring at the others to leave it alone and tend to their duties.

Having no duties to tend to and already happy from the effects of the green goo, Yellow Spandex let his eyes wander about the interior of the piecraft, until his gaze settled on one of the translation devices that the toads used when speaking to shumans and mimes.

An idea popped.

Unhooking his seat belt, Spandex removed his bowler hat and took the translation device and put it on his head. Signaling to the others to watch, he opened his mouth.

"Urrrrk!" the device mechanically buzzed.

Purple Lips smiled.

"Ooook!"

Green Pants silently laughed.

Spandex motioned to the others to watch. Standing, he pretended to walk like Korplash, waddling his fat body around the interior of the spacecraft with a hang-dog look while a huge fat toad dragged him by one vestigial ear, evoking gales of hilarity from the other two mimes.

"Mmmm, it wasssn't me my sweet lily pad," hummed the translation device in a mechanical monotone. The others shook with laughter. The tale of Korplash and his bond-ribbet had reached even Gork's experimental piecraft building.

Spandex got their attention again. Pointing to his imaginary enormous stomach, he blew out his cheeks with his hand over his mouth as if to suppress a burp.

"Croooak!" The translation device reverberated with the sound of his Korplash-like burp.

All three again shook with laughter.

Purple Lips suddenly froze. On the horizon, outlined against the high snow of a peak appeared a phalanx of saucer-shaped crafts. They were approaching quickly.

Exchanging looks of alarm, the three mimes strapped themselves into their seats and prepared to increase speed. Before Purple Lips could manage to do so–frantically inspecting his remaining unsmudged cheat-notes on his palm to learn how–the alien ships swarmed the ribbet's cosmodrone, then lined up neatly behind it. Inside the saucers, muzzles barked and snapped, itching to close with their favorite target.

Siridogs.

Green Pants looked at the others in surprise, and mouthed a silent "How?" Purple Lips shrugged his shoulders. It was a mystery.

Spandex blew his cheeks out again. Quietly he removed the device and hung it carefully back on the wall, and put his bowler hat back on.

Something flashed by.

Purple Lips jerked the guidance lever to avoid colliding with yet another craft, one that appeared from below and seemed incapable of doing anything except to fly incredibly slowly in a monotonous straight line. To avoid collision and evade the fleet of siridogs, Purple Lips punched the Saucer Motion button and immediately the piecraft began to drift and flutter like a leaf. He was not happy when he saw the siridogs immediately do the same and keep pace.

Below and further from Mount Rainier flew the small monoplane that had barely missed crashing into the piecraft. With eyes wide, its pilot removed his radio gear the better to stare at the fantastic sight that presented itself, attesting to the existence of an alien race that had lain dormant in the public consciousness ever since that crackpot Orson Welles had tried to pull the wool over the American public nine years ago back in

1938, and, although soon exposed as a gigantic hoax, had nevertheless awakened the public to the possibility that We Are Not Alone.

Scribbling a few notes on stray paper, Kenneth Arnold replaced his headphones and carefully steered his plane towards Yakima. *Just wait till I tell those reporters!* he thought. *1947 has been a slow year, but this is news even in Seattle!*

As Arnold's plane lost altitude, Purple Lips looked in his rearview mirror and terror again settled on his face. He drained the green goo. The aerial waffling helped a bit, but he was beginning to wonder if the Great Gork's Great Work on Dryland was about to come to an end even before the arrival of his first secret agents.

He noticed a scribbling on his palm which he had forgotten about. It was not an actual scribbling but only a small blue dot which explained why it had escaped his attention heretofore. Looking up at the control panel, for the first time he noticed that adjacent to the two big red buttons was a little blue one, two inches removed. Underneath was a label in small print: 'Siridog Repellent.'

I wonder what this does? he thought, wishing he had studied much better for his cosmodrone pilot's license, one minute having been far too long to retain his attention.

He pressed it.

Instantly a huge rolled up newspaper, a copy of the Galactic Times, extruded from the back of the piecraft and took a swing at the lead siridog saucer. Inside the saucer the barking muzzles shut and whimpered as the craft engaged in frantic evasive maneuvers. This was unnecessary however since the first swing spun the cosmodrone edge over edge until it finally stabilized on the far side of the nearest snow-capped peaks, *sans* saucers and *sans* siridogs.

The mimes directed relieved looks at each other. Jamming the accelerator, Purple Lips guided the craft deftly down the slope of the mountain and over the foothills where he took temporary refuge in the morning's fogbanks. After pausing long enough to make certain they had not been followed, he punched a disengage button to eject the newspaper, which even the mimes realized with some resentment was not the greatest solution but that they were well and stuck with it, and flew towards the southeast.

Green Pants opened a cupboard below the instrument panel and to everyone's surprise found another bottle of green goo. He and Spandex promptly played Me First, stacking hand-grips over the neck of the bottle. Purple Lips won and seized it from both.

In a rare moment of altruism, Purple Lips took only one swig, and then passed it to the others, who soon were staggering about the interior of the craft, pretending to be drunker than they actually were and laughing at each other's antics.

Spandex sighted the Big Red Button…*not* the good one. With a grin, his hand crawled toward the button, his face transformed with exaggerated alarm.

Purple Lips slapped his hand and scolded him.

Shaking his hand exaggeratedly in pretend pain, Spandex resumed laughing. His hand crawled back and pretended to press the Self-Destruct button a second time. This time Green Pants joined the fun, his hand also hovering over the button.

Again Purple Lips slapped their hands back. Frowning, he pointed a finger at both of them and shook it while his silent mouth jabbered recriminations and warnings.

To no effect. A third time their hands drew close to the Self-Destruct button and pretended to press it, both Green Pants and Spandex laughing uproariously at the increasing look of alarm on Purple Lips' face.

Suddenly the craft braked, sending the two clowns tumbling heads over heels to bounce off the plexiglass window. Purple Lips pointed to his foot on the brake pedal. He laughed hardest.

For a minute Spandex and Green Pants looked offended, rubbing their heads and limping about the cabin like pale-face Igors, stuffing pillows up their backs to create hunches. Then they too broke into gales of silent laughter as Purple Lips joined them, stuffing his own pillow up his back.

Out the window, the ground was closer, presenting a landscape of dry scrub brush and shallow gulleys, the occasional cow pausing to observe the approach of the strange craft, perhaps wondering if it was about to lose its udder.

Purple Lips pulled out a map and unfolded it. He held up a finger as if to say: Just a moment. He took another drink. Glancing down, he noticed his shoe was untied; he put his foot on the instrument panel the better to tie it.

An explosion rent the craft.

Pieces fluttering to earth by the thousand in the hot dry air around them, the mimes plummeted the short distance to the ground. They bounced and lay motionless, metal fragments–both memory metal and Alzheimer metal–raining about them like an autumn shower of leaves.

On the far side of a gully, an old pickup negotiated a series of potholes that the New Mexico county seat called a road. The driver wiped his mouth. *Damn fine meal,* he thought. *Topped off by my favorite food group–gravy. Vintage 3:00 p.m.*

Mack the rancher jammed his brakes.

What the hay?

Peering at the scattered debris that overlay a gulley and several surrounding acres, Mack climbed down from his truck and descended into the gulley. He minced a few steps. He scratched his head. He proceeded to pick up fragments here, pieces there, sheets of pliable thin substances that defied categorization elsewhere.

If this don't beat all to hell? I wonder if this has anything to do with those scientists and their ek-splosions in that little town Alamagordo to the south? Mack paused as a suspicion surfaced. *Might this have somethin to do with that 'national security' I keep hearin bout on the radio?*

Tossing the pieces he had collected in a box, Mack threw the box in the back seat of his truck. He started the engine.

Hesitated.

Down the gulley was a smear of white.

Clicking the motor off, he again climbed from the truck and stepped into the gulley. He walked a piece. Up the gully flashed a glimmer of white amid the torrent of silver and lead metal fragments.

The whiteness moved.

Airplanes have pilots… Mack stood straight. *Americans? Or Russkies?*

He scratched his head again. Rushing back to his truck, Mack grabbed his rifle. Slowly he approached the smear of white, rifle at the ready, creeping with the caution of a red Apache.

The whiteness grew larger and became oval.

Creeping closer he was amazed to see the oval shape crystallize into a face–but a face such as he had never imagined in his worst nightmares. Pasty pale, harsh black diamonds centered on evil staring eyes, purple almost black smudges staining the lips and eyebrows. On its head–if that is what it was–sat the ultimate mark of insult and contempt for humanity: a bowler hat one size too small.

Yurp!

The rancher clapped one hand over his mouth to prevent hurling his favorite food group. Of one thing he was certain: such affronts to public peace and welfare could not be of this Earth. Not even Russkies could be so white.

He startled.

The thing had moved!

To his shock, the rancher saw two more ungodly entities stir, one with green pants and red suspenders, the other wrapped in yellow spandex. As if waking from a deep sleep, the two yawned and stretched human-like limbs. Glimpses of black and white horizontal stripes, stars, and bow ties deepened the shock to his sensibilities.

God in Heaven! Such offenses to good taste must be put down. No human with dignity and self-respect could suffer such freaks to live. I'll give each a bullet–after all, it's the humane thing to do.

Mack lifted his rifle. He focused the sight and glared down the length of the glinting barrel, determined to end the freaks' lives before they could implement their evil purpose, whatever that might be.

The cross-hairs in his scope shifted. Mack blinked and rubbed his eyes. No, the cross-hairs were not in his scope, but on the white-face thing itself, having appeared on a red circle on the chest of the alien with the purple lips. He peered down the barrel again. The cross-hairs were plain as day–or rather plain as early morning–indeed the cross-hairs expanded the longer he looked. He blinked in surprise. He saw no cross-hairs, but a round red bulls-eye target held chest-high by the alien with purple lips.

As Mack stared, a hand appeared on the side of the bulls-eye and slowly and deliberately shifted the target from Purple Lips to his companion in yellow spandex. Staring back at Mack through the rifle scope, Purple Lips grinned and pointed to his companion Yellow Spandex. Looking directly in Mack's eyes, Purple Lips mouthed the words: 'Fire away!'

The alien in green pants also pointed at the bulls-eye and at Yellow Spandex, and also laughed silently at his companion's imminent demise, Purple Lips joining in the hilarity.

Yellow Spandex ignored them; he produced a bottle of green goo and took a drink. While the other aliens watched in silent wonder, Yellow Spandex tied a white cloth around his eyes and began to march blindly toward Mack, his elbows behind as if inviting death, the red bulls-eye clinging to his chest.

Mack lowered his rifle. Such bravado! So brave a fellow! For the nonce, he felt he could not visit death on any creature, even an alien, after so brave a performance–but his glance fell once more on the grease-painted corpse-white face with the ugly black marks above and below the eyes as if insulting the intelligence of all the world, the combination of yellow and red a grotesque unhappy medium between all-clown and the merely inane.

He squeezed the trigger.

With a thud the bullet hit.

The thing kept coming…

A second time Mack fired.

A silent guffaw escaped the yellow creature's throat as it disengaged the bulls-eye target from its chest. It held the target overhead.

This time Mack aimed directly at the thing's white-face itself, ignoring the round target. Anticipating Mack's aim, the devilish face distorted with a feigned look of outrage.

The gun fired…

Mack's bullet missed the alien in yellow but hit the painted bulls-eye right in the center!

Frantically, Mack reloaded, re-aimed, and re-fired at several parts of the ugly creature's body–each time he fired, wherever he aimed, the bullet missed the creature but hit the thing's round bulls-eye.

The thing was coming nearer...

The yellow alien rolled the target across the ground. Up the side of the gulley it rolled until it came to Mack's truck, where it bounced in the air and landed on the vehicle's windshield.

The creature came close. One last time Mack aimed and fired at the alien's yellow spandex chest–point-blank. His truck's windshield shattered, his bullet again mysteriously diverted from the yellow alien to the bulls-eye.

Scrambling up the side of the gulley while the thing rushed behind him like a nemesis, Mack leaped into his truck. He gunned the engine.

Directly in front of his truck the thing halted, evil on its face, its yellow spandex clashing insanely with the grisly white greasepaint and vertical black marks above and below its glowing eyes. Mack raised his rifle once more in warning–but he knew the rifle was useless. With a disdainful smirk, the white-face retrieved the round target from the truck's hood and grinned as if to say: Fire as you please! Your bullets will always hit the bulls-eye instead of me!

Mack let the rifle drop. He revved the engine louder. He had his own message: Step aside–or else! In response, the thing in yellow let loose another of its arrogant silent laughs. It thrust out its spandex-covered chest. Do your worst!

The truck lurched forward.

The thing made no effort to move–the truck slammed it into the dirt, the body rebounding in the dust behind Mack as he rocketed past.

Mack braked, scattering dust. *Whew! I finally got him...*

Mack watched his rear-view mirror in horror as a blur of yellow slowly rose up from the road under the growing glare of the early morning sun. Rising to full height behind his truck, the thing in yellow flashed its evil grin. Again it placed the offensive too-small bowler hat on its head.

The grin faded. It strode forward, the red star over its heart glinting with anger.

Mack leaped from the vehicle. He stumbled down the gulley, now well beyond Plan B and trying to form Plans W, X, and Y. He broke into a sweat–the other two white-faced devils were floating through the air swinging baseball bats. Mack stumbled and fell. Propping on one elbow, he grasped a sheet of memory metal from the crash in a desperate attempt to use it as a shield, his last line of defense.

Plan Z.

The metal promptly refolded into a paper airplane. *What comes after Z?* Mack wondered, dropping it, the sweat pouring off his neck in a waterfall.

Like an angel of death, the yellow alien hovered over Mack, its glowing eyes fixed on Mack's own terrified eyes. It halted. Grinned. Stretching out a white-gloved hand, it reached behind Mack and withdrew a bottle. Turning to Purple Lips and Green Pants, Yellow Spandex showed the bottle of green goo–all three white-faces lit up. They dropped their baseball bats. Converging in the center of the gulley, the three joyfully gulped its contents and commenced to dance to the beat of invisible jazz trumpets.

Thump.

The trumpets went silent.

An enormous rolled up newspaper had fallen from the sky, ending the party, leaving three pairs of legs outthrust beneath.

Mack wiped the river of sweat from his brow.

He turned–doubled over–blew gravy.

Finally he wiped his mouth and gasped a breath. That was close! Clambering up the slope of the gulley, he jumped in his truck and drove like a banshee back to his ranch. His eye inspected the windshield that had been shattered by his own bullet, and peered at the strange white paint smeared over the front of his truck, and he thought: *Who in hell would believe this? Since the bulls-eye has vanished they might think I shot up my own truck then tried to paint it white. I'd better tell everyone I rode my horse today.*

Bursting into the ramshackle split-level house he called his ranch, he whipped off his clothes and snapped on new ones, then propelled his glass-strewn pickup through the labyrinth of potholes till he arrived at the nearby town of Roswell, this time not to complain about the roads but to alert the world to the threat from alien white-faces.

Twenty-four hours later, a phalanx of military trucks converged at high speed on Mack's New Mexico ranch, where they expelled over several square miles a host of uniformed soldiers with hard silent glares who proceeded to retrieve every item that could conceivably be a fragment of the crashed saucer, half rushing to the corner of the gulley where Mack (strangely smelling of turkey gravy and bile) had described the horrific creatures that had crashed their alien craft on his New Mexico ranch.

Soldiers with rifles and machine guns; medical staff in biosuits; officers strutting in dark glasses; German Shepherds straining leashes–all swarmed the vicinity, desperate to avert what, from the anxious and fearful testimony of the simple rancher, could only be the first scouts of the most diabolical plot ever to threaten decent human beings on an innocent planet.

One of the newest military instruments in the American roster, a helicopter, descended next to the ravine, and two polished shoes sprang to the dry brush-strewn ground. Hands quietly checking earlobes, the diminutive suit leaped to the ground and, despite the bulky overcoat that was large enough to conceal a second set of clothing underneath, quickly negotiated the downward slope to arrive before three figures lying motionless on the ground, their closed eyes set in the midst of the most repulsive physiognomy imaginable, bespeaking alien modes of thought beyond anything that could possibly be native to Earth. Over their torsos lay a tangled mass of paper, all the ink of which had run off from the previous night's rain.

Edgar looked to General Ramey in triumph. "We got em."

For a long moment, Ramey stood and stared in silence, then struck a match on his shoe for his cigar. "We'll take them to the Wright-Patterson Air Base basement and put them in permanent cold storage. That's the only thing to be done with these...*monsters*. And God help us if they ever wake up and get loose." As he looked, a crane lifted the newspaper off the aliens and the armada of soldiers and medical personnel carefully placed the creatures in three plexiglass containers stronger than steel and sealed the containers. They eased the tubes into a heavy military truck. As the truck barreled down the stony track escorted by jeeps with heavy-caliber guns, General Ramey looked at his watch.

"I've got to get back to Roswell. There's a young officer there who didn't get the word in time and he told reporters about the saucer crash."

Hoover took a step back. "You mean–he told the *truth?*"

Ramey nodded. "Yeah. I can't believe it either. But we're holding a news conference today to set the reporters straight." He gazed down on Hoover, wondering silently why the head of the F.B.I. would wear an overcoat in the desert. "All this crap–" Ramey's gaze swept about them at the acres of debris that stretched into the distance being collected by hundreds of soldiers, "–was just a weather balloon." He winked and walked away.

Edgar turned to a companion in a dark business suit standing silently behind him. “Take a note, Clyde.” Clyde paused pen in hand ready to record for posterity whatever the renowned Director of the F.B.I. might say.

For a long moment Edgar stared up at the vast expanse of sky with its millions of orbs of light. Finally he spoke. Not to Clyde, but to the firmament. “For the moment the Earth is safe…but for how long?”

END PART 1

ADVENTURES OF THE RADIATED LESBIAN NUN

Don't MISS THE NEXT ADVENTURES OF MAGGIE, THE RADIATED LESBIAN NUN..

PART 2:

CROSS-DRESSERS FROM PLUTO

'THE JELLO BROTHERS MAKE THEIR MOVE & MAGGIE GETS HER SQUATCH'

If you enjoyed this
Dark Lotus Book
please post a

REVIEW

on the
following websites:

www.amazon.com
www.goodreads.com
www.siriusreviews.com

Thank You!
–Glenn Lazar Roberts

www.ingramcontent.com/pod-product-compliance
Lightning Source LLC
Chambersburg PA
CBHW072353110726
47909CB00003B/688

* 9 7 8 0 9 6 7 5 8 0 9 5 1 *